Sense &
Second Chances

OTHER BOOKS AND AUDIO BOOKS

BY BRITTANY LARSEN

Pride and Politics

Sense & Second Chances

a novel

BRITTANY LARSEN

Covenant Communications, Inc.

Cover image: *Young Couple Exploring the City* © CasarsaGuru, courtesy of istockphoto.com.

Cover design copyright © 2017 by Covenant Communications, Inc.

Published by Covenant Communications, Inc.
American Fork, Utah

Printed in the United States of America
First Printing: May 2017

23 22 21 20 19 18 17   10 9 8 7 6 5 4 3 2 1

ISBN 978-1-52440-161-0

For Emma, Tess & Jane—
one day you will love Jane Austen, I just know it.

Acknowledgments

WHO TO THANK? THE LIST is long, but first and foremost, let's start with Covenant Communications. Thank you for taking a chance on me and giving my stories a home.

Melanie and Kristine, thank you for seeing me through to the end of this manuscript. It wasn't an easy journey, and I'm grateful for all of your input and suggestions. This is such a better story because I had you with me while I wrote it.

Josi, Rachel, and Emily, you were invaluable beta readers. Your suggestions and insight made my plot and my words so much better. I appreciate the hours you devoted to helping me when you each had so few of your own to spare.

Thank you, Hydi, for sharing your knowledge of Judaism and for checking mine. I know an outsider to any religion will never get it right, but I came closer because of your suggestions.

Joey, thanks for the SC burns.

Thank you to my parents, Bruce and June, and to the rest of my Nelson clan: Nathan and Mackenzie, Anna, Morgan, and Ethan; Barrett and Angela, Elly, Liza, and Anders; Amber and J.R., Taylor, Ikes, and Belle. Your encouragement, praise, and love support me in more ways than I can name.

Emma, Tess, and Jane are the best kids ever. Thank you for cheering me on, but also for cleaning the house. One day you will have your own children and your own chore charts for them that they will ignore, but I will come make them do those chores to reward you for your years of servitude to me. Maybe . . .

I don't mean to brag, but I also have the BEST husband. Thank you, Shawn, for having enough confidence in me to believe I'll someday be your Sugar Mama. Thank you for your continual support, patience, and love. And for Kon-mari folding the clothes. There is no one who can beat you in the husband department.

Chapter 1

If I could map out my life with the same accuracy Google maps my destinations, I'd do it. In fact, I tried. When I was sixteen, I wrote The Plan. It outlined everything I would achieve in ten easy steps. Number one, get into UCLA and graduate with honors. *Check and check.* Number two, work at a big marketing firm. *Check.* Number three, buy my own condo. *Check.* Number four, marry a returned missionary in the temple . . .

I had been working on that one when my parents' plane went down. Suddenly, I was left in charge of my younger brother and sister, and The Plan got tossed out the window like a piece of trash on the Mojave Highway. Not that I didn't cling to it as tightly as a Kardashian to fleeting fame. But on the day our half-brother, Jason, kicked Annie, Bryce, and me out of our house, I felt my carefully laid plans slipping away for the first time.

It started like every other morning of the past nine months. In the first few groggy seconds of wakefulness, I wondered why I was back in my old bedroom instead of in my condo. Then the memory of my parents' accident punched me in the gut and threw me back into reality. As much as I wanted to drift back into a forgetful sleep, I had a ten-year-old brother to sweet-talk into going to school and an eighteen-year-old sister whose floundering acting career I had to save.

Waffles were the one sure way to get Bryce out of bed, but Annie was another story. None of us, including Jason, had recovered from the shock of losing our parents, but we'd forced ourselves through daily routines until we didn't have to force ourselves anymore. They became normal again, and so did the emptiness.

Not for Annie though. She didn't have a normal routine to get back to, so the emptiness and the sadness consumed her. Most days I didn't see her until noon, and then it was only for a few hours. So I was more than surprised when she came downstairs for breakfast. This. Was. Huge.

"Good morning!" I said, too cheerfully, as she plopped down in a kitchen chair. I knew I shouldn't make a big deal about her being there, but I couldn't stop myself. "Can I make you a waffle?" I leaned against her and rubbed her shoulder in a kind of awkward cross between a hug and a pat.

"You can have the first one, Annie!" Bryce couldn't play it cool any better than I could.

"I'm not hungry." Annie's loose topknot of dark hair teetered back and forth as she shook her head.

"You don't have to eat a whole one, only as much as you want." I got the waffle out of the maker and put it in front of her before she could say no again. She was too skinny, and with her long hair piled on top of her head, her cheeks took on a hollowed look that swallowed her dimples and made her green eyes look too big for her face.

I put Nutella, sliced strawberries, syrup, whipped cream, and chocolate chips in front of her, hoping something would tempt her into eating. Then I hovered until she glared at me and Bryce sent me a look pleading for his own waffle.

I loaded the waffle maker and tried to look busy while sneaking glances at Annie. Nutella was her weakness, and I smiled to myself as she spread a thick layer of it on her waffle. One small scoop of Nutella felt like a giant victory for breakfast.

The green light flashed, and I pulled Bryce's waffle out and handed it to him. He stared at me with a grin spread on thicker than Annie's Nutella as he poured around a gallon of syrup over his breakfast, daring me to tell him no. The doorbell rang before I could.

"I'll get it!" Bryce shoved a quarter of the waffle in his mouth and bolted for the door.

"Ask who it is first." I followed him with zero expectations he'd listen.

He made it to the door before I caught up to him, flinging it open to a man with three-day stubble and a tool belt.

"Hi." The stranger's smile reached his eyes, made bluer by his short, dark hair that looked more finger-combed than actually brushed. All things I shouldn't have noticed—along with his perfect jawline—but I'm only human.

"Hi!" Bryce answered.

"Go eat your breakfast." I scooted Bryce out of the way and blocked the entrance. "Can I help you?"

"I'm Joel." He stuck out his hand, but instead of taking it, I pushed Bryce back behind me. "Rachel's brother," he added before dropping the rejected hand.

I was about to ask "Rachel who?" when a car pulled up and Jason's on-again, off-again girlfriend stepped out. *That* Rachel. Jason climbed out of the driver's side and met her on the sidewalk. She held his hand, and with each step they took down the long walkway, my stomach folded in on itself.

"Bryce, go eat your breakfast," I said in my sternest voice and pointed him back to the kitchen, watching until he was out of sight. When I turned back around, Rachel and Jason were on the porch.

"You beat me here!" Rachel said to Tool Man—I'd already forgotten his name—and offered him her cheek. He pecked it lightly, and she turned to me.

"Annie," she said.

"Emily," I corrected her. Rachel and I weren't close. Obviously.

"Emily. Sorry. You look so much alike."

We didn't. I stood half a foot taller than Annie, and my hair, barely reaching past my shoulders, was significantly shorter than hers. Not to mention the fact my eyes were too far on the blue side of the color spectrum to ever be mistaken for green. The only thing the same about us was the chestnut color of our hair.

"This is my brother, Joel." Rachel rested her fingers on his broad shoulder, and he stuck his hand out again. I shook it this time, but I didn't like it. I had a bad feeling about why he was here.

"Hi, Emily," Jason said and leaned in for a hug but changed his mind—probably due to my icy expression—and patted my back instead.

"Hi. Why the surprise visit?" I didn't try to be polite. Jason wasn't the "pop in" type, so I figured I'd cut right to the chase.

"We came to tell you we're engaged." He smiled and put his arm around Rachel.

"Congratulations." I wished I could be happy for him, but I was pretty sure I knew what his engagement meant. "It was nice of you to come over to tell us in person, but I've got to get Bryce to school." I glanced at Rachel's brother, who, feeling the tension, shifted his weight slightly.

"Actually, we wanted to discuss the house." He ushered Rachel and her brother inside, then followed behind them.

"Joel is a contractor. Do you mind if he takes a look around?" Rachel asked me. She said it politely but didn't wait for an answer. The house was already hers, and all I could do was follow them into the dining room.

"What's going on?" Annie walked out of the kitchen carrying a plate piled high with whipped cream, a forkful of it nearly to her mouth. Rachel looked from Annie to her plate, her brow crinkling. I *assumed* there was a waffle under the white fluff somewhere, but as long as my sister was eating, I didn't really care.

"I thought actresses were on perpetual diets," Jason said to Annie, then smiled at his own joke.

Without a word, Annie dropped the fork on her plate and retreated back into the kitchen. I heard the plate hit the sink, and seconds later she reappeared long enough to brush by Rachel and glare at Jason before stomping up the stairs.

"Did I say something wrong? I was just trying to make conversation." Jason looked genuinely confused, if not genuinely sorry.

"Hi, Jason!" Bryce ran from the kitchen and threw his arms around Jason's waist. Jason responded with a gentle pat on the back before unlatching Bryce's arms and stepping away from him. Bryce didn't seem to notice, but I did.

"Can I have Annie's waffle if she's not going to eat it?" he asked, oblivious to the mounting tension.

"No. I'll make you another one in a minute," I said. "After I talk to Jason." The last thing Bryce needed before school was a breakfast of whipped cream. I looked at my watch—did I have time for a "discussion" and to get another waffle into Bryce before I drove him to school? Why was Jason here now? Why couldn't he have come after Bryce was gone for the day?

"I can make him a waffle," Rachel's brother offered, surprising me. "I'm a waffle expert."

Bryce looked at me for an okay, and I looked at the brother to see if he was for real. *What was his name again? Joe?* His smile reassured me that he wasn't some kind of waffle-making pervert, and I nodded at Bryce. He picked up his plate and swirled it across his tongue.

Rachel grimaced, but her brother smiled at Bryce. "I like your style," he said with an approving nod.

"Thanks . . . Joe?" I guessed. I chose to ignore Bryce's bad manners and Joe's encouragement of them.

"Joel," he said.

I nodded, too worried about what Jason was going to say to get bogged down in Tool Man's name.

"I can make them myself, but Emily always complains I fill it too full," Bryce said as Joel followed him into the kitchen, the door swinging back and forth behind their exit.

"Let's talk upstairs," I said to Jason, turning so Rachel stood behind me and was very obviously *not* invited to the conversation.

"I'll be in here," she said and pointed to the kitchen, to my relief.

Jason followed me up the stairs into my bedroom. "What's with the contractor?" I asked as soon as I'd shut the door.

"That's what I came to talk to you about." He looked around my room, which hadn't changed since my freshman year at UCLA when I decided to move out and live in the dorms. "Is there anywhere to sit?"

I pulled up the covers on my unmade bed—a testament to just how overwhelmed I was—and he sat down. I took a seat at my old concert-sticker-covered IKEA desk that wobbled as much as my stomach and knees.

"Rachel needs a kosher kitchen, so Joel's seeing what he can do to ours," he started, and for a second I was relieved he thought of this house as mine too. Then I realized "ours" meant his and Rachel's.

"Kosher?" I interrupted, switching my focus to the other word that had caught my attention. Why, I don't know. Maybe because, beyond not eating pork, I didn't know Jason had decided he was Jewish. I mean, his mom was, so technically he was, but he'd never been religious. Dad had joined the LDS Church when he met my mom, but Jason never had. His grandparents had held a bar mitzvah for him, and he occasionally attended synagogue with them, but that's as religious as he got. Or so I thought.

"Yeah. Meat and dairy can't touch, so Rachel has to have two of everything: fridges, sinks, counter spaces." He started to explain the law of something or other about what animals and foods were unclean and why certain foods couldn't touch, but I was so shocked at his sudden commitment to keeping kosher that I didn't listen.

"I know what *kosher* means, I'm just surprised you're doing it. What I really want to know is when you're getting married and if we have to be out before then." There was no sense in either of us beating around the bush.

"We haven't set a date yet, but I'll move into the guesthouse while Joel does the kitchen and you look for another place," Jason said so bluntly I was glad I was sitting down. My insides were Jell-O.

"You're moving here?" I thought I'd at least have until they were married before we had to move out.

"It doesn't make sense for me to pay rent somewhere when I have a house here. Plus, Rachel wants to be here a lot to help Joel with the kitchen. She'll need somewhere to stay." He talked slowly, as though that would help me understand. It dawned on me that just because he was intent on following a Jewish law about food didn't mean he had the same feelings about premarital . . . *relations*.

"I gave up my place to move in here with Annie and Bryce. We don't have anywhere else to go. Annie still hasn't recovered from losing Mom and Dad. Moving is going to devastate her and Bryce. Do you really think that's what Dad would want? For you to kick his children out of their own home?" My words spilled out in a jumble of half-formed arguments as I tried to grasp onto one that would convince him to let us stay.

"I lost him too, Emily." His eyes flashed, and I could see the hurt in them. "But the house was never Dad's to begin with. My mom left it to me. It's all I have left of her."

The stranglehold that anger had on my heart loosened. I had forgotten Jason lost as much as the rest of us. More, really. His mom had died when he was the same age as Bryce, and although he and my mom had never been close, she'd raised him through his teens. Deep down, he loved her. But recognizing his loss didn't make things any easier.

"We won't be able to live anywhere around here." I picked at the loose corner of a Coldplay sticker. Mom and I had both gone to that concert, except I insisted that she sit as far away as possible from me and my sixteen-year-old friends. That was stupid.

"You've got Dad's ranch, you've got insurance money to turn it into the bed-and-breakfast thing he wanted, and you've got the job experience to do it. That would give you some income—maybe even enough for some place around here. Or, worse comes to worst, you can live there."

I glanced up at him, knowing he was right, but not liking it. Jason got the house, but Dad had left me the ranch in Utah he'd bought as his retirement project, the fixer-upper he wanted to turn from "dried-up" to "dude."

"I've got to get to work," he said when I didn't answer. "Rachel and Joel are probably going to be here a lot over the next few months. You don't have to move until the school year is over, even until the end of summer if you need it." Jason smiled. "But be thinking about your options." He walked out, closing the door softly behind him.

Bryce needed a ride to school, but I couldn't face Rachel or her brother yet. Hugging my knees to my chest, I rested my forehead on them and squeezed my eyes shut. I couldn't think what to do, and after a few minutes, my back end hurt.

I lifted my head and looked across the room. Tiny green leaves peeked at me through the slatted shutters on my window. I walked to the window and pulled open the shutters to get a full view of the jacaranda tree outside my room. The branches were close enough that if I opened the window, I could pluck off a handful of the tiny purple-blue flowers covering the whole tree.

I used to wake each morning and look at that tree from my bed, watching its progression from bare to budding to full bloom as the seasons changed. I never got tired of its beauty. Dad hated the seedlings it dropped and would have cut it down, but Mom said anything beautiful is worth the mess. "The trick," she'd say, "is to keep your eye on the beauty and not what has to be cleaned up."

I closed the shutters and pushed the slats down so nothing showed through. The flowers were blooming early this year due to heat and drought. I should have been grateful for the splash of color when everything else looked brown and wilted, but they reminded me too much of myself, forced by uncontrollable circumstances to bloom before they were ready. Even at the height of their beauty, all I could see were the messy parts.

Chapter 2

AFTER DROPPING BRYCE OFF AT school, I did what I'd taken up the habit of doing lately when I needed someone to talk to. I went to the cemetery.

I found Mom's newly placed headstone and sat down next to her. Dad lay fifty feet away, next to his first wife, where his name had been on their joint headstone for twenty-five years. His recently carved death date stood out against the weathered stone like red lipstick on a bare face. For the first time, I was glad my parents weren't next to each other. I needed to talk to Mom alone.

"Jason's kicking us out," I told her in a whisper.

I knew exactly what she'd say, so I answered her. "I know it's his house, but where are we supposed to go?"

She didn't have an answer for me. I stayed anyway, hoping to feel her presence. I knew she wasn't there, but the cemetery was quiet and peaceful, two things in short supply in LA. I picked a blade of grass and ran it through my fingers, considering my problem. *Problems.*

"I'm not saying it was a bad idea for Annie to do those anti-porn ads, but they haven't helped her career. She's not getting any offers, her agent is about to drop her, and I have no idea how to be her manager. That's before dealing with her bipolar."

Again, Mom didn't have anything to say, which made her absence even more pronounced. I had no one to go to for advice. Of course, if Mom were still here, I wouldn't need advice on how to be a manager. Mom would still be doing it, and I'd still be working as a social media manager at a marketing firm that specialized in the hospitality industry—a job I loved, by the way.

I split the grass blade in two and plucked another. "I'm not mad at Dad for putting Annie's earnings in a trust fund, but it would make things a lot easier if she didn't have to wait until she was twenty-five to access them. There's not enough insurance money to buy a new house, and if she's not earning money, I'm not earning money. I don't know what to do."

I wasn't expecting an answer, but this time I heard her voice in my head. "Emily, you have the ranch," she said in the tone she used when I'd peppered her with questions to the point of exasperation. The tone that said, *You're not stupid; figure it out.*

I wanted to ask what she meant. Should I sell it? Should I live in it? But I knew I wouldn't get another answer. I'd put off making any hard decisions for nine months. It was time to step up and figure things out.

I pushed myself up off the ground then stared at the words on the headstone.

Caroline Carter
wife, mother, friend
April 15, 1965 – July 26, 2015

I still had trouble connecting the words in front of me to the smiling face I expected to see every time I walked through my front door. Nine months had passed, and her absence still didn't feel real, even just weeks away from her first birthday we'd be celebrating without her.

"Bye, Mom. Love you."

I brushed a tear away and walked to my car. I didn't have all the answers I needed, but I had a place to start. The ranch.

*   *   *

I drove home from the cemetery thinking through my options. If I wanted to stay in LA, I'd have to sell the ranch. I knew Dad would have hated that idea. Before the crash he'd planned on spending most of the summer there with Bryce to start fixing it up. But what did I know about fixing up a ranch?

I could use some of the insurance money to hire someone for the repairs, but I'd have to get back at least twice what I put in to make it worth the effort. Annie had a GED and few marketable skills beyond act-ing. She would have to work for the next seven years until she could tap into her trust fund. Bryce still had another eight years of school and then a mission and college to pay for. Basically, I needed enough money to support a family.

I drove down the windy road from the freeway exit to our house—Jason's house—considering what I should do. The safest, smartest thing seemed to be selling the ranch. But every time I came to that conclusion, Dad's dream of turning it into a small resort/retreat kept coming back to me.

By the time I walked in my front door, I was so overwhelmed, my brain felt like the rope in a tug-of-war. A noise coming from the kitchen caught my attention and put an end to the back and forth in my head.

"Hello? Annie?" I called out. But instead of my sister, Joel stood in the doorway between the dining room and kitchen. I hadn't realized the first time we met how short he was. His head was level with the mark Dad had made the last time he measured me, the day I graduated from high school. Of course, I'd been almost five ten then, so maybe Joel wasn't that short.

"Hi." He tucked a tape measure into his belt. "She left a little bit ago."

"Thanks." He had a slight frame, but his T-shirt hugged his chest in all the right places. Maybe it was his occupation or maybe it was the gym, but the guy had some nice pecs.

"So are you starting?" I pointed toward the kitchen.

"Not yet." He followed my finger over his shoulder. "Just measuring."

"Okay." I looked around, searching for something else to say. "I don't suppose you know where my sister went?"

"She mumbled something about your brother."

"Oh no." A wave of panic hit me, and I grabbed my phone from my purse. I scrolled through the increasingly worried texts from Bryce. I didn't bother listening to the voice mails both he and Annie had left.

"I was supposed to pick him up from baseball. He's going to be so mad." I crumpled into a chair, dug my elbows into the table, and planted my forehead in my hands.

"Your sister's got him. He'll understand," Joel said after a silence almost as awkward as the pat on the back he gave me.

I pulled my head up and glanced at him, debating whether or not to explain before letting my words spill out. "My parents were supposed to pick him up on the day they—the day of the accident. He waited for an hour before anyone figured it out. He gets a little panicky now when people don't show up."

He sucked in his breath. "Oooh, understandable."

"Was Annie at least dressed?" Bryce would be even more upset if she showed up looking the way she did on her brief forays back into the land of the living.

"She wasn't . . . *naked*," he said with trepidation.

I let out a sound somewhere between a growl and a laugh. "Was she wearing something besides pajamas?"

"Yeah." He tipped his head back and thought. "She had some of those tight pant things with cats on them."

I lifted an eyebrow. "Those are pajamas."

"Uh." His mouth slid into half a grin. "What do I know? I'm a guy."

"You've been very helpful. Thank you," I said, irritated at his smile. "I'm going to go hide in my room now until I can come up with an excuse that will convince my brother not to hate me forever."

"Actually, would you mind giving me a hand?" he asked before I could leave. "I can help you come up with an excuse."

"A hand with what?" I asked, suspicious but willing if it kept me from getting sucked into the black hole of guilt tugging at my heart.

"I need to measure your kitchen." He waved his head toward the kitchen then handed me a pad of paper from his hand and the pencil he had behind his ear. "It will go a lot faster with two people—I thought Rachel was going to be here, and I need to get back to my paying job."

"Sure," I said—even though I wasn't. If he hadn't said "your kitchen" and I hadn't been feeling so bad about Bryce, I couldn't have said yes to the first step in the demolition of "my" kitchen.

"Isn't Jason paying you?" I asked as I followed him through the door.

"Not what I'd usually make. I'm doing it as a kind of wedding present." He handed me one end of his tape measure and walked to the other end of the counter.

"Wow. Way to make the rest of us look bad. I was thinking towels." I lengthened the tape to the spot at the end of the counter he pointed to.

"It was Rachel's suggestion." He laughed and gave me the dimensions to write down.

"And you took it?" I blurted.

"My sister doesn't really take no for an answer." He gently tugged his end of the tape measure, and it snapped back, startling me.

"I thought that was only with Jason."

Joel looked at me and pursed his lips in way that made it hard to tell if he was holding back a smile or his irritation with me. "She can be bossy, but I owe Rachel a lot."

"Sorry, I didn't mean to be critical."

"No need to apologize. I get she's not easy to get along with, but she did convince my father to let me do this instead of practicing law." He glanced over my shoulder at the notepad then went back to measuring. The smell of his soap lingered.

"You were going to be a lawyer?" I could see where he'd nicked himself shaving along his jawline.

"Am. Passed the bar and have the diploma from USC to prove it." He ran the tape along the floor and squatted to read it.

"You went to USC?" I asked, not waiting for an answer before I pulled out my Bruin burn. "Don't feel bad. Lots of people can't get into UCLA."

"Ugh." He stood up, set his shoulders back, and looked me in the eye. "As a third-generation Trojan, I have too much dignity to respond to a cliché *Bruin*"—his lip curled with contempt—"insult."

"Ya got burnt." I let my mouth slide into a smile. "But I'll leave it there. Because Bruins are charitable."

"You do give away a lot of games." He bent back down to measure the base of the sink cabinet.

"See, and I'm going to let that go. That's how charitable I am." I wrote down the measurements he gave to me. "You'd really rather do this than practice law?"

"Meet interesting women—even if they are Bruins—rather than sit in an office reading documents all day? No question." He stood up and tucked the tape measure back in his tool belt.

I ignored his compliment—and his insult—but my cheeks didn't. They burned, and not with embarrassment. "Then why spend three years in law school?" Our fingers touched as I handed him the notepad. It tingled in a way it hadn't the first time we shook hands.

"My parents are both lawyers, Rachel's a lawyer, my grandparents were lawyers. All SC grads. I didn't know I had any other option." The gray in his shirt brought out the blue in his eyes. I had to remind myself to focus on the conversation, not the converser.

"There's always another option to SC."

"Ha. Not in my family."

"When did you figure it out?" I tucked my hair behind my ear and smoothed it.

"That I didn't want to be a lawyer?"

I nodded.

"When I was five and got my first set of blocks. It just took another twenty years to work up the nerve to tell my parents. Construction is not the job most Jewish mothers wish for their sons. Mine usually leaves out the builder part of my job and focuses on the architect part."

"You're an architect?" I asked, but my thoughts were focused on something else he'd said. I knew Rachel was Jewish. I'm not sure why it hadn't occurred to me her brother would be too. Now he was definitely off limits. Not because of his Jewishness, more because of his non-Mormonness. I'd vowed from the time I was eight I wouldn't marry someone who couldn't baptize my kids. I loved my dad more than anyone, but he joined the Church for my mom. I don't remember him ever being there. I do remember Mom asking him every Sunday morning if he would be.

"I'm taking some classes so I can design and build, but building is what I really love."

"So when did you tell your parents you were trading in the law for a hammer?" I asked, and he laughed.

"I didn't. Rachel did. She knew I was taking online courses in construction management. She told my parents I could be miserable trying to make them happy or they could be happy letting me do what made me happy." He leaned against the counter, and his easy manner made me want to open up and tell him everything. Like how I didn't know how to help my sister or what to do with the ranch or how to raise a ten-year-old boy. But almost as soon as he finished talking, the back door opened, and Rachel walked in.

"Hi." She kissed his cheek. "Sorry I'm late."

"I would have been more surprised if you weren't." He smiled at his sister's glare then cocked his head toward me. "Emily helped me out, so I'm almost done."

Rachel gave me a quick smile, barely acknowledging my presence before turning back to Joel. "Can I show you some things I picked out?"

His eyes darted to mine, the concern in them evident, before he answered. "How about we finish this first?"

I let my breath out, not realizing I'd been holding it. I'd been seconds away from unloading all my worries on this guy I hardly knew. This guy who was Rachel's *brother*. I was impressed—even touched—that he was more in tune than his sister. But he was still her brother, and he was still the guy who was changing the house from what Mom and Dad had made it into what Jason and Rachel wanted it to be.

"I guess I'd better get some work done," I said, checking my watch. "Nice talking to you, Joel. Bye, Rachel."

"Thanks for your help," Joel said.

"Anytime." I waved and walked into the dining room at the same time Annie and Bryce walked in the front door.

"You forgot to pick me up!" Bryce yelled as soon as he saw me.

"I'm so sorry, buddy." He ducked my attempt to put my arm around him.

"Why didn't you answer your phone?" Annie asked with a protective arm around Bryce. No tears fell, but his eyes were rimmed with red.

"Hey, there's my assistant! Where've you been?" Joel came into the hallway, followed by Rachel.

"Emily forgot to pick me up." He pointed an accusatory finger at me.

Joel shook his head with deep disapproval. "Big sisters are the worst." He winked at me then handed something to Bryce. "I got you this."

"Cool!" Bryce took the shiny new tape measure Joel handed him and turned it over and over in his hands, measuring its weight by hefting it in his hand. "When can we start?"

"Soon, I hope," Rachel interjected with a smile no one returned.

"As soon as your homework's done, you can help me measure the kitchen—if it's okay with your sister." He looked to me for an okay, but Bryce had dropped his backpack and was charging toward the kitchen.

"I finished my homework while I was waiting for Emily!" he said, darting past Joel.

"I'll be upstairs," Annie said to no one in particular and headed toward the stairs without waiting for a reply.

"I thought you already measured," Rachel said to Joel, her lip curled with irritation.

Joel shrugged. "Never hurts to have an intern do some fact-checking for you, right?"

Rachel rolled her eyes, but I thought I saw her almost grin before she turned to leave. Joel followed Bryce into the kitchen while I sat down at the table and flipped open my laptop. I would have taken it upstairs to work, but I liked the sound of him and Bryce joking around as they took measurements.

They were done in less than twenty minutes, but those minutes made a huge difference to Bryce. He ran out of the kitchen, past me, and up the stairs, yelling, "I'm going to measure my room now!"

"You saved me. Thank you," I said to Joel as he came through the door.

"No big deal." He set his tool belt on the table and looked down at me.

"It was to him." If his eyes were only less blue, I might have had an easier time thinking of something else to say.

He shrugged, and a few seconds of silence passed. "I guess I better get going." He picked up his tool belt again and headed for the door.

"I'll walk you out." I jumped up from my seat and followed him. "It really was nice of you to give him a tape measure and make him feel important. He needs that right now. Plus, he would have given me the silent treatment for the rest of the night. I owe you." We went down the walkway to where he'd parked his car in the street.

His *car*.

"Shouldn't you have a truck?"

He looked at his Prius then back at me. "My parents gave it to me for passing the bar. I have to take this whole construction thing one step at a time. Once Mom's used to this"—he held up his tool belt before dropping it on the floor of the backseat—"I'll move onto the truck."

"Makes sense." An embarrassing quiet followed. "Well, anyway, thanks again. Bryce will be occupied for hours—or at least minutes." I turned to walk back to the house.

"Hey. Would you be interested in seeing that Book of Mormon musical?" he asked before I got far.

I walked back. "Are you asking because I'm Mormon?"

"You are?"

I nodded.

"No." He took two tickets from his back pocket. "Rachel gave them to me. She and Jason are going. I thought you might like to go with us."

He was cute, and I was tempted, but no. "Thanks. I'd like to go with you, but I think I'm too much of a prude to enjoy it." Like I had time to go on dates anyway.

"Okay." He slid the tickets back in his pocket, his ears looking a little red. "Maybe another time."

"Yeah. If you've got any Mormon questions after you see it, feel free to ask," I joked. Sort of. I hoped he'd use it as an excuse to hang out with me again. As a friend, of course.

Chapter 3

A WEEK PASSED BEFORE I saw Joel again, which was both good and bad. Good because it meant we still had a kitchen; bad because I kept wondering when he'd be back. I chalked up my thoughts of him to feeling anxious about the impending construction. But a part of me wanted to hang out with him again. He was easy to talk to and definitely easy to look at, and the fact he wasn't Mormon meant there was zero pressure to fit some Eternal Companion ideal so he'd ask me out. He wasn't marriage material.

So I was a little irritated on the day he dropped by, when, as soon as I saw him, my pulse picked up speed. It never went all Usain Bolt on me around my other guy friends, but as I opened the door and saw Joel, my heart pounded.

"Hey." He smiled, and I couldn't help but notice the color of his T-shirt made his eyes look more gray than blue. "Is Rachel here yet?" He looked past me for her.

I shook my head.

"She wants to show me some stuff. Is that going to be weird?" His eyebrows creased with concern.

"No." I lied. I stepped back and opened the door wider. "Do you want to come in?"

He wiped his feet and stepped inside. "Are you sure? Rachel isn't always very sensitive to other people's feelings." He leaned against the wall and eyed me carefully.

"Thanks, but I'll be fine. It's Jason's house." I brushed aside my feelings with a wave of my hand, but Joel's eyes narrowed.

"Really?" He cocked his head to the side and leaned closer. "I tried to talk her into waiting until you move out, but she wants it done before the wedding. I'm afraid with all the structural changes she wants, it may take me that long to do it."

"Do you want a sandwich?" I asked to change the subject. "I was about to make myself a PB&J." I busied myself pulling the bread and peanut butter out of the cupboard.

"Sure."

"Can you grab the jam for me out of the fridge?" I took four slices of bread out of the bag, successfully avoiding any eye contact with him—until he handed me the jam and my fingers brushed his as I took it.

"Sorry for butting in. You don't have to answer," he said as we touched.

"I'm okay, really." I paused, spreading peanut butter on the bread. I tried to hold back my words, but in nine months no one had really asked me anything about my feelings. They just assumed I was okay. But the thing was, I didn't know how much longer I could do everything on my own. So I took a chance and unloaded a fraction of my load on Joel.

"I think it's worse for Annie. . . ." I handed him his sandwich but kept my eyes on his shoulder.

"Jason mentioned she doesn't go out much since . . . the accident." He took a bite of his sandwich and leaned against the counter.

"If by 'doesn't go out much' he means 'stays in her room all the time,' then I'm impressed he's actually noticed what's been going on." I tore the corner off my sandwich and popped it in my mouth to keep from saying more. I hadn't meant to say as much as I did; I was just surprised to hear Jason ever said anything about us.

"Does she only hide out when he's around, or is she really holed up in her room?" His mouth curved into a smile. "Sorry. I'm getting into your business again. You don't have to answer that."

I hesitated, but it was too hard to hold back when I had someone actually willing to listen. "No, it's a problem even when Jason isn't around—which is most of the time." Not that I was bitter or anything. "Before we couldn't get her to stay home. She's an actress. She thrived on being around people. Not that she hasn't been depressed before, she has; it's just never been this bad."

"She's been through a lot. You all have." He cleared his throat and lifted his sandwich like he was going to take a bite, then didn't.

Pushing back the lump in my throat took so much effort I couldn't say anything, so I was glad when he did.

"Is she working right now?"

I shook my head and handed him a napkin. He set his sandwich on it and brushed his hands off on his jeans. "It's good." He nodded toward his PB&J. "I'll save the rest for later."

"Uh huh." I nodded, unconvinced, and raised my eyebrows.

"Really, I will." A grin threatened then won, but it only spread to his left cheek. "I don't think I've had peanut butter and jelly since I was twelve years old."

"Between waffles and peanut butter sandwiches, you've experienced the entire range of my culinary skills." I set my own sandwich down and sucked a smudge of peanut butter off my thumb. "At least for now. I've signed up for a cooking class so Bryce will quit complaining I don't cook like Mom and maybe Annie will eat something. Mom tried to teach me, but . . ." I shook my head, unable to finish the sentence.

Joel laughed. "Well, until then, I guess I better not miss out on the full experience." He picked up his sandwich and took a huge bite. Like a half-a-sandwich bite.

"Now, tell me why Annie isn't working." His words came out sticky and jumbled as he worked his way around them with his mouth full of peanut butter. "Her Disney show wasn't my thing"—huge swallow—"but it's obvious she's got talent." He forced the last of his bite down and smiled wide, a spot of grape jelly stuck on his front tooth.

I bit back my own grin then took a huge bite of my sandwich before answering him. "I don't know if youb seen the Stop Porn campaign she did." I stopped to brush the bread crumbs I'd sprayed off his shirt. "But dere haben't been a lotta offers since she did that."

"That stinks. She did a good thing; she shouldn't be punished for it, but it doesn't surprise me that she was."

If there had been any weirdness left between us after our sandwich eat-off, it would have been wiped away with those words. He understood, and that's all I needed.

"She had a part in a movie, but when the ads came out, the producers started looking for a way to fire her. She shut down after my parents' accident, and they had the perfect excuse. Her agent hasn't dumped her, but she might as well have. I don't think she's even tried to find Annie any roles. Not that she could. I know I haven't been able to." I licked my teeth, even though the jelly was on his.

"Neither of you have been able to find *anything*? Not even supporting roles?" He leaned against the wall and crossed his arms.

"It's hard enough to find good parts when you won't do nudity or sex scenes. I think her agent decided it would be impossible to get work for someone who attacked an entire industry that Hollywood may think they're better than but still doesn't mind getting mixed up in. I doubt the producers wanted the challenge of trying to sell a movie starring 'Angelic Annie.'" I made air quotes around the name the tabloids had dubbed her with.

"She's Mormon too, right? Would she be in trouble with your church if she did sex scenes?" he asked.

I had to think how to answer that. "It's not that she'd be in trouble as much as she'd be uncomfortable doing something that goes against what we believe about our bodies and . . ." my face went red, and I couldn't say the word I was going to. "Procreation being sacred." *Procreation?* I was such a prude. And to make matters worse, Annie walked through the door at the exact moment I said it.

"Procreation?" Joel forced back a smile. My face burned hotter.

"Did you just use the word *procreation* with Jason's contractor?" Annie's eyes were wide with horror. "What is happening here?"

Joel let out a loud HA! But I couldn't make a sound.

"Never mind." Annie held up her hand and eyed Joel up and down. "I don't even want to know. I'm just going to get my water and go."

She opened the fridge and took out a glass bottle, eyed Joel again, then left, but not before Joel grinned and said, "Nice to see you again, Annie."

Once the door shut behind her, any hope that we could move on to a different topic shattered when Joel spoke.

"So procreation? Is that in those gold plates Joseph Smith got?" There was a hint of sincerity behind the teasing in his question, which helped relieve some of my embarrassment.

"The Book of Mormon?" I asked, setting him straight. "Well, kind of. But it's also on those stone tablets Moses got." I could tease too.

"Noted." He smiled. "So is that story really true? About Joseph Smith? It's not just in the musical?"

"I don't know how it's depicted in the musical, but, yeah, an angel directed Joseph Smith to where some gold plates were buried, and those were translated into the Book of Mormon." My face felt fine now. I wasn't embarrassed to talk about what I believed. Why should I be? Growing up with a dad who wasn't active meant belief had always been something I had to choose on my own. I'd made my choice the first time Dad told me

I didn't have to go to early-morning seminary if I didn't want to. I went every day. Occasionally I even made it on time.

"So you *really* believe that happened? Angels and gold plates?" Despite his voice sounding incredulous, there was a hint of hope in his eyes.

"How is it so different than the story of Moses being given the Ten Commandments on stone tablets? You believe that, don't you?" I don't know what made me play on his Jewishness. A feeling, I guess.

He raised his shoulders slowly. "I don't know. I used to. My parents do."

"Well, can't God give His word on gold plates too?"

Before he could respond, I heard a car pull into the driveway. I knew it had to be Rachel. "No offense, but I think I'll go before I have to talk to your sister." I threw the crust from my sandwich in the garbage and brushed the crumbs into the sink.

"It's fine. I get it." A car door shut, and he glanced out the window. "You said I could ask you Mormon questions, right? Could I take you for a coffee some time?" He asked, his eyes darting back to the window as heels clicked on the walkway to the back door.

I smiled. "First thing you should know is Mormons don't drink coffee." I should have left it at that, but I didn't. "How about ice cream?"

"Right." He smiled back. "Ice cream's good too." He pulled a pen out of his back pocket and grabbed my hand. "Here's my number. Text me yours." He scrawled seven digits across my palm. Before I could stop the thought, I found myself wishing his number was at least seven digits longer.

I liked the way my hand felt in his.

Chapter 4

I texted Joel my number before the ink could smear. Waiting would feel like I was playing games, and playing games would mean I liked him as something more than a friend.

Which I didn't—wouldn't.

So when Saturday rolled around and I found myself checking my phone every half hour to see if I'd missed a call or a text, I decided I needed a distraction. And what better distraction on an unseasonably hot March day than the beach?

Bryce didn't need any convincing when I suggested it and had invited a friend by the time I'd talked Annie into coming too. She had taken more convincing than Bryce, but not nearly as much as I thought she would. Within an hour, we had our chairs set up on the beach and Bryce and his friend Tanner were in the water.

"I'm glad you came," I said while Annie and I watched the boys ride a wave on their boogie boards.

"Me too." She closed her eyes and faced the sun. "I don't even care about wrinkles today. It feels so good to be out here."

"Yeah, right," I said and tapped her arm with the sunscreen I knew she'd be asking for soon. If there were other eighteen-year-olds besides Annie who actually believed the science behind sun and skin damage, I hadn't met them. But I also didn't know any other eighteen-year-olds whose road to fame started with a dermatology ad.

Annie took the sunscreen from me and spread it over her face. "Is it all rubbed in?" she asked and leaned close to me.

I used my thumb to wipe a white streak off her cheek and a spot on her forehead. "Are you feeling better?" I asked, more gentle with my words than with my touch. Annie would talk about anything, except her depression.

"Yeah, I'm getting there." She turned her back to me, and I lathered sunscreen on her shoulders.

"Good. Your medication is working?" I'd finally convinced her to see her psychiatrist a few weeks before, but it took time for the prescription he gave her to start working.

"Yeah." She sank slowly back into her chair and covered her face with her hat, leaving only her mouth exposed. "Things don't look as black. But I'm still sad."

"We all are." I dug my feet into the sand then pulled them out, letting the sand run between my toes.

Annie lifted her hat and looked at me. "Really?"

"Well, yeah." Her question surprised me.

"Sometimes it's hard to tell with you." She leaned her head back, keeping the hat pulled up so I could see her face. "I know I'm too emotional. Exhibit A: the meds I'm on. . . ." She opened her eyes wide as she said this, and I snorted. "But at least I'm expressing my emotions, not just holding them in. That can't be any healthier than staying in bed. At least that's what my therapist says." She covered her face again, not waiting for an answer. Or maybe she knew better than to expect one.

I started to reply but bit back my words. There was no point in getting into an argument over whether or not I expressed my emotions. How could I explain to Annie that I didn't have the luxury of staying in bed when everything was crumbling around me? Someone had to keep things from completely falling apart. She'd be offended, and I didn't want her shutting down again. Instead of letting her words get to me, I decided to go for a swim.

"Come on; come out with me." I grabbed her hands and pulled her out of her seat. At first she was reluctant to get up, but once I started running toward the water, she had to beat me. We made it to the water at the same time, but we didn't stop until we had to dive under a wave.

"Oh, this was a bad idea!" Annie squealed when she popped up. LA may have been hotter than usual, but the Pacific was still freezing.

"I know. Wanna see who can stay in longest?" My teeth were already chattering as I dove under another wave.

Annie hated to lose, which meant the longer I stayed in the water, the longer she would. And the longer I focused on ducking under waves, the longer I could go without thinking about all the problems I couldn't duck—or the one person I should duck but didn't want to.

I made it about two minutes—Annie a few seconds longer—before running back to shore and wrapping up in my beach towel. I rubbed the water off my shoulders and legs then spread the towel on the warm sand and flopped down on my belly, resting my head on my hands.

"I'm sorry I'm not working right now, Emily," Annie said a few minutes after lying down next to me.

I sighed. "I'm sorry I can't find any work for you. I'm not very good at the manager thing."

"That's not true!" she protested. "It's my fault for doing those Stop Porn ads. I never would have done them if I'd known they'd keep me from getting hired again."

I rolled over and sat up to make sure she heard me. "Yes, you would have, and you shouldn't question your decision. Even if you never work again, you did the *right* thing, and that's what's important."

"You don't think I'll work again?" Worry lines etched their way across her normally flawless brow.

"That's not what I said." I shook my head.

"Remember when Bryce came home totally traumatized by what his friend had shown him on the computer? I wanted to do something to protect my little brother. Then when the Stop Porn people contacted me around the same time, it seemed like God had given me a way to help Bryce and every other little kid." She raced through her explanation without taking a breath even though she knew I was on her side.

"You don't need to explain anything to me. What do you think will have a better lasting impact on people? Your TV show or your fight against pornography?"

"My fight against porn." She wrapped her arms around my shoulders and squeezed. "Thanks for putting things back into perspective for me."

I patted her arm then stood up to find the boys. I spotted them farther down the beach, but they didn't look like they were coming in from the water anytime soon, so I lay back down on my stomach and pulled a book out of my bag. "Can you keep an eye on the boys?" I asked Annie. By the time she answered yes, I'd put my book down and closed my eyes.

I woke up in the middle of a dream about someone poking me with burning icicles. I opened my eyes to Bryce's feet inches from my nose. The burning icicles were actually bullets of icy water shooting from his hair as he leaned over me shaking his head, purposely spraying Annie and me.

"Stop it!" she yelled.

Similar words were on the tip of my tongue, but in the split second before I let them out, I saw the ear-to-ear grin on Bryce's face. He *needed* to tease his sisters again.

"You little . . . !" I didn't know what to call him, so I laughed and jumped up to escape.

Before I could, he shook his head again and sent more cold water flying my way. I ran, and he chased me. The wetsuit he had stripped down to his waist kept him from catching up to me, and when I saw a stray bucket full of water, I grabbed it. I turned to face him and held up the bucket, stopping him in his tracks.

"Truce?" I raised the bucket, ready to douse him.

"Okay, but only because you're sunburned." He stepped closer and poked my shoulder with his finger, then pulled it back, leaving a white spot surrounded by bright red.

"You are too." I poked his shoulder, only harder to get him back for the shower. "Which means it's time to go." I dropped the bucket and walked back to our spot with Bryce following.

"Your phone dinged while you were playing chase." Annie held out my cell, pursing her lips to keep from smiling. She'd read my text.

The words *Ice cream tomorrow?* spread across the screen. My heart pumped faster, and suddenly my shoulders weren't the only things burning. I took a deep breath and reminded myself Joel wasn't asking me out, we were just friends. And *tomorrow* meant Sunday, so that put an end to any hopes of seeing him this weekend.

Would love to, but it's Sunday, I typed.

Is that a problem? Joel replied.

The Sabbath. Gotta keep it holy.

Got it. I think. . . .

"Who are you texting?" my sister asked. The smile she'd tried to hold back had moved to her eyes. She knew who it was.

"Nobody." I shoved my phone into my beach bag, then dropped a towel on top of it.

"Your face is pretty red for a text from nobody," Annie taunted, making my face even hotter.

"I'm sunburned." My phone dinged again, and I resisted the urge to dig it out of my bag.

I folded my beach chair, hoisted it onto my back, and picked up my bag. The chair banged against my knees with each step, sending hot rays of pain across my burned skin, but still I took my time walking to the car. My bag bounced against my hip, reminding me it held my phone and the text from Joel that was on it.

I drove below the speed limit all the way home to prove to myself I wasn't in a hurry to read Joel's message. I unpacked the cooler and the beach bags, I took a shower, I even vacuumed the sand out of my car. Zen masters had nothing on me and my self-control. Three hours after my phone had dinged, I allowed myself to read Joel's text.

Adding this to my Mormon ??? list.

I smiled and gave myself permission to answer. I'd waited long enough to prove to myself I wasn't falling for him.

Making a Jewish ??? list of my own.

Once I'd sent my text, my Zen moment was over. I spent the rest of the night slathering aloe vera on my sunburn and chastising myself every time I checked my phone for Joel's answer. Under threat of torture, I will never admit how much self-chastising it took before I finally put my phone away and went to bed.

Chapter 5

THE NEXT AFTERNOON WHEN JOEL still hadn't texted and it was time for me to go to church, I felt like a sixteen-year-old girl waiting to be asked to prom. Ridiculous. I grabbed my scriptures and left my phone behind before I yelled goodbye to Annie and Bryce, who were going to our family ward later, and headed to the YSA ward.

I came home four hours later to a moving truck in the driveway. Jason had told me that he and Rachel would be moving into the guesthouse within a few weeks, but I wasn't prepared for it to be that day. With them in the guesthouse, it increased the pressure I already felt to find a new place to live.

I was about to find somewhere else to go until they were done, but then I saw Joel. Shirtless. Which gave me an even better view of the shoulders and pecs I'd admired through his T-shirt.

"It's a nice day to sit in the park," I told myself, even as I was putting my car *into* park. "You could join Annie and Bryce in your old ward. See all those familiar faces."

I didn't listen.

I sat in my car and watched Joel help Jason carry a sofa to the back of the house then around the corner toward the guesthouse. When I couldn't see him anymore, I told myself to get out of the car and go inside before he saw me.

I didn't listen.

I gathered up my scriptures and my purse . . . and then any trash I could find in my car. I double-checked I hadn't forgotten to turn off my lights and that I had my registration in the glove box. When I heard voices, I opened my door and walked slowly up the walkway toward our porch, ignoring the voice telling me, "You're not wearing heels; you're not carrying anything heavy. WALK LIKE A NORMAL PERSON!"

But when Joel came around the corner and his face broke into a smile when he saw me, I had no regrets.

"Hey! I'm sorry I never answered your text," he said, while I ignored the look of surprise on my brother's face. "Jason and Rachel conned me into slave labor."

"So I see." My eyes wandered to his bare chest before I could stop them, then they shot back up to see a grin tugging at the corners of his mouth. He'd busted me.

"Do you, um, need help?" I stumbled over my words, trying to recover.

"We could use some more muscle." He cupped his hand around my bicep and squeezed. "But I guess you'll do."

His touch pretty much ruled out any possibility of recovery, but somehow I managed to laugh and say, "That sounds like a challenge."

"We're okay without you. I know you don't like to work on Sunday," Jason interrupted, killing the moment.

"No, it's fine. I'd say this is an ox-in-the-mire situation," I answered, to which I was greeted with two quizzical faces.

"I don't know what farm animals have to do with moving, but ignore Jason and come help," Joel said at the same time Rachel's voice drifted from the backyard, yelling, "Are you on your way with more stuff?"

"Please," Joel added—no, begged.

"Sure, let me go change." I glanced at Jason, who shrugged. Not that I needed his approval.

I went inside questioning whether I'd only decided to break the Sabbath because a cute guy was involved, but I convinced myself I was actually doing service and that the cute guy was a blessing of that service. Yeah . . . that.

I changed into jeans and picked out a top that brought out the blue in my eyes. It looked good. Too good. Like I was trying. I slipped it off and threw on an old UCLA T-shirt without checking myself in the mirror. I couldn't check the smile that spread across my face though. I doubted Joel could resist saying something about my shirt.

By the time I got back downstairs, Joel was helping Jason carry a dresser down the truck ramp.

"Oh good, you wore something not worth saving," he said as he passed me, and the smile I'd just tucked away popped out again.

"How can I help?" I asked as Rachel started down the same ramp with a large box. She glanced at me then lifted up a leg to try and balance the box while she got a better grip. I ran and grabbed the other side.

"Thanks." She smiled at me around the box, and we backed down the ramp.

For the next hour, I helped Rachel unload boxes and arrange the furniture. And it wasn't so terrible. Rachel and I didn't talk much, but Joel joked a couple times about my muscles. I didn't say anything about his, but I definitely noticed them. They were hard to miss. But not in a body builder kind of way, more like an I-come-by-these-naturally kind of way.

After we finished unloading and arranging as much as we could, the four of us collapsed on the front steps of the guesthouse. Jason brought out waters and passed them around. The smell of sweat mingled with the sweet scent of the jasmine blooming in the flower beds, and I was hyper aware of Joel sitting behind me. His knees brushed my back whenever I moved, and it took an epic amount of self-control not to just lean back into them and make myself comfortable.

"So eating ice cream isn't okay on your Shabbat, but unloading moving trucks is?" Joel leaned forward as he asked his question, and his breath tickled the back of my neck.

I turned to face him and put the cold bottle of water against my neck. I was hot from working, and having him so close wasn't cooling anything down. "*Eating* ice cream is fine. *Buying* it isn't because someone else has to work to sell it."

"I'm joking. Trust me, I know what is and isn't okay on the Sabbath. I've got eleven years of Hebrew school under my belt." He held the water bottle to his mouth and took a long drink.

"I may have bent the rules a little with the unloading." I blew my bangs out of my eyes and watched his Adam's apple bob while he swallowed.

"I'm glad you did." Jason almost smiled.

"Yeah, thanks." Rachel leaned back into Jason's chest and let him rest his arms on her.

Jason slapped Joel on the back and stood up. "We better get going if we're going to return the truck and make dinner at your parents'." He pulled Rachel up, and they walked down the steps. "See you later, Emily," he said without looking back. "You coming, Joel?"

"In a minute." He scooted down to sit on the step next to me.

Rachel looked back and raised an eyebrow. "Don't be late. Mom won't want to wait for you."

They climbed into the truck, and once Jason had it started, Joel spoke. "Why isn't Jason a Mormon?"

"His mom was Jewish. Even though she wasn't observant, when she knew she was dying, she asked my dad to let Jason go to synagogue with her parents. I think she was trying to make amends with her parents for marrying a non-Jew. They loved my dad but always wished he was Jewish or that he'd convert."

"That makes sense."

"Does it? All my dad said when I asked him why Jason went to church with his grandparents instead of with us is, 'That's what his mom wanted.' I'm kind of making assumptions about the rest from what my mom told me." I propped my elbow on my knee and rested my head on my hand.

"Your dad didn't care if Jason wasn't raised Mormon?" A crease divided Joel's brow.

I sat back, stretching my legs in front of me. "Dad got baptized before he married Mom, but I don't think he ever really converted. Even if he had been a more active Mormon, I think he loved Jason's mom—Leah—and respected her parents too much to go back on his promise."

Joel nodded. "Does active mean observant?"

I laughed. "Yeah, sorry."

"Mormons have their own Yiddish."

I laughed again. "Kind of."

He stood up, stretched his arms, and twisted back and forth. "I'm going to feel this tomorrow." He hesitated. "Do you want to come to my parents' for dinner?"

His question came out of nowhere and knocked me off balance. I hadn't anticipated it, so I had no idea how to answer it. I wanted to go, but I didn't want *to want* to go. I blinked and bit my lip.

"I totally freaked you out, didn't I? Going from 'let's have ice cream' to 'come meet my parents'?" He closed his eyes and shook his head. "Let me try again. You're hungry, I'm hungry, my mom can feed us."

My lips crept into a grin, and I was about to say yes when I heard a car pull into the driveway. Bryce and Annie were home from church. "I'd better not."

A whisper of disappointment crossed his face, and I almost changed my mind, but I couldn't. Sunday dinner was a thing at our house—Mom made sure of that. But now it was my job, even if peanut butter sandwiches were the best I could do. Annie and Bryce needed me, and I didn't need anything that would make my life more complicated than it already was. And Joel was the equivalent of advanced calculus when it came to life-complicating problems.

Chapter 6

AFTER WE'D EATEN DINNER, WATCHED our traditional cheesy Sunday movie (Disney's *Wilderness Family* for the win), and I'd put Bryce to bed, I pulled out my Binder o' Goals. Every New Year's from the time I was eight until eighteen, I wrote down my personal long-term and short-term goals. Mom put them in a binder along with erratic journal entries about how I was doing. She did it for Annie and Bryce too once they turned eight.

When I turned eighteen, I kept setting goals and adding to the binder myself. Every once in a while, I'd look back through it for a laugh or a reminder of how much I'd changed in sixteen years. Even though Annie, Bryce, and I had forced ourselves to keep up the tradition this past New Year's, I hadn't been able to bring myself to really look through my binder since my parents' accident.

Tonight, I worked up the courage. As much as my goals had changed over the years—I never did become a dog trainer—the one at the top of my long-term list never had. Temple marriage. I'd wanted it when I was eight, and I still wanted it now. Except it wasn't so long-term anymore. I had to think about it every time I went on a date with a guy, and especially if I got all the way to the Define the Relationship phase.

It hadn't really been a problem before. I'd gone on dates with non-members, but I'd never been drawn to any of them like I was to Joel. And unless my radar was way off, the attraction wasn't one-sided.

I went to bed with my head spinning more circles than an Olympic skater. It's not like I could avoid him since, one, he'd be working in my house, and, two, he would soon be my brother's brother-in-law. I was bound to run into him sooner or later. The only real solution was to keep him in the friend zone. I could do that. . . .

I had to.

I went to sleep resolved to keep my feelings in check, but my first test came with a text the next morning. I picked up my phone when I heard it ding, and read Joel's name.

Working at your house today. Ice cream tonight?

Before I could stop myself, my mouth stretched into a smile, and my fingers were itching to type yes. Then I remembered I had FHE that night. I could skip it, but I had talked Annie into going, and she needed it. Although . . . there would be ice cream at the activity. I considered for a minute before texting back.

How do you feel about board games? My heart pounded as I pressed send.

They don't taste as good as ice cream.

I laughed out loud. *What about in addition to?*

Loser buys? I'm in, he replied.

I chewed my lip and considered how to break the news to him he would be hanging out with a bunch of Mormons without it sounding like I was trying to convert him.

Good news! The ice cream is free, and you'll have plenty of people to answer your Mormon questions :)

He took a long time to respond. Long enough for me to take a shower, get dressed, change, get dressed again, and put on full makeup. Finally my phone dinged. I nearly knocked it off my desk as I scrambled to read Joel's text.

Is this a church thing?

Five simple words that could be read so many ways. I decided to keep my reply even simpler.

Yes. Might as well be up front, but I also had an out. *I talked my sister into going, and I can't bail on her. Ice cream another night?* I hoped I sounded casual enough to keep him from bolting.

He responded right away, which I took as a good sign, but my nerves were bouncing off the walls, and seconds passed before I worked up the courage to read it.

Will there be missionaries there?

No, I typed then deleted. I had to be realistic. Missionaries were masters at showing up when you least expected. *Maybe,* I wrote then deleted again before settling on a way to put the ball in his court. *Do you want there to be?*

Ha ha. Way to avoid the question.

You know what's really funny? In Mormon Yiddish, you may actually be the only Gentile there.

How can I pass up the opportunity to see what it's like to be a Gentile?

My heart slowed to its normal pace. I read back through our texts to make sure I didn't sound like he was my missionary project. Or that I was into him as anything more than a friend. I probably should have just said no to the ice cream and left it at that. But, honestly, I needed Joel. He'd never met my parents, so his eyes didn't fill with pity when he saw me. I could talk about them without him looking away, wondering what to say. Or I could not talk about them without a weird weight hanging over us, threatening to drop.

Everything got lighter with Joel around. Maybe because he tried to make things easier for me in little ways, like being nice to Bryce. Or maybe because he was the kind of guy who would do that for anybody. Whatever it was, I wanted to keep him as a friend.

At the same time, I had to keep him as *only* a friend. Nothing more than that.

Which meant that if he were going to be working at the house today, I needed to work somewhere else.

I'd been putting off springing a visit on Annie's agent, but today was the perfect day. I had some leads on projects we needed her agent to follow up on. I hoped the possibility of work would be enough to get my sister out of bed. If not, then the threat of being stuck at home listening to the kitchen being demoed would have to do the job.

And it did. Within an hour Annie was dressed and looking almost like herself again. *Almost.* She'd made a minimal effort to dress up by putting on a floral shift dress and sandals, but she kept her face even simpler with only a touch of mascara and lip gloss and her hair pulled back in a ponytail. A year ago she wouldn't have left the house without full makeup, let alone gone to see her agent as bare faced and dressed down as she was.

"She probably won't see us anyway, so it doesn't matter what I wear," she said, guessing what I was thinking about her outfit before I could say it.

She still looked beautiful, but she'd never gone this long without work since she was six years old and shot her first commercial. The last nine months had done a number on her confidence.

We dropped Bryce off at school then headed downtown to the highrise with the gleaming office of Sharon Lynch, who worked at one of the best-known talent agencies in Hollywood. The agency itself represented some of the biggest names around, and the top agents had offices that made Sharon's look like a cubicle.

We rode the elevator to the eleventh floor and stepped into the marble-and-glass foyer. The walls were lined with promo shots from TV shows and movies, including one from Annie's show. I was glad to see they still had it there. I'd take it as a good sign they still wanted her.

I walked past the couches lined with people to the receptionist desk and smiled at the borderline-anorexic blonde who had to be my age but so obviously had already started Botox. Her failed attempt to raise her eyebrows when she saw us was a dead giveaway.

"Hi. Will you tell Sharon that Emily and Annie Carter are here to see her?" My lips felt plastic, they were pulled so tight—almost as plastic as the receptionist's face would look in another twenty years. Sometimes I hated Hollywood. Like, most of the time.

"Is she expecting you? I don't see you on her calendar." She scrolled down her iPad looking for our names, her eyebrows once again trying to move but failing.

"She's not. We just haven't heard from her for a while, so I thought we'd pop in," I said loudly enough for the other people—Sharon's prospective clients—in the foyer to hear. "It's been a while since she's been able to get any work for Annie, so we wanted to make sure everything was okay." My voice dripped with more artificial sweetener than a sixty-four ounce Diet Coke. Annie's stardom may have been on the decline, but she was still orbits above the potential stars seated around the room, who, as I glanced around, were all listening intently.

"I'll see what I can do. It may be a while though." Anorexic Receptionist dipped her chin and stared me down.

"That's okay. We've got time to wait." I leaned over the chest-high partition to get closer and whispered, "Looks like there's plenty of people for Annie to talk to. She loves talking craft with fellow actors." I stood back, and, as if on cue, Annie sat down next to a little girl and her mom, signed the paper the girl handed her, then started chatting.

"I'll tell her you're here." The receptionist frowned and picked up the phone.

"We'll wait over there." I tilted my head toward Annie, who, whatever she was saying, had the full attention of the little girl's mom.

When I sat down next to them, it turned out the intense conversation was about the best hair products for little girls, but Skin and Bones didn't need to know that. She could go on sweating over what Annie might say about Sharon's ability to find work for her clients.

The receptionist watched us closely for the next hour before Sharon finally came out herself to lead us back to her office.

"I'm so glad you stopped by," she said, motioning for us to sit down on the plush white sofas in her office. "I think I've found some things you might be interested in." She sat down across from us and crossed her legs, smiling confidently as though it had been a few days since we'd last talked instead of a few months.

"Not commercials?" I asked, but it was a preemptive strike. Annie had started in commercials, but we had decided going back to them after her successful TV series and movie would be a step backwards. She didn't have the star power to do them without losing the credibility she had.

"No, but I wish you'd reconsider. The parameters for what she's willing to do on film or TV are pretty narrow. She'd have a lot more work if she'd do commercials." Sharon directed her comments to me even with Annie only two feet away.

"But that would kill my chances to work on bigger projects. I don't want to be stuck doing commercials for the rest of my career," Annie interrupted.

"I understand, but you've made it very difficult for me to find anything else for you." Sharon scolded her like a kid who'd been sent to the principal's office.

"What about the new Spielberg project? Can you get her an audition for any parts in that?" I asked and, feeling a little Mama Bearish—or at least Big Sister Bearish—scooted closer to Annie.

Sharon shook her head. "I tried. They've already cast the part that fits Annie's description. I'm telling you, directors and producers are afraid to use her because of that porn thing she did."

"I'm right here. You can talk to me." Annie sat up straighter and lasered in on Sharon. "And it's called Stop Porn. I'm sorry I ever did it, but at least get the name right."

I reeled back. "Don't say that," I exclaimed at the same time Sharon sighed and said, "Me too."

"If Russell Brand can make a YouTube video about how bad porn is, what's the big deal about Annie's thirty-second spots?" If Annie didn't feel like defending her decision, then I would.

"The difference is he knows from experience, and he hasn't given it up. For better or worse, Annie doesn't have the experience to back up her message."

"So only addicts should warn kids about drugs?" I shot back.

Sharon shrugged. "The point is no one is interested in a grown-up Annie Carter right now. Except for one project . . ."

"What is it?" Annie asked.

"It's a period drama BYUtv is producing," Sharon said hesitantly.

"BYU?" *Weird.* I doubted I had heard her right.

"You mean like their *Granite Flats* show?" Annie perked up for the first time.

"You've heard of it?" Sharon's shoulders fell into a more relaxed position.

"Well, yeah. Parker Posey guest starred. I've watched all the episodes, but isn't it ending soon?" Annie's interest surprised me, but her eyes had a tiny spark in them. Not the fire they used to have when it came to acting, but I'd take a spark.

"It is, but they're casting for a new project they're hoping will be bigger than *Granite*. I didn't think you'd be interested because even though they had a lot of success with *Granite*, its viewership is still smaller than what you're used to." Sharon picked up on Annie's growing excitement, changing her tone from brush off to business. "Filming will also be in Utah, so you have to take that into consideration, but they're very interested in having you play a lead role."

"Really?" Annie's spark got fire, but I still had some questions.

"How long would she have to be in Utah? When you say 'smaller viewership,' how much smaller are we talking? And do they expect viewership to increase with this new series?"

"*Granite Flats* got good reviews, and it's been picked up by Netflix. This could be exactly what I'm looking for, Emily." And there was Annie's fire. I didn't want to put it out, but I also had to control it.

"Let them know we're interested, but we need to see a script first. How soon are the auditions?" The more I thought and talked about it, the more excited I got. Except about the Utah part. That could be a problem.

We stayed a little longer, talking over the details, then left with Sharon's promise to call me that night with audition and script info. Annie practically tap-danced back to the car, forgetting all the complications attached to the job. I hadn't, but that was okay. My job as Annie's manager was to let her live in the clouds while I stayed grounded in the details of her career.

Chapter 7

AFTER STOPPING FOR LUNCH AT The Grove and killing some time window-shopping, Annie and I headed home. Her original excitement from having a director interested in hiring her had morphed into anxiety about whether she'd like the script, or if she'd even get the job if she did like the script, and how much it would pay, and whether she'd have to move to Utah without Bryce and me, and a thousand other worries.

By the time we got on the freeway, all Annie wanted to do was get home, soak in a lavender bath, and go to bed.

"We have Family Home Evening tonight," I reminded her. "Joel is coming, and I already got a sitter for Bryce."

"I don't want to go. I'm too stressed out to be any fun." She rested her head against the seat back and squeezed the bridge of her nose.

"Take your bath and a short nap, and you'll feel better. You've got to go with me though. Please." My own spool of anxiety wound itself around my stomach. For a few hours, I thought Annie was better, but if this job didn't pan out, I worried she'd get worse. And in the immediate future, I *needed* her to go with Joel and me tonight. Otherwise, we'd totally be on a date.

We got home and walked through the front door into a cloud of dust. Bryce was in full Thor mode swinging a hammer at the wall. He grunted every time he made contact, and his face broke into a smile.

Mine didn't. My heart crashed to the floor with the same velocity as the flying plaster. Annie took one look and walked silently upstairs. I rushed toward Bryce, ready to grab his arm and make him stop destroying Mom's house. The grin that stretched across his face stopped me. It radiated pride, but even more than that, I could see him letting out every emotion he'd been keeping in for nine months.

"There you go, dude!" Joel yelled as Bryce yanked a chunk of plaster off the wall.

"Awesome!" Bryce pulled his arm back and took another swing.

I picked up my heart, took a deep breath, and forced my own smile. "Whoa! Aren't you breaking some child labor laws here?" I yelled to Joel over the pounding, startling both of them.

"Emily! Did you see what I did?" Bryce pointed to the section of wall that was now just two-by-fours and the chicken wire stuff used in plaster walls.

"Bryce wanted to get in on the demolition. Hope that's okay." Joel stuck his safety goggles on top of his head and walked over to me. The closer he got, the easier smiling got for me.

"It's too late now if I did care." I quirked an eyebrow and put on a stern teacher face. "I doubt you'll ever get that hammer back from him, and I for sure won't be able to get him to go to school if he knows you're going to be here destroying things every day." I put my hand on my hip and bit back the smile that threatened to return when Joel answered with a long slow shrug and a grin tugging the corner of his mouth.

"He's a natural. I may take him on as a partner. How important is grade school anyway?" Joel's cheek twitched, and the grin won, spreading across his face.

"Don't joke. This is doing him more good than the grief counselor I'm paying."

Joel's blue T-shirt was covered in white flecks of plaster, and before I could stop myself, I reached out and brushed a few off his shoulder. Shock waves traveled from my fingertips to the rest of my body, and I jerked my hand back. Accidentally touching him was one thing, but doing it on purpose? No. Just, no.

"Sorry." I glared at my traitorous hand to keep from looking at him. My fingertips still tingled from touching him. I had to get control of myself.

"No worries. I'm a mess."

My eyes were drawn to his, and the look I saw there sent a second round of shock waves all the way to my toes. The softness of his gaze told me I wasn't the only one on unsteady ground.

"How about we call it a night and grab some dinner? I promised Bryce a double-double." Joel brushed more of the plaster off his shirt, and I took a step away from him. Partly to keep from getting hit by the flying dust but also to catch my breath. The closer I stood to Joel, the faster my blood pumped, my heart beat, and my breath . . . breathed?

"And a shake! You promised me a shake too." Bryce took a last swing then set his hammer down and stood back to admire his handiwork. I hated to look at the piles of plaster and open walls, so I looked at Bryce's beaming face instead.

"Whatever you want. You deserve it." Joel patted him on the back, sending up a cloud of dust.

"I think you better shower first," I said.

Bryce scowled. "Joel's not showering."

"Yes I am. I'll go over to Rach—the guesthouse," Joel said, glancing at me as he stopped himself from calling it Rachel's house.

"See? Joel's not too manly to shower and neither are you. Now go." I clapped Bryce on the back and pushed him toward the stairs. He responded by using both hands to shake the plaster out of his hair. I clamped my eyes and mouth shut as I got a faceful of dust. Bryce laughed and ran upstairs while I wiped the debris off my skin.

"I guess I'll get cleaned up too," I said to Joel as I wiped plaster off my shirt. "Little brothers are the worst."

He laughed. "I wouldn't know. I can give you my opinion of older sisters though."

"Only if you say they're the best," I teased.

Somehow we were within touching distance again. I stuck my hands in my jean pockets to keep from brushing away a tiny piece of plaster at the corner of his eyebrow. The one with the scar running through it.

"Obviously." His lip twitched.

"Good. Because they are." I kept a straight face, but my breath caught when he stepped closer and brushed his thumb across my cheek.

"Plaster." The corner of his mouth pulled up, and he dropped his hand. "I'm going to get cleaned up." He jutted his head toward the back door.

I nodded and watched him as he walked out the door and down the path toward the guesthouse. Once he went inside, I could breathe again.

I could also see again. I mean, *really* see.

The wall that separated the kitchen from the dining room and the two doors it once held—one for going in, the other for going out—were gone.

Mom had wanted to take down the same wall for years. She hated being "squirreled away" in the kitchen cooking while everyone else was in the dining room or family room together. She also didn't love that Annie and I, when we were younger, chased each other in circles through the two doors until we were dizzy.

Dad had refused, not wanting to alter the original craftsman architecture. Our home had been built in 1914 by a renowned architectural firm for Jason's great-grandparents, and Dad had worked hard to maintain most of its original features, including the wood doors that were now covered in plastic and propped up on the front porch.

The dark wood wainscoting and baseboards also lay in plastic-covered sections on our front porch. I was grateful Joel was being as careful with our old house and its history as Dad would have been. I only hoped those pieces would be used somewhere else.

But it wasn't up to me. My house had never been mine at all. It had never really even been Mom and Dad's.

I turned away and walked to the wide staircase. I took my time climbing up it, running my hand along the wood railing, soaking in the feel of the grain like I'd never done before. I didn't know if it would still be there in a few months, but I knew for sure I wouldn't be.

Chapter 8

GETTING ANNIE OUT OF THE house for a second time in one day was no small feat, but somehow I convinced her to be ready for YSA game night by the time Joel, Bryce, and I were done with dinner. I hadn't pressed my luck trying to get her to In-N-Out with us.

Joel and I took Bryce for his double-double then dropped him at his friend's house. In the two minutes Joel and I were alone between dropping Bryce off and picking Annie up, I kept my fingers crossed that she'd actually get in the car. Our limited alone time was all I needed to show me I couldn't be trusted to keep Joel in the friend zone.

But my relief when Annie got in the car quickly turned to annoyance when she opened her mouth.

"I know how I got suckered into this, but what happened with you?" she asked Joel after practically throwing herself into the car.

"Wow. Attitude," I said.

"I said I'd go. I didn't say I'd be happy about it," she grumbled. "But really, Joel, do you know what you've gotten yourself into?"

"All I know is I get to be a Gentile for a night. I don't know what that means, but I'm guessing there will be a lot of pork," Joel replied, making Annie laugh.

"Just how Jewish are you, anyway? Like, if you eat bacon, will you go to hell?" She settled into the seat and waited for an answer as I pulled away from the curb.

"Don't beat around the bush or anything, Annie." I would have been more annoyed if I hadn't been dying to ask the same questions.

"It's fine," Joel answered. "We're Reform."

"What does that mean? You're not, like, delinquents or something anymore?" Annie had Jewish friends—she worked in Hollywood, after all—but I guess she'd never really asked them about their beliefs. I hadn't done any better with my own Jewish friends.

Joel laughed again. "It means a lot of different things depending on how each person believes. But when it comes to food, in my home we ate kosher, but we didn't observe kashrut when we went out or to someone else's home who didn't observe it. That's pretty much what I still do."

"So you've had bacon before?" Annie asked.

"Yeah. I don't go out of my way to eat it or anything, but I've had it."

"You like it, don't you?"

"Annie! Would you leave him alone?" I still wanted to know the answers to her questions, but I knew they wouldn't stop. I didn't want to date Joel—or, at least, I didn't *want* to want to—but I didn't want to scare him off either.

"No comment. My turn for a question. How many Mormons am I going to be up against here?"

"A lot," Annie answered at the same time I said, "It's not really you against us, you know."

"So says the girl who called the nice Jewish boy a Gentile," Joel said over his shoulder to Annie, looking for a conspirator.

"She called you a Gentile?" Annie asked, wide-eyed and open-mouthed. Joel had found the perfect ally.

"Oh sure, gang up on me with my sister." I pretended to be mad, but it had been a long time since Annie had put any effort into teasing me. It was a good sign her meds were working.

The teasing didn't stop until I pulled into the full church parking lot and waited for a large group to cross in front of us as they laughed and talked on their way to the doors. I glanced at Joel, who looked more nervous than I expected.

"How often do you all get together?" he asked and bit his lip as I parked the car.

"Every Monday," I answered.

"*Every* Monday?" Joel unbuckled his seat belt but held onto it like he might strap himself in again rather than face all the Mormons.

"Well, yeah. Not everyone shows up every week, but we usually get a pretty good crowd." For the first time, I was seeing a BMG (Big Mormon Gathering) through a non-Mormon's eyes. It made sense he might feel a little intimidated.

"That's cool," he said but didn't pull the handle to open the door.

"Don't you do stuff like this with your synagogue?" Annie asked. "I'm pretty sure you're not the only young, single Jew in LA. I thought I heard about a huge dance for Jewish singles that's on Christmas Eve every year."

I got out of the car.

Annie and Joel followed slowly while he answered her question. "Yeah, there're events like that, but they're not organized by synagogue. It's mostly big Jewish organizations. At least that's what they want us to think. . . ."

"What do you mean?" Annie asked.

He made a show of checking to see if anyone else was listening. "I have a theory about who's really running them."

"Oh, yeah? Who's that?" Annie whispered loudly. I'd pretty much been shut out of the conversation, but I didn't mind. It was good to see her act normal.

"I think the organizations are just a front for a secret group of Jewish mothers in Brooklyn called 'Find a Nice Girl, and Settle Down Already,' FNGSDA for short."

I snort-laughed, and Annie smacked Joel on his arm. "That's terrible!"

"So I take it you haven't been to a lot of them?" I asked.

He raised his shoulder. "They're just big matchmaking things."

"News flash!" Annie interrupted. "What do you think this is?" she asked loudly and pointed to the building.

"Yeah? I doubt there are as many hookups after a rousing game of Scattergories as there are after a dance with an open bar. There's always way too much booze at the events I've been to," Joel said and held the door open for us.

"Hmm. Well, the booze part you don't have to worry about here, but dancing sounds like a lot more fun than Scattergories," Annie answered as she went through the door.

"Yeah, but it gets old being the only person who doesn't drink. When you don't have religion as an out, people put a lot of pressure on you." His eyes had lost all of their laughter.

"You don't drink?" I asked.

He shook his head again.

"Ever?"

"Never."

"How do you say no?" Religion wasn't the only reason I didn't drink, but telling people I was Mormon usually shut down the drink offers before I even had to say no.

"Sometimes I tell them about my brother, but mostly I avoid situations where there might be alcohol." He stopped at the fountain, bent down, and took a long sip of water.

"What happened with your brother?" Annie was never afraid to ask a question, even when she shouldn't. I wanted to know too, but as Joel's water stop dragged on, I took it as a signal. He didn't want to talk about it.

"I don't want to be a downer," he said when he finally straightened and stepped back from the fountain. "I'll tell you another time."

We walked the last few feet to the cultural hall, and he opened the door, all smiles again. I was relieved. Whatever happened with his brother couldn't be good, and I wanted him to have fun. More importantly, I wanted Annie to have fun. She *needed* to have fun.

Round tables were set up around the room, each with different board games on them. Most already had a group of people at them ready to play, but the Scrabble table lay lonely and deserted in the far corner.

"Should we kick it old school?" Joel asked, pointing to it.

"I'm out." Annie rolled her eyes then waved to someone she recognized and ditched us.

"I love Scrabble. Be warned, I've devoted a lot of hours to playing Words with Friends. And I usually win." I sat down in the chair he pulled out for me and opened the box.

"Does anyone still play that?" he teased.

"Only people who are better at making words than lining up candy." I dumped the letter tiles in the box and flipped them letter-side down.

"Hey, Candy Crush takes a lot of hand-eye coordination," he said, flipping tiles with me.

"I think I like my odds of winning this game." I lined up my letters and squinted at them until a word popped out at me. I laid the letters down one at a time, enjoying the *clack* each little piece of wood made as I set it on the board. "Thirty points," I said, gloating.

"Nice. Too bad there's nothing to keep score on." He grinned.

I dug through my purse until I found a scrap of paper and an old pen, then dropped them on the table with dramatic flair.

"Your turn." I raised my eyebrows, daring him to beat me.

And then my phone rang, totally ruining the moment. I looked at the screen and saw Walt Holland's name. "Ugh. I should take this." Instead, I silenced my phone and stuck it back in my pocket.

"That's not really how you take a call."

"I know, but I don't want to deal with it right now."

"You want to tell me about it?"

"It's Dad's—my—property manager." I sighed. "He's taking care of the ranch Dad left us, and I'm sure he's calling to tell me something's wrong or ask me what I'm going to do with it or ask about something else I need to figure out."

He looked at his letters and shuffled them around. "So what is it you're trying to figure out about this ranch, Cowgirl?" He laid his tiles down and counted his points. "Forty."

"What the heck I should do with it." I looked at the letters he'd set down. They didn't make me nervous the way his eyes did. The letters were only asking to be read, not reading me. "*Bupkes* is not a word," I said, meeting his gaze with a challenge.

"You've never heard *bupkes*? As in, 'All that work and for what? Bupkes.'" He broke out a thick Jewish New Yorker accent. "Your mother never said that?"

"Um, no. What does that even mean?"

"It means for nothing or . . . very little. Except maybe not as polite."

"So it's Yiddish? Because the rules clearly state you can't use words from other languages." I pulled the rules out of the box to show him.

"Not Yiddish. *Yinglish.* People use it all the time." He grabbed the paper and pen and wrote down his score.

I narrowed my eyes. "I'll let you have this one, but I'm not taking it easy on you anymore. And no more Yiddish."

"Yinglish. And it counts. Now tell me about this ranch."

"There's not much to tell. It's in Utah, and my dad left it to me, and I don't want it. Right now it's operating as a bed-and-breakfast, but he wanted it to be an eco-resort kind of place. He had enough experience in the hospitality industry to make it work, but I was just getting started when I quit." A mixture of guilt and relief flooded over me as I put into words for the first time what I'd been feeling since we read the will.

"Your dad wanted you to be a cowgirl? Remember how my dad wanted me to be a lawyer?" he asked. "Cowgirl beats that any day. Nobody pretends to be a lawyer when they're a kid."

"True." I laughed, letting go of a sliver of my guilt. "I don't think he ever expected me to be a cowgirl, but he did think I had a talent for management and marketing. I have a degree in business management, and I worked in social media marketing, specializing in the hospitality industry.

I guess he thought if his dude ranch idea worked, at the very least, I'd know how to do the marketing and managing side of things." I'd asked myself for months why Dad left me the ranch. Answering Joel's question answered my own, and something happened inside me. Whatever had my heart in a vice grip loosened. It didn't let go, but I could breathe a little easier. And with that loosening came a flicker of hope that one day breathing wouldn't hurt.

"But you don't want to be the one to turn it into a dude ranch?" Something about his eyes kept me from saying no. It's like he was telling me to really think about the question, without actually saying the words.

"I don't know. It's already halfway there with the caretaker we've got running it, but it would still be easier to sell it." The answer obviously should have been no. I didn't know anything about ranches. I barely knew anything about dudes.

"What exactly did your dad want to do with it?" He reached past me to grab a cup and the water pitcher in the center of the table. He poured me a glass then poured himself one and took a long drink, his Adam's apple bobbing with each swallow.

Suddenly my mouth felt dry. I took a drink of my own water to give me something to do besides stare at him. "He wanted to tap into what he called the 'tree huggers with money crowd,'" I answered when I could talk again. "He had this vision of turning it into an eco-resort where we'd grow most of the food or get it from local sources, so we could bill our food as farm-to-table. Walt and his wife are already doing that part of it, plus they've got a support staff in place. Dad planned on rehabbing the ranch itself so it was environmentally friendly and energy efficient. You know, all those things."

"As a matter of fact, I do know." He spun his empty cup. "Kosher kitchens are not my only area of expertise. I focused on green building in my construction courses."

"Really?" My pulse quickened, like it knew something big was coming, even if I didn't.

"I could help you out if you decide you want to make his vision a reality." He shrugged like he hadn't cleared a hurdle I had no idea how to get over.

"Seriously? My dad was so passionate about this idea I hate to see it die with him." In nine months, I hadn't used the "d" word. The sound of it brought a rush of emotion that made me quake with the effort it took not to break down into tears. Dad and I had done a lot of research before he bought the ranch. It had huge potential to make money, but I'd been too overwhelmed since the accident to do all the things Dad hadn't. Joel's offer of help gave me the confidence I needed to take a swing at my Goliath. If I could make the ranch work, a part of Dad would still be alive. I just had to figure out how to do it from LA.

"It sounds really interesting. I'd love to see what we can do," he said and glanced at me. He had to know I was about to burst, but all he said was, "Your turn."

I rearranged my tiles while I gained my composure and figured out a better word than his. Jell-O was all I had.

"That's a proper noun."

"No, it's a type of salad."

"I'll let you keep it, but you know you're a cheater, right?" He didn't let me reply before putting down his next tiles. "Do you have pictures or anything of this ranch? I'll need to see it before I can work my magic."

I shook my head and bit my lip to keep from smiling. "I've got to make a trip out there. I can take some then."

Joel laid down his tiles and counted his points. "Ten."

I wrote it down. I was ahead but had lost the motivation to play.

"When are you going?"

I shrugged. "As soon as I can find time to make the drive and be sure Annie is okay enough to stay alone with Bryce." I bit my lip again, but this time to keep from telling him any more of my problems. If I kept spilling the way I was, he'd need to bring a therapy couch and a notepad the next time he saw me.

He opened his mouth, reconsidered, and shut it. He picked some tiles out of the box and rearranged the tiles on his rack. I stared at my own tiles, my mind blank now.

"What if I went with you?" His words came out slow and uneven.

My head jerked up.

"It would be easier to tell you what needs to be done and give a guesstimate of what it would cost if I see it in person. Then you can decide whether you need a contractor or a realtor." He moved his tiles around while he talked, his eyes darting from me to them.

"You'd do that?" My instinct was to say no to be polite, but his offer was too generous. I needed him. "It would be a huge help to have someone's opinion I trust," I blurted and felt my face color. "It's kind of a long drive though. Can you take the time off?" I carefully measured each word this time.

He shook his head. "I can fly us," he muttered and looked down, staring intently at his letters.

"What do you mean, you'll fly us?"

"I have my pilot's license, and I have a plane. Or, my family does. We share ownership with a couple other people." He laid down his tiles but bumped the others in the process. It took more than one try for him to straighten them back into perfect position.

"You know how my parents died?" My search for tickets on a commercial flight had been hard enough. The thought of getting on a small plane made my chest tight and the air heavy.

Joel nodded and kept his eyes down.

"I think I'd rather drive."

He waited a while before answering. "So you're not going to fly ever again?"

"I don't know." Mentally I knew how impossible that would be, but emotionally I couldn't imagine doing it again.

He took a deep breath. "If they had been in a car accident, would you have stopped driving? Or riding in cars?"

"No, but that's not really an option. I don't *have* to fly anywhere because I can drive." My voice rose with defensiveness.

"Not to Hawaii or Europe or a lot of other places." He spelled out *pizza* using a blank tile and a triple word point square, effectively shutting down any chance I had to beat him.

"I don't need to go that far." I wrote down his points.

"We do need to get to Utah fast. We can spend our time driving there, or we can fly and spend our time solving the problems that need to be solved." Now he did look at me, keeping his eyes locked on mine while he waited for my answer.

"I get all of that, but it's only been nine months." I put down the word *it* and said goodbye to my lead. I couldn't block out the conversations around me anymore. Every time someone laughed, it sounded like when Bryce holds down the volume button on the TV remote to see how loud he can make it.

"I'm not trying to push you. I know how hard it is to lose someone you love." Joel shuffled his tiles then pushed his rack aside. "I also know it's easy to let fear take over when you're grieving."

I closed my eyes and took some deep yoga breaths. The pounding in my head quieted. "Who did you lose?" I opened my eyes and asked.

"My brother."

"How?"

"Car accident. He was driving drunk and hit a family. He killed himself, the mom, and two of the kids." His eyes met mine, and I got why he was taking his time with our kitchen, why he was so nice to Bryce, and why he knew I was afraid.

"Were you close?"

He nodded and tapped his fingers on the table.

"And that's why you don't drink?"

He nodded again. "He had a lot of problems with alcohol before he died. My parents sent him to treatment, but when he didn't want to stay, they checked him out."

"I'm sorry." I put my hand on his and the tapping stopped. He turned it over and interlaced his fingers with mine. Everything went quiet. Time stopped. All I could feel was the warmth of his hand in mine. But as much as I wanted to keep my hand there, I pulled it away.

"You gave up something dangerous because someone you loved died doing it, but you don't think I should do the same?" I rubbed my hands on my thighs. The hurt written on his face made me stop.

"Sorry. I didn't mean to be rude," I stammered.

"I think it's a little different." He took his hand off the table and leaned back in his chair, away from me.

"You're right. I appreciate your offer; I really do." Embarrassment washed over me in hot waves. I'd been rude when he'd gone out of his way to help in more ways than his offer to fly us to Utah. "I am scared," I whispered.

"I don't want to push you or anything, but think about it. It would make things a lot easier." He leaned back in and moved his tile rack back in front of him. "Your move."

"Okay." By some miracle, my last letters spelled out *sorry*. The tips of his mouth curved into a slow smile and mine followed. "Can I think about it for a few days? Your offer, not my move."

He laughed. "I don't have anything for a couple weeks that my crew can't handle without me, but I do have a new job at the end of the month. We should go before then."

I nodded then scanned the room for Annie. "We should probably get going," I said and stood up. I had to look at something besides him, and if

I didn't put some space between us, I wouldn't be able to stop myself from holding his hand again. Mine felt empty without it.

Chapter 9

"LET ME MAKE SURE I heard you right," Annie said with the same satisfied grin of a cat who had cornered a mouse but wasn't hungry enough to eat it. And I was the mouse. "You're going to Utah? With Joel—a guy you barely know. On his plane, alone," she continued, making me regret pulling her out of bed that morning.

I took a bite out of my toast and nodded.

"But it's not a 'date'?" Annie did that annoying air quote thing when she said *date*, and her mouth morphed from a teasing grin to an outright smirk, which was even worse.

"It's not a date. He's just doing me a favor. I have to figure out what to do with the ranch. And we're not going alone; you and Bryce are coming with us." I took another bite of toast and chewed on the words that had popped, unplanned, out of my mouth.

I hadn't really thought about the fact Joel and I would be alone for days until Annie said it. Considering the effort it had taken me to keep my hands to myself when we were surrounded by other people, being alone with Joel probably wasn't a good idea. If Annie and Bryce came along, not only would that problem be solved, but I also wouldn't have to worry about Annie being left by herself to take care of Bryce.

And, as much as I didn't want to, we had to fly. Only an hour before, I'd called Walt, who told me the city council was on the verge of passing an ordinance requiring the owners of small lodgings to live on the property unless the neighborhood was zoned strictly for commercial properties. If the ordinance passed, I wouldn't be able to keep the property as a bed-and-breakfast unless I moved there. And living there meant not living in LA.

But I also couldn't afford to keep the ranch except as an income property. The taxes and upkeep on it were too high. I was staring a conundrum right in its crazy face. I didn't have time to wait for a cheap commercial flight or spend the hours driving to Utah when Joel was offering to fly me for free. Practicality and expediency won over fear.

"Take Bryce if you want to, but I'm not getting on that plane." Annie put her bread in the toaster—the one appliance we could still use now that we were kitchen-less—and pushed the lever down. Hard. "And good luck convincing Bryce to go either. I can't believe you're even thinking about it. What's wrong with a normal flight on a normal plane that's not going to crash?" She stuck her shaking hands behind her back.

"Nothing. Except it's not as flexible or as free as what Joel is offering." I looked at Annie, wanting to do something to make her feel better, but I couldn't move without giving away the fact that my hands weren't any steadier than hers. Then, what I needed to say came to me. "We can call Sharon and tell her to set up an audition while we're there."

She blinked twice then stared me down. "You're trying to force me to get on that plane."

"I'm really not." I shook my head slowly. "I'm nervous about this too, but it's a fear we have to face. I need to get to the ranch, and you need to get to that audition. Neither one of us can afford to take our time getting to Utah."

Minutes passed while she chewed on her thumbnail and stared through me. She switched from chewing her thumbnail to her bottom lip, and more minutes passed. "You think Bryce will get on that plane?"

It wasn't a yes, but it wasn't a no. So, progress.

"I hope so."

"Are you going to make him if he doesn't?"

"Hopefully I won't have to. He's been asking to go to the ranch, and he really likes Joel. Maybe the combination of Joel and the ranch together will be enough to convince him." I put a drop of raspberry jam on my cold toast to avoid looking at her. I didn't want her to see my uncertainty.

"Maybe." Annie didn't sound any more certain than I felt. "If Sharon can't get me an audition, he can stay home with me."

My eyes shot back to hers. She was playing her cat-and-mouse game again. She knew I needed one of them to go so I wouldn't be alone with Joel.

"I think it will be good for him to go." I stood, anxious to get away from the eyes that bored into mine, digging for the truth.

She broke into a smile before I could make my escape. "You like him. That's why you need Bryce to go. You're afraid to be alone with Joel."

"You're both going, and Joel and I are just friends." I doubted she believed me. How could she if my face looked as hot as it felt? Luckily, Bryce's footsteps on the stairs saved me from a full-on interrogation.

"Need me to go where? And why are you afraid to be alone with Joel? He's cool," Bryce said as he jumped over the last few steps into the hallway and ran into the dining room. He could pass for deaf when he wanted to, but if it was something we didn't want him to hear, suddenly he had supersonic ears.

"Where are we going?" he asked again and plopped down in the chair next to me.

"Nowhere," Annie answered at the same time I said, "Utah."

"To the ranch?" Bryce nearly bounced out of his chair as his words came tumbling out. He had been the most excited when Dad bought the ranch. They'd been planning a special "Man's Weekend" to visit it when Dad died.

"Great." Annie stuck a Pop-Tart in the toaster for Bryce. "I guess I'll stay here and worry about another plane going down and taking out the rest of my family."

"We're going on an airplane?" Bryce stopped bouncing. "I don't want to go."

Annie gave me a worried glance that I returned with a glare. She knew she'd messed up. The one thing our parents had been determined to teach us was to be brave. Mom always said, "Faith and fear can't reside together," and any time we said we didn't want to try something new, Dad threatened to tattoo "no fear" on our forearms.

"I shouldn't have said that, Bryce." Annie crossed the room and wrapped her arm around my brother. "If you go, I'll go." She brushed the hair out of his eyes, but he shook her hand away.

"Joel's going too?" Bryce asked me.

I nodded. "He's flying us in his plane."

Worry lines creased his forehead. "Is it a little one? Like Dad's?"

Annie sat down next to Bryce but wouldn't look at me. I glanced between them. I had one chance to say the right thing. "It's small, but not like Dad's. Joel's is sturdier." At least I hoped it was. "It's newer and has better equipment than Dad's." I had no idea what kind or how old it was.

"Dad didn't have good equipment?" Bryce asked.

I'd said the totally wrong thing, and now I had to backtrack. "Sweetie, he had everything he needed, and he did everything right. Accidents just happen sometimes." I reached to touch the blond curls Annie had attempted to brush out of his eyes but pulled my hand back. "Remember how much Daddy loved being up in the air?"

Bryce nodded.

"And Mom and Dad loved being together, right? They hated being apart."

He nodded again.

"It's not fair that we lost them, but they got to go together, and Dad was doing something he loved," I said.

Bryce swallowed hard. "But they're not together now because they weren't sealed in the temple."

Annie's chair scraped the floor as she scooted closer and pulled him into her arms. He buried his head on her chest.

"We'll take care of that, I promise." I wanted to offer more than words to comfort him, but he was just out of reach. The toaster popped, but nobody moved.

"Heavenly Father doesn't want our family to be apart. He loves us. So quit worrying about that." Annie stroked his hair as his little shoulders shook. "And I think Daddy would be very sad if you never went in an airplane again."

Every once in a while, Annie had surprising moments of maturity. I was grateful this was one of those times as I moved closer to rub his back and tried to hold back my own tears.

"You don't have to go, buddy, but I'd sure like it if you did. I think Joel would too." I hoped he would anyway. I had painted myself into a pretty tight corner if he didn't.

"Okay." He sat up and quickly wiped his tears away, his cheeks red from crying as much as from embarrassment at being seen crying.

"If you're serious about going, I'll call Sharon to get your audition set up," I said to Annie then turned back to Bryce. "We'll talk to Joel about everything tonight, okay?"

"Okay," he nodded again. "What's for breakfast?" he asked, and Annie jumped up to grab his Pop-Tart.

Chapter 10

AFTER I DROPPED OFF BRYCE at school, I went back home to call Annie's agent, but I bumped into Jason first. Literally, I bumped into him. Or the front door did anyway. He was about to walk out of the house at the same time I opened the door to walk in, and *boom*, the doorknob caught him right in the stomach.

"Oh, sorry about that," I said as he doubled over, clutching his stomach.

"It's fine." He squeezed the words out as hard as he squeezed his eyes shut. I stepped inside and closed the door, not sure if I should pat his back, help him sit down, call 911, or stand awkwardly by waiting for him to get his breath back. I went with the last option.

"How's the house hunt going?" he asked once he could stand up again.

"Is that why you're here?" I had assumed his unexpected visit was to see the kitchen, which would have been annoying enough at eight thirty in the morning. But I wondered how many more surprise have-you-found-somewhere-else-to-live-yet visits I could expect now that he lived thirty feet away.

"Just checking in. Rachel offered to help if you want her to. She's already found a few possibilities." With that, he handed me a stack of papers. A quick glance at the pages of apartment and rental listings told me Rachel's offer of "help" was much more of a strong suggestion that it was time for us to go.

"I've looked in our neighborhood, but there's not a lot available." I set the papers face down on the entryway table and hung up my purse before walking into the dining room to clean up breakfast.

"Have you tried other neighborhoods?" Jason followed me, chock full of helpful suggestions that had me rolling my eyes so far to the back of my head they threatened to stick.

"I'd really like Bryce to stay in the same school. He's having a harder time than he's letting on. It would be nice to keep one thing from changing so he has some normalcy in his life." I twisted the lid back on the peanut butter Bryce had left open after making his lunch, and then I wiped bread crumbs into my hand. Once I brushed those into the garbage, I didn't have an excuse for not giving Jason my full attention.

"That's not going to be easy." Jason pursed his lips. I knew he had more to say about it, but he changed the subject. "What's going on with the ranch?"

"I'm going to Utah this weekend to figure out what to do with it."

"What do you mean, do with it? You're keeping it, right? That's what Dad wanted." Jason scratched behind his ear, a nervous habit he'd formed as a kid and a clear sign he was worried.

"The city is passing an ordinance that would require me to live there if I want it to be a bed-and-breakfast." I explained everything Walt had told me. "I'm not sure I *can* keep it."

Jason nodded his head and rubbed his chin. "That's a problem."

"Yeah, and that's before all the work that would have to be done to the ranch for it to be what Dad wanted. He had a five-year plan; I don't even have five months."

Dad had planned to make improvements to the ranch over a few years while Walt and his wife leased it from him and ran it as a B&B. Once Bryce graduated from high school, Dad would retire, and he and Mom would move there and run it as a higher end resort, keeping Walt and LaRell on to help. The city's ordinance would make Dad's plan impossible. Plus, I'd been counting on the income from the ranch to help pay the rent on a new place. Jason couldn't have chosen a worse day to put pressure on me.

"How are you getting there?" Jason ran his hand back across his chin then did his behind-the-ear scratching thing again.

"Flying."

He raised his eyebrows. "You got tickets already?"

I shook my head. "Joel's flying us."

His eyebrows shot up even higher, reaching for his hairline. "Joel is?"

I nodded.

"Rachel's brother Joel?"

I nodded again.

More scratching. He was starting to remind me of a nervous dog. "Who's us?" he asked, finally.

"Who do you think? Me, Annie, and Bryce."

"So my whole family is getting on a small plane even though—" he finished his thoughts with an angry sigh instead of words.

I sucked in my lips and shrugged. "What else am I supposed to do? I can't leave Bryce here alone with Annie for three days."

"Why not? She's eighteen." His face folded in with confusion.

"She's depressed. Severely depressed," I said slowly, emphasizing each word. "She's getting better, but I don't think she could handle it. Bryce would be taking care of her. Plus, she has an audition with some producers in Utah who are interested in her." I was stuck between being touched by Jason's concern about us flying and annoyance that he was suddenly taking an interest in his "half-family"—as he liked to call us—when he'd spent most of our lives ignoring us. It was too much, too late.

"Why don't you drive," he demanded more than asked.

"Do you want us to move out or not? Because I've got to get this figured out before we can do anything. I don't have two days to spend driving." My clipped words got him to really look at me for the first time.

"Okay." His head bobbled back and forth, trying to shake all the details I'd given him into a place that made sense. "What can I do to help? Do you want me to go with you?" He swallowed hard. He had taken a step so far out of his comfort zone, sweat beads were forming on his clean-shaven lip.

"No." The last thing I needed was him coming along making everything awkward. "I don't even know what you could do that would be helpful."

He pulled out a chair and sat down, resting his hands on the dining room table. "I thought this ranch thing was pretty stupid when Dad told me about it—what did he know about being a cowboy, right?" The corner of his mouth twitched, and he shook his head. "But he was so excited about it, I hate to see his dream die."

"I know." He echoed the same words I'd said to Joel. "But I don't even know where to start. Walt's got a list of repairs I need to make if I'm going to sell, and Joel's going to give me some ideas about how to make it the eco-friendly place Dad wanted. After that, I have no idea what to do."

Jason sat up and snapped his fingers. "Here's what I'll do. Rachel's friend Becca is an interior decorator—we would have used her, but she and Joel haven't been broken up very long, so Rachel didn't think Joel would like it—I'll get her to help you do the inside if you decide to keep it. She's done a bunch of boutique hotels and places like that."

Jason's words stunned me. There were so many things to consider. First, he was offering to help—in a helpful way. For the first time EVER. And this Becca person sounded like exactly what I needed.

Except for the second thing to consider: Joel used to date this person. This *Becca*. I already didn't like her. Which was crazy because, one, I needed her, and, two, Joel and I were *not* dating. I'd made that very clear in the lectures I'd given myself about not getting involved with him.

"I'll keep that in mind if we get to that point," I said through gritted teeth. "She sounds perfect."

"If you're worried about the cost, don't. I'll take care of it." He stood and pushed out the chair, a giant smile splitting his face in two. Jason loved solving problems. He'd found the right formula for this tricky equation, and now he could be on his way.

"Thanks, Jason. That's really generous. I appreciate it." I smiled back, and I almost meant it.

I should have meant it. My brother was being super generous, something that didn't come easily for him. I just wished he wasn't being super generous with someone Joel used to date. That could mean so many things, and I didn't like any of them.

*　*　*

I went to my room to call Joel after Jason left. Since I'd told everyone else I was flying to Utah, it was only fair I tell the guy who was doing the flying, and who I'd turned down when he offered to do it. Why I needed that conversation to be in private, I don't know. Probably so Annie wouldn't come downstairs and see me smiling while I talked to him. I didn't need her making any more assumptions about my feelings for Joel.

"This is Joel," he answered, as I sank onto my bed.

All I wanted to do was ask him about Becca, but I kept my cool. "Hi. It's Emily."

"Hi!" He sounded happy to hear my voice, which tempered some of the ridiculous jealousy I was feeling toward a woman I'd never met over a guy I wouldn't date.

"Is your offer still good?" I asked.

"Do you mean the one where I whisk you away to Utah in my trusty plane, then solve all your ranch problems with my super tool belt?" he teased.

My stomach fluttered, a definite red flag if I only wanted to be friends, but I chose to ignore it. "That's the one. I was going to light up the sky with a hammer signal or at least text you one, but I went with calling instead." I laid back on my bed. The smiling had started. I'd made the right call talking to Joel in private.

"See, this is why I switched careers. There's no good signal for lawyers."

"Hey, guess what else?" I had him laughing so it seemed like a good time to bring up my brother. "I've got a sidekick for you."

"A sidekick? Hmm. Tell me more. Does this sidekick know how to use a screwdriver?"

"I'm not sure, but he's a quick learner," I answered.

"He?" His voice went from jokey to serious.

"Yeah. My brother." An air of tension traveled across our connection, and I sat back up. "Is it okay if he comes with us? And Annie too?" I realized then that I didn't even know how big Joel's plane was or if it had enough seats for all of us. "You know, so people don't get the wrong idea that we're dating or something," I spluttered.

"Oh." Two beats of silence. "Yeah, of course they can come. Bryce makes a great sidekick."

"I don't want to put you on the spot or anything. It's really okay if they can't. It's just, Dad promised to take Bryce to the ranch, and I think this might give him some closure he needs. And I was able to set up an audition for Annie while we're there." My arguments sounded more convincing than I felt.

"Of course they can come. You don't need my permission to bring them. I should have suggested it." His voice was back to normal. "And you're right. We don't want it to look like this is anything but business."

Business sounded so cold, even with the warmth of his voice.

"When should we leave?" he asked.

"Is Friday okay? After Bryce is out of school? That would give us Saturday, and we could fly back Sunday." I answered, still spinning the word *business* around in my head. How did we get from *not dating* to *business*?

"That will work. I'll pick you up at three." He hung up, barely saying goodbye.

I crossed my legs and stared at my phone. I tapped my Instagram app, scrolling through words and pictures that were supposed to be a distraction. I couldn't separate them into anything that made sense. Exactly like what was going on with my head and my heart.

Chapter 11

WE MADE IT THROUGH THE flight with no major freak-outs. Joel talked us through takeoff, landing, and every little bump in between. Still, I was glad we'd be in a rental car rather than a plane for the rest of the weekend.

After picking up the car, we dropped Annie off at the home of an old Young Women leader who had moved to Provo and had offered to get Annie to her audition. That left me time to focus on the ranch rather than driving up and down the mountain to get her where she needed to be.

Once Annie was settled, the rest of us headed up Provo Canyon to Park City. I never stopped being surprised by how the mountains shot up out of the valley like a giant, gray-spired crown dotted with emeralds that had been dropped from the heavens.

"This is incredible," Joel said, craning his neck to see the tops of the mountains out his window.

"You should see it in the fall. All the leaves turn a hundred different shades of red and orange. It's even prettier." I glanced out the window but then turned my focus back to the road in front of me.

He opened the window and let in the crisp mountain air. "Wow. Smell that. I may not want to leave."

"Really? The mountains make me claustrophobic sometimes." My family had spent a lot of time in Utah when I was younger, and I loved it. But I'd never considered not going back home.

"Are you kidding me? People and cars and buildings make me claustrophobic. I feel like I can breathe for the first time here." He rolled the window up but left it open a crack, looking over his shoulder at the mountains behind us then facing forward again to see what he'd missed.

When we got to Heber, we had to stop so he could see the little town tucked in the mountains. I'd never seen anyone so excited about *Utah*.

Joel would have made a better Brigham Young than Brigham Young if he'd been the first pioneer to enter the valley.

He got even more excited as we turned on a dirt road and drove the last quarter mile to the ranch. "You have thirteen acres here? Thirteen *acres*." He was almost as impressed with the ranch itself as we approached. "It's outdated—the seventies and eighties were not good to architecture— but from here the wood looks good. I think there's a lot you can do to keep the château feel but make it more visually interesting."

I didn't even get the car into park before he jumped out. Rocks crunched under his feet as he walked across the gravel driveway away from the house and toward the lawn. Bryce took off for the pasture to see the horses, and I followed Joel.

Joel stopped at the top of a grassy knoll in the middle of the winter-brown yard and turned around, surveying the ranch from a wider perspective. The sun was setting behind us, making it difficult to see very well, but Joel looked anyway. Lights went on inside and on the porch, but they couldn't match the light in Joel's eyes as he scanned the property.

"Do you think I could sell it without making too many structural changes?" I asked. "I don't have a lot of money to sink into it."

He looked down at me, his brow creased, and blinked slowly. "I think you could do a lot of things with this place. Selling it is the least interesting."

A man with a moustache big enough to be seen in the dim light and a woman with hips big enough to be seen from anywhere stepped out the front door and waved to us. I waved back and walked toward the house, too surprised by what Joel had said to answer.

"Who's that?" Joel asked.

"Walt Holland, Dad's—my—caretaker and his wife, LaRell. Dad bought the ranch from them when they were about to lose it to foreclosure, but then he hired them to look after it so they wouldn't have to move. I've only met them once, but Dad trusted them, and Walt's been a lifesaver the last few months." I kept my voice low to keep them from hearing. "They live in the cabin out back that's been there since before the big house was built."

"We've got your rooms ready, or as ready as we could," LaRell called, still waving as we walked toward them.

"Bryce! Come inside!" I turned and yelled toward the pasture. Bryce reluctantly dropped the grass he'd been holding out to the horses through the lodge-pole fence and ran toward us.

Joel and I walked up the steps to the porch, where I introduced him. Walt shook both our hands; then LaRell hugged us separately. I returned her embrace with an embarrassed one, but Joel wrapped his arms around her like they'd been friends for years.

"Let me grab your bags. LaRell's got dinner for you in the kitchen." Walt went stiff-legged down the steps. Joel moved like he was going to follow, but LaRell grabbed his hand and pulled him inside before he could.

"Let's get you three fed. You've got to be starving." LaRell chattered the whole way to the kitchen, giving us the entire life history of the chicken we were about to eat.

"You're serious about this farm-to-table thing, aren't you?" I asked once we'd reached the kitchen and LaRell had stopped talking long enough to take a breath.

"We've always raised animals for ourselves, but ever since your dad said he wanted to make this place an organic getaway kind of thing, I've been trying out a bunch of recipes using what we've grown here and what we can get local." She took a large pan out of the lower oven and tipped it forward for me to see the herb-covered chicken pieces and potatoes. The smell of thyme and a hint of garlic made my stomach grumble, and looking at the dish was like taking a trip to the Louvre to see a masterpiece. The chicken pieces were carefully arranged with not just red, but purple and yellow potatoes, then topped with sprigs of rosemary.

"Mmmm," was all I could say.

"We should get that in my belly now." Joel breathed in all the deliciousness in front of us.

"That chicken lived here?" Bryce asked, looking worried. "Are there more chickens? Are they going to care if we eat their friend?"

LaRell answered him with a laugh and set the pan on top of the stove, then pulled out another pan of brown yeasty rolls from the top oven. "You'll want some of these to go with it," she said and rubbed a stick of butter across the tops of the rolls.

She made us sit down while she plated the food. I didn't think the food could look more appetizing, but when LaRell set our plates in front of us with the chicken and veggies arranged on them, I was proven wrong. Bobby Flay had nothing on her.

"This looks amazing." Joel took a bite at the same time Walt walked in the door.

"Did we already bless the food?" he asked.

"Not yet, hon. We were just waitin' on you." LaRell's eyes bounced from Joel to the full fork that was on its way back to his mouth. He glanced at me and set it back down.

Walt said the prayer, and we dug into our food. It tasted even better than it smelled. Mom had been a good cook, but I hadn't inherited that talent. The quality of our dinners had definitely suffered since she'd been gone, even before I'd lost the use of the kitchen.

"This is so good. Thank you." I'd never been emotional about food, but suddenly I could barely push the food past the lump in my throat. LaRell's cooking made me homesick for a place and time I'd never be able to go back to.

"This is what we'd serve up for the guests, if you decide to move forward with your dad's resort plan. We could even open it up to people who wanted somewhere quiet or romantic to eat. But that would be down the road a bit." Walt spread a spoonful of homemade jam—there was no Smuckers label on that jelly jar—on his roll and put the entire bottom half in his mouth.

"If everything you make tastes as good as this, you'll have people lining up outside the door." Joel put his fork in his mouth then closed his eyes while he chewed, savoring every bite. Bryce, who never ate anything I cooked without complaining, could hardly sit still while LaRell scooped up a second helping for him.

"I don't know what I'm going to do yet, Walt. That's what I need to figure out this weekend." I hadn't really considered the fact that if I sold the ranch, Walt and LaRell would be out of jobs and a home. Dad didn't pay them much, but they lived at the ranch for free. Would a new owner want to keep them around? They were both pushing seventy, at least. There were also the three maids and other support staff to consider.

"Get settled, and we'll talk in the morning," Walt said and took another bite. Despite his cheerfulness, when he raised his eyes to LaRell, a worried look I wasn't meant to see passed between them.

Joel changed the subject by asking LaRell questions about where she'd learned to cook and then kept a conversation going with Walt about the materials he'd used to build the ranch. By the time we finished eating, it was late, and I was tired. I herded Bryce upstairs to the room LaRell had ready for us and tucked him into bed. I wanted to climb into bed myself, but I had to say good night to Joel and thank him. Not only for getting me to the ranch, but for being there with me.

I found him on the back porch sitting in a swing, rocking back and forth.

"It's freezing out here," I said, and he scooted over so I could sit beside him.

"Look up." He pointed at the sky.

I tipped my head back. We pushed the swing back and forth with our feet while I tried to find what it was he wanted me to see. All I saw were stars.

"What am I looking for?" I asked finally.

"Stars. Have you ever seen so many?"

I glanced at him to see if he was serious. "Yeah. Every time I'm here. Or anywhere not inundated with light pollution."

"I never have."

"You're kidding me. Didn't you ever go camping or anything as a kid?" I'd always lived in LA, but I couldn't imagine anyone having never seen the Milky Way.

"Camping isn't really my family's thing." He kept his eyes on the sky, totally oblivious to the cold.

"But you've gone other places? You've left LA before, right?" My teeth chattered as I spoke even though I had on a thick sweater and jeans.

"I've seen every major city in the world, but I've never seen anything this beautiful."

I took another look and tried to see it the way Joel did. "This is one of the few places I've been. A lot. Even before Dad bought the ranch, he loved coming to Park City. I think I've been to every national and state park in Utah. He couldn't wait to retire here." By this time my teeth were chattering so hard Joel tore his eyes from the stars to see why I was shaking.

"Hold on." He jumped up and ran inside. Two minutes later he was back with the comforter from his bed. He sat down and threw it over both of us, although it wasn't quite big enough.

He put his arm around me and pulled me closer. "Don't get the wrong idea. I'm not putting a move on you, just trying to be a gentleman and keep you warm." He gave us a push, and we started swinging again. I tucked my legs up under the blanket and inched a little closer to him, burying my head in his chest. For warmth, I told myself.

"This is nice," he said. I nodded. His cable knit sweater scratched my face, and I could hear his heartbeat. I knew in my head I shouldn't stay, but no part of my body wanted to leave. Then his lips brushed my crown.

I looked up and met his eyes.

"I'm sor—"

I didn't let him finish. Without thinking, I put my hand on the nape of his neck and pulled him to me until our lips met.

"I brought you two some hot chocolate." LaRell's voice and the sound of the door closing brought me back to reality, and I jumped out of the swing.

"Thanks, LaRell." I grabbed the cup from her. I wrapped my hands around the mug, but they shook too much for me to take a drink.

"I think I'm ready for bed. Good night." I didn't wait for Joel or LaRell to respond, but bolted inside. The way LaRell sucked in her grin told me she'd seen everything.

I set my hot chocolate down on the first table I saw so I could make a quicker get away, but it wasn't fast enough. I only got as far as the stairs before I heard Joel's voice.

"Emily, wait up!"

I ran up the stairs, but he caught me outside of my room.

"I shouldn't have done that." I couldn't look him in the eye, or I'd want to do it again.

"Kissed me? Why?"

"I just . . . I can't do this." I kept my eyes on the worn green carpet. That would have to go.

"I'm not asking you to sleep with me, but if we're interested in each other, why can't we kiss? Or at least spend more time together?" He stepped closer and touched my arm.

Now I did lift my eyes to his. I thought he might have feelings for me, but hearing him admit it made what I needed to say so much harder.

"I like you too, Joel, but you're not Mormon, I'm not Jewish, and I'm past the point of wanting to date someone I can't have a future with."

"*Can't* have a future with?" He blinked, and I realized that sounded a little cultish.

"Not because I'm not allowed, it's just not what I want." I questioned if I were reading way too much into what he said. But I'd already started, so I had to finish. "My parents had a good marriage, but I want a better one. I want to get married in a Mormon temple, and you probably want a Jewish wedding. Why start down a road that's not going to lead in the direction either of us want to go?"

"Are you saying for us to even date I need to be a Mormon?"

I nodded slowly.

"I'm not ready to make that kind of commitment, but I'm willing to try it. I can go to church with you." His blue eyes invited me to forget everything I wanted, everything I'd planned, and just see what happened. But I shook my head no.

"That's exactly what my dad did," I answered. "If you want to do it for you, do it. It doesn't work to do it for anyone else."

"So that's it? You don't want to even try?" He worked his jaw back and forth like he wanted to grind everything else he might say into tiny pieces.

"It's not that I don't want to; it's that I can't. I know we can be great friends, and I'm not willing to risk that for something with so many odds stacked against us."

The paint on the wall behind him was peeling, and I focused all my attention on that instead of the cracking in my heart. I'd only known him a few weeks. If telling him I didn't want a relationship was this hard, how much harder would it be to break up if we were actually dating?

"You're probably right, and if friendship is all we can have, I'll take it." His eyes didn't leave my face, and I had to meet them again. When I did, he took a deep breath and said, "I think you could also be having another 'fear of flying' moment. If you're ever ready to take the next step, let me know."

I shifted my focus back to the carpet and nodded. He crossed the hall and went into his own room, and I went into mine, shutting the door quietly to keep from waking Bryce.

Chapter 12

At some point in the night I finally fell asleep, but as soon as I woke up the next morning, my brain started replaying my conversation with Joel. Everything would have been easier if Joel had agreed with me that we should just be friends. It made the most sense. But what did he mean about my fear of flying?

I wasn't *afraid* of a relationship with him. We just wanted different things. Even if religion hadn't been an issue, right now I didn't have time for anything or anyone else besides my job, my ranch, and my brother and sister. I'd already lost my parents; I couldn't risk losing anything else. And there was way too much risk of losing Joel to even take a chance on him.

Once I'd convinced myself I'd made the right decision, the only thing left to do was roll out of bed, get dressed, and ignore the doubts that kept worming their way into my head. The first two tasks were only marginally difficult. The last? Easier said than done. Especially when I got downstairs and saw Joel sitting at the dining room table. He smiled as if nothing had happened.

"Good morning," he said cheerfully. "Sleep okay?" His ease almost erased the weirdness between us.

"I did." The dark circles under my eyes told a different story. "You?"

"Great." He pulled out a chair for me, and I sat down, a twinge of disappointment rippling through me. Apparently our chat hadn't kept him up all night like it had me. And his lips probably weren't tingling with the memory of our kiss.

Bryce burst out of the kitchen with Walt following close behind, both with plates full of pancakes and bacon. Bryce sat down between Joel and me, breaking the magnetic force that kept drawing my eyes to Joel's lips. Thank goodness. I needed something else to look at. Bryce would do fine.

"Emily said I have to help LaRell instead of hanging out with you," Bryce said to Joel then glared at me and poured half a bottle of syrup over his breakfast, daring me to make him stop.

"We've got a lot of work to do, Bryce." I'd explained days before why he couldn't monopolize Joel's time.

Joel took the syrup away from Bryce and set it down. "If anything exciting happens, I'll come get you," he said, and Bryce almost smiled.

LaRell set plates just as full as Bryce's in front of Joel and me. Joel looked at the bacon, then smiled at her. "Thank you. Looks great."

"You're welcome. Eat up. The hog that bacon came from was raised up the road in Oakley." She stood behind us, waiting.

Joel took a bite of his pancake, and when LaRell turned her back, he put his bacon on Bryce's plate. Walt eyed him, but instead of asking the question written on his face, he picked up a paper at his side.

"Here are the major repairs I've found that need to be done if you want to sell." Walt slid the piece of paper across the table to me. Every line was filled. "Here's the list of improvements if you want to go the eco-resort route your dad wanted." This time he handed me a yellow legal pad. Every page was filled.

I ate while I went over that list. The longer it grew, the less I wanted to eat. I passed the pad to Joel after I finished the last page.

"How many people can you room now?" Joel pushed his plate away and flipped through the pages of repairs.

"We've got six rooms that sleep one to four, but the kitchen isn't big enough to feed that many people if we're filled to capacity," Walt answered. One of the first things on the improvement list was a bigger kitchen.

"But you'd only serve breakfast?" Joel asked. He walked to the back door and opened it to see outside. Bryce got up to follow, but I sent him into the kitchen before I answered Joel's question.

"For now, but we'd like to be able to offer picnic lunches and eventually a limited dinner menu. At least that was Dad's idea." We stepped outside with Walt close behind, and I went on. "Eventually, he wanted to build two or three one-room cabins in some of the more secluded areas of our property. Something more private and high end than the rooms inside but still eco-friendly." I followed Joel's gaze around the property, trying to see everything through his eyes.

Rehashing Dad's dream got me excited about it again. He loved talking over his plans with me. We had mapped out a business plan and how he would market the ranch as an "affordably luxurious eco-resort." A place not just for people who enjoyed skiing but for anyone who loved the outdoors and would appreciate a place that not only blended into its surroundings, but also limited its environmental impact.

As a B&B, the ranch generated enough income for Walt and LaRell to pay the lease and cover the costs of keeping it open, with a little bit of profit left over. But there were weeks when we didn't have any guests at all—like this one. We needed to keep it filled to capacity and charge more in order to really make money. Dad had drummed up a ton of interest in his eco-resort idea, and I knew that's the direction I needed to go if I didn't sell. Aside from liking the idea because my dad had thought of it, I liked it because it was a good one.

We circled the entire outside of the house, and Joel inspected every inch of it. He and Walt talked through the different fixes that *had* to be made and the changes that *could* be made to bring it more up to date. I was glad they were doing most of the talking because I was having a hard time focusing on anything other than the view I had as I walked behind Joel—so focused, in fact, that when he suddenly bent down, I nearly toppled over him. I stopped inches from his curved spine as he leaned over to tie his shoe.

"Sorry. I wasn't watching where I was going," I said when he stood back up. His sideways grin made me wonder if he'd done it on purpose.

"Let's take a look at the kitchen." He opened the back door, and I followed him through the great room into the kitchen, where LaRell had Bryce hard at work on the dishes.

It was big, but it needed to be bigger. Or at least it needed bigger appliances. Even with both of the ovens working, they still weren't large enough to feed the thirty to forty people we eventually wanted to accommodate.

"I think you could rearrange the layout in here to maximize your space without expanding." He pulled out his tape measure and handed the tape end to me, pointing me to the opposite corner. "A good kitchen designer could draw up some plans for you," he said as he unrolled the tape and measured the oven wall.

Suddenly I remembered Jason's offer to contact Rachel's designer friend. The designer friend who Joel used to date. I swallowed hard, debating whether to bring her up or not. Practicality won, as usual. Jason was willing to pay, so I had to take what he was offering. Which meant I'd have Joel and his ex helping me.

"Jason offered to contact a designer friend of Rachel's to help me out. I wonder if she'd be able to do something like that."

Joel looked up from his measurements, suddenly very interested in what I'd said. "Who is it?"

"I think her name is Becca. He said you used to date her." I sucked in my lips and held my breath. I would have turned blue if I had held it for as long as it took him to answer.

"Yeah, she could draw up some plans." He pulled the tape measure, and I let go. It rolled back with a loud snap. Without looking at me, he rattled off a list of recommendations for the kitchen.

I can't lie. I didn't mind the change in subject. I typed notes into my phone as fast as I could get my thumbs to move. The more Joel talked, the less overwhelming and more exciting the ranch-to-resort renovation seemed. The churning in my gut that hadn't stopped since Mom and Dad's accident slowed, and I even felt a tingle of excitement buried deep inside there.

"Those are great ideas," I said when he stopped talking.

"Before you get too far ahead of yourself, we probably oughta talk about what you're up against." Walt's low drawl tamped out the tiny sparks of possibility.

"Yeah, I guess we do have a pretty big problem to solve first." I shoved my phone with all my notes into my back pocket then rubbed my temples.

"Prob*lems*, is more like it." LaRell handed the mixing bowl she'd rinsed to Bryce, and he dropped it with a loud clang into the dishwasher. I raised my eyebrow, and he reloaded it, quietly.

"Where's those letters, LaRell?" Walt asked.

LaRell dried her hands on her apron. "Bryce, clear the dishes off that table, love," she said as she walked out of the kitchen, and he reluctantly followed.

"What problems?" I asked Walt. "Why haven't you mentioned them before?"

"We just got the letter the day you called. I figured it was better to talk in person."

LaRell walked back in and thrust three sheets of paper at me. The address in the corner said they were from the Summit County Planning Commission. I scanned them, but only four words stuck out at me: *conditional use permit tabled.*

"What does this mean?" I asked Walt. I continued to scan them, but my brain jumbled the words. "They can't shut us down unless that ordinance passes."

Joel held out his hand, and I gave him the letters so he could look.

"The neighbors have decided they don't want a road through here. They don't want people in and out of here all the time. They're afraid it'll bring down their property values," Walt answered, his flat vowels scraping my ears like a sidewalk being raked.

"Why do the neighbors get a say in what we do with our property? Dad checked the zoning laws when he bought this place, and there weren't any restrictions against commercial development," I shot back.

"Well, they're trying to sell the lane as a conservation easement—to protect the wildlife. If it goes through, we can't improve the road. Without a road, the city won't let us operate a business here. They've tabled our business permit till things are figured out. We've already had to turn people away." It was the most I'd ever heard Walt say at one time, and it took so long for him to say it all, I had to grip the kitchen counter behind me to keep from shaking it out of him.

"We own the rights to that lane." My voice rose in frustration.

"That's what they're contesting," he replied.

"You need a lawyer," Joel said and handed the letters back to me. "Even if you solve this problem, it looks like you're going to have to live here to operate it as a bed-and-breakfast . . . or anything else, for that matter."

"Yep," Walt said. "Those knotheads on the city council are going to pass that ordinance, and leasing doesn't count as owning. Your only options are to move here or sell." He spit out the word *sell*. Selling would mean he and LaRell would be out of jobs. They didn't have the money to buy the ranch from us.

I turned around, leaned my elbows on the counter, and dropped my face into my hands. I took deep, quiet breaths, reminding myself this wasn't the worst thing I'd been through in the past year. There was no reason to break down now, even as the reality of my situation sunk in. If we couldn't operate the ranch as a bed-and-breakfast, I didn't have a reason to keep it. I'd have to sell. The catch-22? The ranch was worth more as a business than as a residential property, but I couldn't sell it as a business if I didn't develop the road, and I couldn't get approval for the road unless I lived there and operated it as a business.

"You okay?" Joel laid a gentle hand between my shoulder blades. I stood up before his touch could comfort me.

"You're right. I do need a lawyer." I faced Joel and forced a smile.

"My friend Brian does real estate law. He can hook you up with someone here," Joel said, pulling his phone out of his pocket.

"Thanks." I already regretted resisting his touch. He was the one who knew exactly how to help me.

Joel spent a few minutes talking to Brian, explaining my situation. As Brian's voice boomed across the line and Joel paced the kitchen answering his questions, I understood why Joel's parents were so disappointed when he decided not to practice law. He knew his stuff. He was throwing around more Latin than a Catholic priest at Mass.

"I'm going to put you on speaker so Emily can hear." Joel stopped his pacing and set the phone on the counter.

"Hi, Brian."

"Hi," he said then launched right into his advice. "You've got to find the deed to the property and the exact property lines. That's your starting point." His voice filled the kitchen, his words sprinting faster than an Olympic runner. "Then you've got two approaches you can take. You can go in fighting if the lines are on your side, or you can try to make friends with the neighbors and figure out what it is they want."

"Which of those approaches would you recommend?" I asked and pulled my phone back out of my pocket to take more notes.

"It's always better to make friends, but that means compromising. You take a chance they'll want more than you can give, and you're right back where you started. Except you've wasted a lot of time getting there."

"So make friends or not, Brian?" Joel asked, to my relief. Brian's answer wasn't super helpful.

"Find the deed so you have the upper hand. If you've got documents to support your position, the neighbors and the city council have more reason to be your friends." This answer was clearer cut, though not necessarily easy. I had no idea where Dad had the deed, which meant I couldn't put off going through his files and personal things any longer. It also meant I'd need more than the couple days we'd planned on being in Utah to work this mess out.

"Let me ask around, and I'll get you some names of attorneys there." A quick tapping kept rhythm with Brian's words, and I pictured him with a pencil, drumming the papers on his desk, anxious to move on to the next important thing.

"Thank you for all your help," I said.

"I'll call you back soon with names." He hung up, and I looked at Joel. "Now what?"

At that moment, Walt—who I hadn't noticed leave—walked back in the kitchen with a large roll of paper. He dropped it on the counter with a loud smack, then unrolled it. I looked closer at the blueprints and noticed the name Winter Lane.

"That's our lane." I pointed at the white lines, and my pulse quickened.

"This is the property line." Walt pointed at a line parallel to the lane.

"So we have rights to it?"

"Sure as heck looks like it." He clenched his fist and rapped his knuckle on the blueprints. "Your dad got these when he bought the place."

"So this is all we need, right? This shows the lane is on our property." It wasn't a title or a deed, but it had to work.

"If they have documents showing they bought the same piece of property, then it's not," Joel said.

We studied the plans some more and talked through my options but didn't get much further until Brian called back.

"John Walker can meet with you at one o'clock today. He's in downtown Salt Lake." Joel repeated to me what Brian had told him, even though I'd heard most of it.

I looked at my watch. Ten o'clock. "I have to leave now if I'm going to get there," I said to Joel, who said a quick goodbye to Brian.

"Do you want me to come too?" he asked after he'd hung up.

I did. Very much. But there was one problem. "I don't know what to do with Bryce."

"I'd help you out, but I've got a lot to get done. And I doubt he'll want to hang out in the kitchen with LaRell all day." Walt stuck his hat on his head. "Sorry about that, but let me know how it goes."

I nodded my goodbye to him, and he left.

"We'll go with you. There's got to be something we can do in downtown Salt Lake while you meet with this guy," Joel announced, totally oblivious to the one obvious sightseeing option in downtown Salt Lake City, Utah. But after our conversation last night, I wasn't going to be the one who pointed it out to him.

"I'm sure you can find something." I could have had him stay at the ranch with Bryce. It didn't make much sense to drag either one of them all the way to Salt Lake if Joel wouldn't even be in the lawyer's office with me. But knowing he would be close by made me feel better about the whole thing.

And maybe a part of me hoped he would find his way to Temple Square. I wasn't exactly sure where Walker's office was, but when I saw the address was on South Temple, I figured it had to be somewhere near the temple.

Turned out, it was even harder to miss than I imagined. Walker's office was smack dab in City Creek, directly across from the temple.

"Hey, it's Temple Square," Bryce pointed out helpfully as I pulled into the underground parking. "We could go there, Joel."

"Whatever you want, bud. What do you do there?" Joel asked.

"You sure that's what you want to do, Bryce?" I butted in before Bryce could answer. "You've been there before." Not my greatest missionary moment ever.

"I haven't been there for a long time," he said to me before turning to Joel. "You just look at stuff, but it's cool. There's a big statue of Jesus in one building and there's the temple. But we can't go in there."

"Is it closed today or something?" Joel asked, and my heart beat faster.

"You have to be twelve or older. And you have to be Mormon," Bryce answered.

Joel looked at me for clarification.

"You might like the history of it. It's pretty amazing what the pioneers did to build it." I didn't exactly answer any of the questions I imagined were running through his head, but at least it was more missionary-ish than my last answer. Sort of.

"I guess it's a good place to start if I want to know more about Mormonism, right?" His eyes widened with a genuine interest that made my heart beat faster and brought the kiss we'd shared to mind. Maybe Joel did want to learn more on his own. Maybe that wouldn't be a bad thing. *Maybe* it could turn into a really good thing.

"You definitely won't have trouble finding people to answer your questions; that's for sure." I parked the car and gathered my purse without looking at him. Heat swept up my neck to my cheeks, partly from the memory of his lips on mine and partly from guilt over not giving him a fairer warning about the people so willing to answer his questions.

"All right, Bryce. Let's go learn some Mormon stuff." Joel let Bryce out of the backseat then looked across the top of the car. "Call me when you're done."

"Thanks. Have fun." I forced a smile. I was glad he'd come with me, but now I was almost as nervous about what he'd think of Temple Square as I was about meeting with the lawyer. Somehow my quick trip to Utah had the potential to be a major crossroads in my life in so many ways.

"Your lawyer will figure this out," he said.

"I hope so."

"What's the worst that can happen? You have to sell the ranch." His words weren't super comforting, and the look on my face must have told him so. "You've lost more than that and survived."

That reminder, while not necessarily pleasant, was helpful. It gave voice to the feelings I'd been trying to ignore since we'd driven away from the ranch along the lane that held my fate in its rutted, rocky path.

"I don't want to lose it," I blurted.

"Then fight for it," he said with enough enthusiasm to motivate a snail to win a marathon; then he smiled wide.

Those words gave me courage as he turned to catch up with Bryce, and I went in the opposite direction to prepare for battle. I was going to keep the one thing that was Dad's to leave behind. The one thing that was mine now.

Chapter 13

FOUR HOURS LATER I CALLED Joel, feeling a lot more hopeful about my chances of keeping the ranch but also a lot more certain I'd have to live in it too.

"Hi, where are you?" I asked when he answered.

"Standing in front of a building with a Star of David on it with Sister Cameron and Sister Kim," he said then asked, "What's this called again?"

I heard a voice in the background, and Joel spoke again. "The tabernacle. We're at the tabernacle."

"I'll be right there." I hung up my phone and sped up to a fast trot. *Joel was with missionaries.* Why that thought sent me into a panic, I don't know, but I had to get to him. I weaved through the shoppers coming in and out of the stores surrounding Walker's office and ran across the street to Temple Square.

I was out of breath by the time I found my brother and Joel. Joel was shaking hands with the sisters and saying goodbye.

"How'd it go today?" I whispered to Bryce.

"We've been here *forever*." He tipped his head back and let his arms dangle at his sides.

Joel, on the other hand, looked like a kid who'd spent the day at a candy store. "That was cool," he said when he joined us. "Did you have a good time, Bryce?"

"You asked a lot of questions," he sighed.

"Thanks for hanging in there with me, dude." He patted Bryce on the back and smiled.

I wanted to know what he'd learned, but I didn't want to ask, and before I could, he started on his own questions for me. "How did it go? You look happier than you did this morning."

"I am, but I'm hungry. Should we eat?" I pointed to a restaurant as we crossed the street back to City Creek.

"Yes, I'm starving." Bryce ran ahead of us to get in the line winding out the door.

"John did a title search, and the preliminary documents show we have rights to the easement, which means we should be able to develop the road. He has to do more research." I explained everything I could remember the lawyer telling me as we caught up with my brother.

"Sounds like good news," Joel replied.

"We choose what we want then order at the counter," Bryce interrupted, waving a menu in my face.

"He's also looking into filing an appeal with the city council so we can get our conditional use permit back." I took the menu from Bryce and moved him to my side so I could continue my conversation with Joel.

"So you'll be back in business soon?" he said with excitement I couldn't muster. We'd gotten to the place I wasn't so sure about.

"Maybe . . . if I move here." I scanned the menu intently without really reading it.

"You're moving here?" His excitement had turned to confusion.

"He's pretty sure I'll have to make the concession to live at the ranch if I want the city council to okay giving us our permit back." I turned the menu over and read the back, staring at letters I knew should form words but wouldn't seem to cooperate.

"And you're going to do it?"

I looked up to meet his eyes. "I don't think there's another way if I want to keep the ranch."

"Oh." The line moved, and he stepped forward with it before turning all of his attention to the menu. I should have been hurt he wouldn't look at me. Instead, I was relieved. I had to make a decision in the next few days about whether to sell the ranch or move to it. Joel's eyes would only make that decision harder.

I stepped up to the counter and realized I had no idea what was on the menu, so I ordered the first thing I saw. After making Joel let me pay, we found a table and sat down across from each other.

"Can I play a game on your phone?" Bryce asked, something I never let him do, but I made an exception. I wanted Joel to myself.

Once Bryce was absorbed in his game, Joel started on his questions again.

"So if you move here, would it be permanent? Or would you be able to move back to California?" He tapped his empty plastic cup on the table, still not making eye contact.

"I don't know. Maybe I could split my time between the two and keep Bryce and Annie in California. That might depend on whether Annie gets this job or not." I unrolled my napkin and smoothed it on my lap. "But if I've learned one thing over the past year, it's that plans have a funny way of changing."

"When we make plans, God laughs. My rabbi said that once," he said and stopped his tapping. He raised his eyes to me and smiled, almost melting my resolve to just be friends.

"That sounds about right." I tore my eyes away from his. "Although, if I'm going to move here even temporarily, I've got a lot of plans to make." I thought back to the list Walt had given me that morning. Thinking about everything on it started my heart racing.

"You want me to get your drink?" Joel stood up and grabbed his cup and mine.

"Coke," I answered and watched him all the way to the soda fountain and back.

"And what do you do for work? Become a cowgirl full-time?" he asked as he set my drink in front of me.

"I don't think so. I'm a lot better with numbers and marketing than with horses. That's why Dad thought I could handle running the ranch." I took a long sip of my drink. The rush of caffeine only made the anxious pounding in my chest worse.

"Those are both better skills for running a business than being able to work with horses—even if horses are part of that business. Your dad knew what he was doing."

"Thanks." I was torn between loving his encouragement and wanting him to beg me not to move to Utah. And I wasn't sure if the carsick rolling in my stomach was from the thought of everything I'd have to leave behind if I moved or just the thought of leaving him.

The waiter came out with our food and set it down. I held my hand out for my phone, and Bryce passed it over. I'd ordered a chicken sandwich and fries, but now my appetite was gone.

"Are we moving to Utah?" Bryce asked, his mouth full of fries.

"I don't know, sweetie. Maybe." His supersonic hearing was back at work.

"I think we should move. If we live on the ranch, can I help take care of the horses? And can I learn to snowboard? You could visit, Joel. I could teach you how to fish like my dad taught me." He ate as fast as he talked and got more excited with each bite until food and words were flying out of his mouth.

"Mouth closed please," I said and wiped crumbs and spittle off my arm. "You wouldn't miss your friends if we moved?"

"I would. . . ." He shrugged. "But the ranch reminds me of Dad. It's easier to feel like he's with me at the ranch than at home."

"Do you feel Mom with you at the ranch?" I asked. Bryce had barely said anything about our parents since the accident.

"Mom's always around. I dream about her all the time, and sometimes I hear her voice. Like when I'm doing something I know she wouldn't like." His mouth slipped into a smile that just as quickly slipped away. "Besides, if we can't stay in our house, then I want to live in the other place Dad and Mom wanted to live."

I hadn't really considered Bryce in my plans for the ranch. I'd assumed he wanted to stay in California as much as Annie and I did. But seeing how happy the thought of moving to the ranch made him caused me to look at the possibility in a whole new light.

"That seems like a pretty good reason to live there," Joel said.

"Maybe we could stay there for the summer. Would you like that?" I wasn't ready to commit to moving permanently, but staying there for a few months would mean I could get started on the renovations and figure out if splitting my time between Utah and California might be an option.

Bryce shook his head. "No, I want to move there, not just stay for a few months." He squirted ketchup on his plate even though he'd finished his fries.

I looked at Joel, who raised an eyebrow.

"How about when we get home, we write down all the pros and cons of staying in California or moving to Utah? Then we can make a plan for what we want to do—"

"Did you hear that?" Joel cupped his hand behind his ear.

"What?" Bryce and I asked at the same time.

"I think I hear someone laughing," he said, staring pointedly at me.

"I don't hear anyone." Bryce looked around. There were plenty of utensils clinking and people talking, but no one laughing.

I looked at Joel, who was still staring at me, and then I got it.

"I think he means God," I said to Bryce, and Joel smiled.

Chapter 14

BY THE TIME WE FLEW home Monday morning, I was no closer to knowing what to do than I had been when we left. In fact, there were only two things clearer to me than they had been four days before, and both of them only made things harder for me. The first was I had to accept the fact I wasn't in control of my life. The second was I liked Joel a lot more than I should.

Before I could make any decisions of my own, Jason pushed me along. He made good on his promise to help me with the ranch, and Monday afternoon I had a call from Rachel's designer friend. (I had decided to think of her only as a friend of Rachel and Jason's, not Joel's ex.)

"Hi! This is Becca Lewis. Is this Emily Carter?" The cheerful voice on the other end surprised me. I guess I was expecting someone more reserved and less—I don't know—friendly.

"Hi, Becca." I held the phone an inch away from my ear where her voice was still ringing.

"Jason told me about your ranch project, and I'd love to help you with it. It sounds really exciting."

I got the feeling Becca wasn't too hard to excite, but who cared? If the ranch made it on to her list of really exciting things, I could only benefit.

"How about you come to my office tomorrow? E-mail me all the measurements and pictures you have. I'll use them to draw up some plans, and we can talk options."

"That sounds great." A little whirlwindish, but great.

She gave me her address and told me to "take a peek" at her website, then hung up, leaving me breathless. I did take that peek but only to see what *she* looked like, not her designs. Tiny with sleek dark hair and beautiful, despite her too-big features in her tiny face. Already I could see what Joel saw in her.

The next day I got to her downtown office building right on time but waited in the marble floored foyer for ten minutes before her secretary led me back to her office.

"It's so great to meet you!" As soon as she saw me, Becca held out her small hand and greeted me with a warm smile. She motioned me to a white sofa, and I sat down, noticing a photograph on the table next to it. Luckily I was already sitting because my legs felt shaky. She and Joel were on a beach with their arms wrapped around each other and the sun setting in the background. I was 90 percent sure it wasn't a California beach either. It screamed Hawaii.

"So you're Jason's little sister?" She sat down in a chair across from me. All I could do was nod.

"He's talked a lot about you. I'm so sorry about your parents. I know that's been hard on all of you." Her face wrinkled with genuine concern.

"Thank you." Her mention of Mom and Dad momentarily distracted me from the picture of her and Joel, but only until she said his name.

"Jason said Joel went with you to the ranch, so I gave him a call. I hope that's okay, but we speak the same language when it comes to renovation and design, so I figured it would be more helpful to talk to him before I got started on any plans."

I nodded while she rambled, and I wondered how long it had been before that since they'd talked.

"He told me about the structural changes he said need to be made," she went on while I tried to focus on what she was saying instead of speculating about their relationship. "Based on all of that, I went ahead and drew up some plans. Joel said you need to get this done quickly in order to open, so I didn't want to waste any time." She opened an iPad sitting on the table between us and pulled up her work. I scrolled through her pages of ideas, becoming more impressed with each one.

"Wow. I never would have thought to rearrange the kitchen like this," I said.

"I'm excited about this project. It's such a great idea—the whole eco-resort thing is getting so big. I can't believe there's not something like it in Park City already." Her movements were small but quick, and energy spilled out of her tiny body even when she sat still.

"May I?" She leaned over the table and took the iPad from me. "I want to show you an idea I had for the great room." She handed the iPad back to me, its screen filled with a rendering of the room that included giant windows and sliding glass doors. As soon as I saw it, I knew Joel had to have been in love with her. I'd known her fifteen minutes and already was.

"I love it. It will make that room so much lighter and offer an incredible view of the mountains." If I could make her plans a reality, there was no way I was getting rid of the ranch.

"I'm so glad!" She dropped the iPad in her lap and clapped. "Joel actually suggested it."

"Really?" He was even better at what he did than I realized. "It's beautiful. I just hope the price is in my budget."

"Girl, we'll make it work. I know how to get what my clients want for the lowest price possible." She leaned over and put her hand on mine. "And Jason's paying me, so that means your budget is all materials. Plus," she glanced around and lowered her voice, "I've been dying to call Joel and didn't know how to do it—we had kind of a bad breakup. You gave me the excuse I needed." She leaned back and lifted her eyebrows. "I owe you."

"You really don't." I shook my head, not knowing what else to say. Clearly she wanted to tell me something. I had a feeling it was something I wanted to know but didn't necessarily want to hear. Still, I bit. "That's a great picture of the two of you." I pointed to the picture on the table, trying not to look at it.

"Thanks. We took it on the night we got engaged." She picked up the picture, smiling sadly, which gave me almost enough time to realize I needed to shut my gaping mouth.

"You're engaged?"

"Were." She set the picture back down, and the nausea creeping toward my chest sank back to my stomach. "Biggest mistake of my life breaking up with him. I've regretted it for months but didn't know how to reach out to him. When we talked yesterday . . . I don't want to call it fate, but I don't believe in coincidences either."

"Oh." I hoped my smile didn't look as fake as it felt. "Maybe." I swallowed. "How long ago did you break up?"

"A little over a year ago. I kind of freaked out and didn't think I was ready to commit. I mean, *marriage*. That's huge, you know?" She picked up the iPad and tapped the screen.

I nodded, still in shock.

"But I think I'm ready now, so maybe his call is fate giving me another chance." The printer started, and she flipped the iPad case closed.

"It could be." I surprised myself by how much I hoped it wasn't.

"Anyway, sorry to get all personal on you. I don't usually spill my guts to potential clients, but I've known Jason forever. We're practically family." She stood up, walked to her desk, and took papers from the printer.

"Here are the designs if you want to look them over some more. If you don't like them, I'll come up with something different." Becca handed me the stack of papers.

I wished I didn't like them—or her—so much. The only thing I wanted different was to work with someone who hadn't been engaged to the man I couldn't quit thinking about.

Chapter 15

I LEFT BECCA'S OFFICE CONFLICTED. I loved the plans she'd drawn up but hated the jealousy gnawing its way from my gut to my heart. I didn't have any claim on Joel, so I had no right to be mad he hadn't told me about his engagement. But I was. I tried to talk myself out of being hurt as I drove home, but it didn't work. The only thing I'd convinced myself of by the time I walked in the front door was that I'd been right not to get involved with him. I only wished I'd been able to convince myself not to fall for him.

Annie sat on the couch in the family room staring at her phone. She was still in pajamas, but her hair at least looked combed and she wasn't in bed, so I called it a win for the day.

"Hey, what's up?" I sat down next to her and tossed Becca's plans on the table.

"I just got a call from Sharon," she answered with a lot less enthusiasm than a call from her agent usually generated.

"That's a good thing, right?"

"Yeah . . . sort of."

"What do you mean?"

"Well, I got the job in Utah—"

"You did? Yay!" I wrapped my arms around her, ready to do a hugging, happy dance, but all I got was a pat. "Why am I the only one excited?" I let go and pulled back to make eye contact.

"She also gave me the name of a new agent. A woman in Utah who represents a lot of actors and models who are members of the Church, so she only finds work that won't ask them to compromise their standards." She looked down and turned her phone over and over in her hands.

"Why do you need a new agent?" I asked, even as the pieces started falling into place.

"Sharon can't find me work, but she thinks this new agent will be better able to get me into the 'clean' market," she answered with a shrug.

I waited for more, but when it didn't come, I asked my own question. "Are you going to take the Utah job?"

"I don't know." She shrugged again. "I don't think I have another choice if I want to keep acting."

"You don't want to give up acting, do you?"

Half a second passed before she shook her head.

"But you're afraid you won't be able to come back, aren't you? You'll be stuck only doing Mormon stuff."

Her mouth pulled to one side before she glanced at me and nodded. "I know I should be grateful, but all I feel is scared. I think I'd have to move there, and I don't know if I'm ready to do that." She set her phone down and sank back into the couch cushions.

"Is that the only thing scaring you?"

She wagged her head back and forth. "It seems like a step down, and I won't be making nearly as much money."

"Yeah, but are there good things about it?"

"It would be nice not to worry about what I'm going to be asked to do and whether turning down a part for moral reasons is going to ruin my career. Plus, it's a growing market, so the Utah agent says there'd be plenty of work for me." She sat up a fraction of an inch as though the act of stating the positives was, literally, pulling her up.

"Those are all good things. Do they outweigh the negatives?"

Annie swallowed hard twice before raising her red-rimmed eyes to me. "I don't want to live there by myself."

I glanced at the plans on the table then back at Annie and knew I had the answer I'd been searching for. We were moving to Utah.

*   *   *

I called Jason that night to give him the good news that we'd be moving out. Annie had to be in Utah within the month, and Bryce would be out of school by then, so it was perfect timing. After months of worrying about where and how we were going to live, it seemed strange that the question resolved itself within a few hours.

Joel texted me the next day, but I didn't answer. I wasn't ready to tell him I'd be moving soon and knowing he'd so recently been engaged to Becca made me question how genuine his feelings for me were. How could he be close to marrying someone less than a year before and be ready to move on already? And if Becca wanted to get back together with him, what would keep them apart?

He tried calling a few times too, and each time it got harder not to pick up. I forced myself to focus on calls to my lawyer about the ranch and finding a contractor to do the work. After checking those things off my list, I turned my attention to Becca's plans. She'd attached fabric swatches to them so I could see the color scheme she was thinking and get some ideas about what kinds of upholstery to use for seating. She also gave me the names of stores in the fabric district, and since I knew Joel would be working at the house the next day, it seemed like a perfect excuse to go shopping.

I knew I'd have to see him. I *wanted* to see him. Looking at the angles of his face and the curve of his smile sounded so much more appealing than studying fabric texture and durability—which was exactly why I needed to focus on anything that had to do with the ranch. Too soon I would have to tell Joel goodbye, and I didn't want it to hurt any more than I already knew it would. I'd had enough goodbyes to last a lifetime.

It was seven o'clock that night when I turned on to my street, exhausted from going store to store examining thousands of fabrics, until I couldn't distinguish pink from orange or herringbone from tulle. I wanted nothing more than to plant myself in front of the TV, catch up on *The Good Wife*, and pretend I was back in my Santa Monica condo a year ago when my life was normal. But as I pulled into my driveway, I saw Joel's car still parked on the street. A surge of energy shot through me. The thought of seeing him revived me, but it also made me want to run. I'd thought all day about how to tell him I was moving and we shouldn't see each other anymore, but I couldn't formulate any ideas that didn't split my heart in two.

Which was why I tried to hide from him. I parked my car and shut the door softly. I could hear pounding, so I figured it would be easy to sneak upstairs without him seeing or hearing me. I held my breath as I opened the front door and crept up the stairs. Before I reached the top, I heard his voice.

"Are you ignoring me?" he yelled over the pounding that hadn't stopped. I guessed he'd put Bryce to work. I should have known.

I turned around. "I've been pretty busy today." My eyes darted to his, before I forced them to the dark outline on the wall behind him where a picture of my family had hung. Annie had promised to start packing. She must have started there.

"Have you eaten?" He moved up two steps and leaned against the railing.

I nodded.

"How about ice cream?" His eyebrow and the corner of his mouth went up.

I shook my head, unable to stop my own grin.

"I'm taking that as a 'No, I haven't had any' and not a 'No, I don't want any.'" He climbed the stairs between us and grabbed my hand.

I let him lead me down the stairs and out the door, pep talking myself into taking this chance to tell him I couldn't see him anymore. Not even as friends. It would be too hard.

The problem was he talked first. "Have you been to Milk?" he asked as we walked toward his car, my hand still in his.

"No. The line is always too long."

"Doesn't matter. You have to try it before you move."

I stopped and took my hand away from his. "How do you know I'm moving?"

He turned to face me. "Jason told me."

Seconds passed while we looked at each other. I didn't know if my eyes looked as sad as his, but I guessed they did, and my resolve crumbled.

"Is it really worth the wait?" I asked, breaking the silence.

His mouth crept into a slow smile. "Doesn't matter. It's the hip thing to do, so you have to try it." He took my hand again, but this time I wound my fingers in his as he led me to the car.

"Hip? Do people still use that word?" I asked as he opened the door.

He sighed, shaking his head with pretend disappointment. "You haven't even left LA, and already you don't know what's cool." He shut the door and jogged to his side.

"I know standing in line isn't cool." I said as soon as he climbed into his seat.

"Tell that to the five hundred people who will be in line ahead of us."

"Five hundred? Seriously? Do they milk the cows right there? How can anything be worth that kind of wait?"

"Trust me. If nothing else, you get to spend some time with me." He took his eyes off the road long enough to give me his crooked grin that made me hope the line would take forever.

"I guess that's not the worst thing in the world. The ice cream still better be good though."

"Have you got everything settled with the ranch?" he asked suddenly, his mood turning more serious.

"Not yet," I answered. "Things are looking good. My lawyer seems to think the property rights fall in our favor. The fact I'll be living there will be a huge bargaining chip with the city council. They're more willing to grant us the permits we need once I'm there."

"How soon can you start operating again?"

"As soon as we get the permit to improve the road and the construction is done. Six months maybe?"

"You found a contractor?" A BMW cut us off, and Joel hit the brakes before saying a few choice words about the other driver. "One thing you won't have to deal with anymore is this." He waved his hand at the cars.

"Yeah, I won't miss traffic; that's for sure." I pulled on my seatbelt to unlock it. "Walt found a contractor for me. He'll start once I get there."

"Are you going to work or just focus on the ranch?" He sped up and changed lanes to get to our exit.

"I don't think I'll be able to do both. I worked out the finances today, and I've got enough insurance money left to get us through the year, as long as I keep construction costs down. Annie got the job in Provo, so with her working again, she can pitch in for expenses too." Once I'd made the decision to move, things had started falling into place easily.

"That sounds great. I'm glad you're keeping it. . . . I wish you didn't have to move though." Joel kept his eyes straight ahead, driving down the 101, passing signs for Echo Park and Historic Filipinotown, places I'd passed a thousand times and never been.

We talked about the plans Becca had drawn up—without actually talking about Becca. We entered Koreatown, passing houses with barred windows, strip malls advertising in symbols I couldn't read, homeless people sleeping on the piles of their possessions, and Asian women tottering in stilettos. I'd lived in LA my entire life, and always there was something new. Still so much I hadn't seen.

"Sounds like you've got things all figured out." His words were tinged with sadness as he pulled into a parking spot.

"As much as I can from eight hundred miles away."

He got out of the car, and I waited for him to open the door for me. I stepped out, and he pulled me aside as a group of tipsy diners from the

Korean BBQ place passed us. He didn't let go of my arm even after they'd gone by, and we didn't move. "I'm going to miss you," he whispered.

I lifted my shoulders in a slow shrug that asked what else I could do. He trailed his fingers down my arm then let his hand drop. I turned to continue our walk to the ice cream line wrapped around the building, but he grabbed my hand.

"Wait." He sucked in his lips. "I want to tell you something, but I don't want you to freak out."

"What is it?" My first thought was he was going to tell me about his engagement, but what he said surprised me even more than that news had.

"I had the missionaries over."

"Why?" I blurted, confirming me, once again, as the worst missionary ever.

"I don't know." He laughed. "I thought you might be a little happier about it than that."

"It's not that I'm not happy. I'm surprised."

He dropped my hand, leaving me feeling awkward standing in the middle of the sidewalk. I moved to a bench and sat down.

"They want to come back," he said, sitting down next to me.

"Do you want them to come back?"

He leaned forward and clasped his hands then sat back up. "I do if it means keeping you in my life as more than a friend. Even if it's long distance." His knee bumped mine, sending as many sparks up my leg as his words had sent down my spine.

"You can't do it for me. It has to be for yourself." I moved my leg so we weren't touching anymore. I couldn't let a few sparks burn out of control.

He pressed his lips together and let out a long breath before looking at me again. "You have to understand what I would be giving up if I became Mormon. My family, my friends . . . my life. Isn't it enough that, right now, I'd be willing to lose everything for you?"

"I don't want you to lose anything. Especially for me." I met his gaze but couldn't hold it without caving.

He slid his hand into mine and held it. "As long as I have you, I have everything I need."

"You barely know me."

"That doesn't matter," he said, shaking his head.

We sat in silence while I tried to convince myself to take my hand out of his, but it felt right there. As hard as I had tried, I couldn't deny my feelings for him. And why should I? Here was a man who was willing to give up everything for me, and I wasn't even going to give him a chance?

I took my hand out of his and stood up. His eyes followed me as I placed my hands on his cheeks and leaned down, drawing his face to mine. Our lips brushed in a gentle kiss before I pulled away and whispered, "Let's go get some ice cream."

Chapter 16

ICE CREAM NEVER TASTED SO good. I ordered a Citrus Vanilla Float, and Joel got the Milky Way Malt after changing his mind about the Coffee Toffee Crunch he originally wanted.

"We'll want to share, right?" he asked.

"Of course." I hadn't asked him to change his order; he just did. *This could work,* I kept telling myself, and I actually believed it.

We left the hipster-crowded shop with our drinks plus some cookies and a slice of blue velvet cake. It had taken us so long to get from my house to the front of the line that we had to try more than one thing. Walking back to Joel's car with our hands full, our arms touched with each step. He set his shake on the car roof while he opened the passenger door and let me slide in. I caught a glimpse of my shining eyes and love-sick grin in the rearview mirror. I bit my lip but couldn't stop myself from feeling as happy as I looked.

Joel slid into the driver's seat and held his shake out to me. I scooped a spoonful out and passed my float to him.

"Mmm, that's good," I said. "You could have ordered the coffee flavor though."

"I'd rather share." He stuck his spoon into my perfect scoop of vanilla. "Now tell me what's so bad about coffee."

"It's just that Joseph Smith received a revelation that said we should avoid hot drinks, tobacco, and liquor. Later prophets defined hot drinks as coffee and tea. It's really a Mormon health code thing . . . kind of like your kosher laws, right?"

"Yeah, sort of." He took a few bites of his own shake, his brows still creased with unasked questions. "The missionaries told me about modern prophets, and we talked about prophets from the Torah—like Abraham—but . . ." He shook his head. "I don't know."

I jabbed the ice cream in my float and took a bite without really tasting it. "What else have you talked about? I mean, how many times have you met with them?"

"Just once—they're so young—but I've done some studying of my own." Joel poked at his own ice cream then turned his head to look at me. "They started by asking me if I believed Jesus Christ was my Savior."

"Probably not the best place to start with a Jew."

"Not really." He stirred his shake with his straw and took a long drink. "It's a huge divide to cross, this idea of Mormons' that God has a body and takes the form of a man. That's not something I've ever been taught."

I twisted the cup in my hands, not sure how to answer.

"I've studied the Torah; I spent a lot of years in Hebrew school. I see how Mormons can read scriptures about God having hands or walking and think He has a body, but Jews don't read those verses literally."

Now I was confused. "How do you read them then? Doesn't it make more sense that, if we're God's children, we look like Him?"

"That's man trying to make sense of God by giving Him human traits. God isn't male or female." Joel waved his spoon as he spoke, flicking a drop of ice cream on my cheek. "Sorry," he said and wiped the spot gently with a napkin.

"So you don't believe anything the missionaries told you?" I lowered his hand from my face.

"Maybe," he said and stuck his keys in the ignition. "I want to because you do, but it's hard." The blue of his eyes invited me in, so I concentrated on the light scar that cut through the middle of his right eyebrow, under-lining it below.

"Give it time, Joel." I swallowed hard. "Pray about it," I added softly.

"That's another thing." He pulled out of the parking space where our time on the meter had run out. "Jewish prayer is different from Mormon prayer."

"How? We talk to the same God, right?"

"In a different way. Mormons ask God to tell them what to do. Jews ask God why He does what He does. We're taught what prayers to say when. From what I can tell, you just say whatever."

"Couldn't you try our way? Is it so bad to have a personal conversation with God?"

"No. But having ritual prayers means we're always praying. We have a prayer for everything, and we acknowledge that we can't change God's path, only accept it with joy." The light changed, and a car honked behind us.

"You're always praying?"

"Well, ideally that's the purpose. I've recited Shema—the prayer we say morning and night—so many times, those are the first words that come to my mind when I wake up." We left Koreatown, and he pointed out his favorite Mexican place. "We should go sometime."

I nodded. "As long as it's in the next month."

"Tomorrow?"

"I'll pencil you in," I teased, but really I wanted to get back to our conversation. "So reciting the same prayers helps you remember God all the time?"

"Yeah, I guess so." He smiled at me like he'd had an epiphany.

"Does it help you to *know* God?" The question came out before I knew I was going to ask it, and his smile shrank.

"Hmm. I've never thought about that. Are remembering and knowing different?"

"I think so."

"That's something to consider."

He took a sip of his shake, and I did the same with my float. Our conversation lagged but not in a bad way.

We got off the freeway and passed Dodger Stadium. I'd never liked baseball, but suddenly I felt my loss. I didn't even know if Utah had a professional baseball team.

We drove by the same strip malls and run-down apartment buildings I'd seen a million times. There was a comfortable silence between us, but that silence didn't extend to my thoughts. Had I made a mistake in letting things move forward instead of stopping them? It made sense to my heart, but things weren't adding up in my head.

"You okay?" Joel reached for my hand and held it lightly in his.

"Yeah." I nodded and flashed a quick grin. I hadn't realized how much of a divide there was between our religious beliefs. Mom had always said Mormons and Jews had a lot in common because both religions focus on Abrahamic covenants. But the differences in mine and Joel's understanding of God and my belief in Jesus—were those too wide to be bridged? And would I be okay dating him—possibly marrying him—if we couldn't bridge that gap?

I didn't think so.

Joel parked in front of my house behind a car I hadn't seen before. We walked up the steps and the long pathway to the front door. The lights were on inside, and voices floated through the open windows.

"I wonder who's here," I said more to myself than to him.

Joel slowed down and let go of my hand. As we drew closer, I could tell one of the voices was Rachel's. The front door opened, and she stepped out followed by someone I couldn't see.

"There you are! Look who's here." Rachel stepped aside, and the woman behind her stepped forward.

"Hi," Joel stuttered with surprise and stepped away from me.

"Hi! Hi, Emily." Becca raised her hand in a half-hearted wave, and her eyes bounced between Joel and me before landing uncertainly on him.

"Hi, Becca." I took Joel's lead and increased the distance between us.

"Where have you two been?" Rachel eyed us with suspicion. "I told Becca to come see what you've done to the kitchen." Rachel stepped off the porch and looped her arm through Joel's. She led him back up the steps to Becca, leaving me behind.

"It's good to see you." He leaned over Becca's petite frame to peck her cheek, but when she pulled him in for a hug, he returned it.

"It's great to see you." She held him close after he'd let go.

"Are you all ready to get started on the ranch?" she said brightly to me after she'd released Joel. Her eyes only rested on mine for a second before she turned her gaze back on him.

"Yeah. I'm looking forward to it. I spent the day in the fabric district." We talked lightly about what I had found, but her eyes kept flitting back to Joel. Our conversation fizzled out, and I wasn't sure where I should look. I only knew it couldn't be at Joel.

But I couldn't help it. I knew Becca still had feelings for Joel, but all my doubts about him being over her came flooding back as I watched them together. He may not have felt the same as Becca, but as minutes ticked by, he quit fidgeting and his voice smoothed out.

"The kitchen looks like it's really coming together. Rachel showed me the before pictures. You've done an amazing job." Becca craned her neck to look up at him.

"Thanks. I've still got a lot of work to do, but Rachel picked out some really nice material to work with," Joel said then glanced back at me.

"I'm going to go in," I said. I stepped between Rachel and Joel to get to the front door. She didn't return my forced smile. "Good night." I waved and met Joel's eyes. He looked caught between a question and a hard place.

"Wait. I'll walk you." He lunged forward, but I shook my head and stopped him.

"I'm already in."

"Becca's coming over for a drink." Rachel hooked her arm around his again. "Come around back, and we can sit on my porch with a glass of wine."

Joel looked back at me. I shut the door and walked up the stairs, listening to their footsteps and Rachel's chatter as she led them around back to the guesthouse.

If I'd needed a sign that I'd made the wrong decision about a relationship with Joel, I'd received it. Loud and clear.

Chapter 17

JOEL WAS AT MY DOOR early enough that I wouldn't have had time to leave even if I'd wanted to. He was there so early, in fact, I'd barely rolled out of bed. Bryce opened the door to let him in at the same time I was walking down the stairs in the ratty In-N-Out T-shirt and old soccer shorts I'd worn to bed.

"Joel!" Bryce yelled and raised his hand for a high five.

Joel slapped his hand while I attempted to scramble back upstairs before he saw me.

"Is that what you're wearing to breakfast?" he asked.

I stopped and turned back around. I wanted to stay as mad at him as I had been all night, but the sheepish grin on his face knocked the bricks out of the wall I kept trying to build.

"I'm saving my formal wear for lunch." I bit my lip to keep from breaking into my own smile. He'd been inside for thirty seconds, and any thought I'd had of not spending every free minute with him until I left was washed away in a flash flood of excitement.

"Good thing I brought breakfast to you then." He held up a brown paper bag with a bagel logo on it. "Can we go for a drive?"

"Can I go too?" Bryce asked.

"Not this time, buddy. Your sister and I need to talk." He tousled Bryce's hair, but the playfulness had left his voice. "We'll bring something back for you."

I nodded. "Let me go change." There was no smile to hold back now. His sudden seriousness had me drowning in doubt. Seeing Becca again had probably reignited some sparks, and he had realized she was a much better fit for him than I was. That should have quieted the debate that had raged in my head all night over whether to cut him off now or friend-zone him when I left. Things would be a lot easier—in a hard way—if he were the one making the decision about when to end things.

I went to my room and shut the door. I knew I shouldn't keep Joel waiting, but the synapses from my brain to my feet had stopped firing. All I could do was sit on my bed and wait for feeling to come back to my limbs. My heart was the only part of my body that could feel anything, and it just hurt.

I took a deep breath and pushed myself up off the bed. As much as I wanted to put off the even deeper hurt that was coming, I couldn't make Joel wait forever. I stared at my closet, feeling grateful most of my clothes were packed. Even choosing something from the few things left was overwhelming.

I finally settled on some jeans, a T-shirt, and my favorite comfy cardi. I slipped on my flip-flops and pulled my unbrushed hair into a little pony, finger combing my bangs. After brushing my teeth and putting on a touch of mascara, I was ready to go. At least physically.

I went back to my room to grab my purse. I picked it up off my desk and noticed the blue, softcover Book of Mormon under it. We'd been challenged at church to give a copy away. To be polite, I'd taken one out of the basket that was passed around during Relief Society. I hadn't really thought I'd give it away, but now I slipped it in my purse.

Joel was in what was left of the dining room with Annie and Bryce when I came downstairs.

"Joel says he's going to come visit us in Utah," Bryce said, on the verge of running in circles with excitement.

"You can totally come stay with us," Annie said. She smiled wide, glancing in my direction like she'd done me a favor.

I couldn't help but look at Joel. His lips twitched between smiling and frowning, seemingly as uncertain about which direction they should go as I was.

"Ready?" The words squeaked out of my mouth.

He nodded his answer and waved goodbye to Bryce and Annie.

Walking down the long pathway to Joel's car, my heart pounded. I was torn between fear he wanted to end things with me and indecision over whether I should break things off first. I couldn't have been close-to-retching dizzier unless I'd been on the teacups at Disneyland. The yo-yoing going on in my stomach was the exact reason I'd never been on a roller coaster bigger than Space Mountain.

Joel opened the car door for me, and I slid in. A toolbox took up most of the backseat, and there were tile samples stacked on the floor.

"It really is time to get a truck," I said after he closed his door and handed me the bagel bag.

"I know. I've already committed to the job; I should commit to the lifestyle," he said, peeking over his shoulder at the mess behind him.

We laughed, and for a second the tension disappeared. But like ants to crumbs, it didn't take long for it to creep back.

We didn't say anything until Joel pulled into the park a couple blocks from my house.

"Do you want to get out or sit here?" he asked.

The grass under a leafy maple looked inviting, but there were kids laughing and playing on the playground nearby. The sound of their laughter made everything harder. It didn't seem fair that there were people not worried about their future, even if they were kids.

"Let's stay here."

He rolled down the windows, shut the car off, then took the bagels out of the bag. "I took a chance you'd like lox. It's the best one they have."

"I've never tried it." I unwrapped the sandwich, hoping it wasn't gross.

"Never tried lox? How is that even possible?"

"I don't know. It's good." I swallowed the bite I'd taken and wiped my mouth before taking another bite. It was good, but eating also gave me the excuse I needed not to talk.

"So that was awkward last night." Joel broke the silence between us.

"A little bit." I took another bite.

"I'm really sorry. There's nothing between Becca and me, but seeing her took me by surprise. I didn't know what to say." He handed me a napkin as I was about to ask for one.

"There's nothing to apologize for."

"I feel like there is. I'm over her, you know."

"Are you?" I met his gaze for the first time. "I know she's not over you."

"We were together for a long time, but I'm more interested in seeing where things go with you than getting back together with Becca." He reached for my hand, and I let him take it.

"The thing is"—I took a deep breath—"I don't know that we should keep things going after I move."

"I was afraid you were going to say that." He dropped my hand and fiddled with his keys still hanging from the ignition.

"I really like you, Joel. I just think the best thing for us is to enjoy the next few weeks and then agree to be friends after that." I touched his arm, and he let go of the keys.

"You're wrong." He met my eyes and smiled a sadder version of his crooked grin.

I shook my head. "Think about it. Neither one of us is going to convert, and I don't think either of us is interested in something that won't end up being long-term."

"What makes you think I wouldn't convert?"

My head jerked up. "Would you?"

He shrugged and dug something out of his fingernail. "It's not out of the realm of possibilities."

The excitement I'd felt vanished almost before I realized it was there. "A lot of things can be in that realm and still be pretty far from reality. I know your family would cut you off. Plus, what would it do to your business if your clients knew you'd traded in Judaism for Mormonism?"

"I'd still be Jewish."

"Yeah, emphasis on the -ish. I doubt the Jewish Federation would be excited to keep you on their networking lists."

"I could get new clients."

"You couldn't get a new family."

He wrapped his hands behind his neck and leaned forward, resting his forehead on the steering wheel before letting out a deep sigh. "I'm not ready to give up on us," he said finally, sitting back up and dropping his hands.

I put my hand on his. "I don't want to either, but do we really want to do the whole long-distance thing until everything fizzles? Or worse, we end up using the distance to let our friendship die too."

"If you think we couldn't last long distance, you've already given up. You couldn't wait until you were gone to tell me all this?" he asked with a sigh of resignation before dropping his head on the seat back with his eyes closed.

I pulled my hand back. "This isn't easy for me, Joel." My voice was laced with the same hurt his had held. "I feel like I found the perfect guy. The only problem is I'd have to give up a huge part of who I am—and what I want—to be with him. I'd rather be realistic about our chances than peel the Band-Aid off a little piece at a time."

"Serious relationships are always about giving up some of who you are and what you want. That's what it takes to make any marriage work, no matter how different two people are. The difference between you and me is I'm not afraid to do it." His hurt had turned to anger, but I was stuck on the fact he'd said "marriage."

"That's because you don't know what it would be like. I lived it with my mom and dad. There are worse ways to grow up, but I want something different for my kids. I want something different for my marriage."

I'd said it too. *Marriage.* Had he thought about what it would be like if we got to that point the way I had? Or was he projecting his feelings about Becca—what had happened with their relationship—on to me? Either way, the fact we'd both mentioned it meant making a clean break before things got any more serious—the smartest thing to do.

"I get it." He nodded but without conviction.

I reached into my purse and pulled out the Book of Mormon.

"I don't think you do, but you might if you read this." My heart hammered inside my chest. "Let's not talk religion anymore. Let's just have fun and make the most out of the time we have left together. But I want you to have this, just in case."

His forehead creased as he took it.

"You don't have to read it, but if you decide to, start by writing down questions you have, then see if it answers any of them." I spit words out, knowing I had to say them but wanting to get it over with quickly.

"Start with 2 Nephi, chapter twenty-nine. There's a shout out to Jews in there," I said.

"Right." A laugh slipped out. "Second Wi-Fi."

"Nephi. Now you'd better take me home so I can shower and get some packing done before you take me to that Mexican place tonight."

"You still want to go?"

"Yeah." I took his hand. "I want to spend every second I can with you so I don't regret anything. Then I want to leave and know we're still friends and that you'll call me every once in a while and maybe come visit me and Bryce when you have a chance. And when you find a nice Jewish girl, I want you to send me a wedding invite and know that I probably won't come, but I'll wish you the very best."

He nodded and with his free hand tucked a loose strand of hair behind my ear, then pulled me close until our lips met.

A shower and packing would have to wait.

Chapter 18

I WOKE UP THE FIRST morning at the ranch before the sun was up. I was buried under a down comforter, but the chill in the room had nudged me out of my dream. At the halfway point between being asleep and awake, my first thought was what Joel had planned for us that day. Then I remembered I wasn't in California anymore.

I peeled back the covers to look at the time. The alarm clock read 5:02 in too-bright numbers. I tucked my head back under the covers and attempted to go back to sleep, but all I could think about was Joel and the last two weeks we'd spent together.

When he wasn't at work, he tried to fill every moment with things I'd never done in LA. We hiked to the Hollywood sign, ate at an Ethiopian restaurant, and went to the Time Travel Mart and the Electric Dusk Drive-in. We went to a Dodger's game and a roller derby. I preferred the roller derby.

If I hadn't done it, we did it. Of course we did some old favorites too, like a sunset walk on the beach and a moonlit hike in Griffith Park. Every day was something different, but it was always packed full.

The realization that I'd have to face the day without Joel scooped out a giant hole in my chest. I squeezed my eyes shut, determined to put him out of my head and get some more sleep.

Before I could, I heard my bedroom door open then shut. I peeked out to see Annie running tiptoe across the carpet. A blast of cold air hit me as she climbed under the covers into my bed.

"It's freezing!" Her teeth chattered as she nuzzled close to me.

"I know. I couldn't get the windows shut last night."

"Add that to the list of things to fix."

"I think it's more of a book now."

"Then make it the first chapter. I'm never going to get warm."

It had been eighty degrees when we left LA. By the time we got to Park City, the temperature had dropped forty degrees due to an unexpected cold front.

"If it's this cold in June, will it ever get warm?" Annie had asked Walt as he helped us with our bags.

"We were hoping you'd bring some of that California sun with you." His mouth spread into a smile that quickly disappeared when he didn't get any in return.

"There's some chili on the stove you can heat up. I'll be by Monday with the contractor so we can get to work." He tipped his hat and left.

We tried to eat the chili, but none of us had much of an appetite. Reality had set in, and even Bryce couldn't muster up his usual excitement for our new life.

After checking all the rooms, we decided the empty guest rooms were warmer than our quarters, and each of us took one. We would have been better off sharing one. My bed was a lot warmer now with Annie's extra body heat.

"Why is it so cold?" She scooted so close our noses almost touched.

"I don't know, but don't you dare put your feet on me."

It was too late. Her icy toes were already resting on my calf.

"Seriously, keep your feet off me, or I'm kicking you out." I stretched my legs across the bed away from her.

"I hate it here already," she said, giving up on using me as a heater and instead rubbing her feet together.

"We've got another few hours to sleep before church. Leave me alone." I clenched my eyes shut, determined not to wake up.

Annie's feet stopped moving, and minutes later her breathing turned heavy and content. Her ability to fall asleep at a moment's notice never ceased to amaze me. I, on the other hand, was wide awake. After half an hour, I threw back the covers and climbed out of bed to face the cold. For half a vindictive second, I left Annie uncovered, then got over it and tucked an extra blanket around her.

After putting on a couple pairs of thin socks—the only kind I owned—I went to turn on the heater. It didn't take long to realize I had no idea where it was or if we even had one. My first official day as a bed-and-breakfast proprietor was not off to a good start.

The great room was even colder than upstairs, but a neat pile of logs was stacked next to the fireplace along with some newspaper and long matches. I doubted they'd be there if the fireplace didn't work, but I was less sure about my ability to light an actual fire.

Fortunately, my years spent at Girls Camp didn't fail me, and within fifteen minutes I had a decent fire going. I pulled one of the big chairs closer to it, its feet scraping the wood floor. I sank into its soft leather.

A thin layer of frost covered the wide expanse outside the window. Light reflected off its icy crust as the sun rose. "This isn't so bad," I said aloud. My voice echoed through the empty room, almost convincing me. "You can do this." I raised my voice enough that this time the echo really did boost my confidence. Then I curled my legs under me and rested my head on the arm. I resisted the urge to text Joel at five in the morning and dreamt about him instead.

*   *   *

I don't know how long I slept, but I woke to the sun on my face. Beams of light shone through the windows, and the frost had melted. Already the fire was too hot combined with the heat from the sun.

I sat up, stretched the kinks out of my neck, and checked the clock. It read eight o'clock, and the family ward started at nine. I would have preferred to go to the YSA ward for Annie's sake, but with Bryce we didn't have much choice. I doubted it would be very easy getting the two of them to church at all if they were as nervous as I was.

And it wasn't easy, but we made it on time. Or close to on time anyway. Of course everyone made us feel welcome, and I was pleasantly surprised when a tall man with a long face and thin nose stopped me in the hallway after Annie and I introduced ourselves in Sunday School.

"You're Emily Carter?" he asked and held out his hand. "I'm Luke Johnson. Walt hired me as your contractor."

"Nice to meet you." I shook the offered hand. "I'm excited to get started."

"Me too. Walt's shown me around the place a little bit, but I didn't want to draw up any estimates before you got here."

His eyes drifted from me to Annie, where they stayed. She was used to people recognizing her, but when Luke didn't say anything, she did. "Hi. I'm Annie Carter." She held out her hand, and he shook it, but without the usual gushing Annie got when people met her.

"Nice to meet you." Luke didn't take his eyes off her, but he also didn't give any indication he knew who she was, which meant Annie lost all interest in him. She shifted back and forth, not meeting his gaze.

"So you're in this ward?" I asked to break the awkward silence.

"Usually I go to the singles' ward, but I needed to attend earlier today." He glanced at me as he spoke, but his gaze kept drifting back to Annie.

"Well, I'm glad you did so we could meet you."

"Yeah, I guess I'll see you tomorrow," Luke stammered and dragged his eyes back to me.

"That was weird," Annie whispered as Luke walked away.

"He seems nice."

"He seems *old*."

I held back a smile. "He can't be more than thirty-one if he's in the YSA ward, and he doesn't look any older than me."

"You're not that young."

I rolled my eyes. "Only if you're closer to twenty than thirty."

"He's the perfect guy for you then," she smirked before sashaying down the hall.

Chapter 19

JOEL FACETIMED ME THE NEXT morning. Bryce grabbed my phone off the kitchen counter and answered it before I could stop him. It's not that I didn't want to talk to Joel face to face—or, rather, screen to screen—but I'd rolled out of bed five minutes before and hadn't combed my hair or changed out of my pj's.

We had texted a few times since I left LA—okay maybe more than a few—but we hadn't talked. On our last date, I had made the case again that we should just be friends rather than try a long-distance relationship. He agreed, but only if I'd let him come visit me before the end of the month. It didn't take much convincing for me to say yes. But friend or not, I didn't want him seeing me with bedhead and in scroungy pajamas. "I'll be right back!" I yelled and bolted for the stairs, hoping Bryce wasn't giving Joel a shot of my behind.

I ran to my room, threw on some yoga pants and a hoodie, broke the sound barrier brushing my hair and putting on some mascara, then ran back downstairs to take the phone from Bryce.

"Hi!" I said, breathless as much from my sprint as from seeing Joel's face again. "What are you doing?"

"I couldn't wait two more weeks to see your face." His face broke into a teasing smile.

"You're breaking the rules." My heart thumped, but I had to stay practical. "Keep it friendly." As much as I liked hearing his words, they were way too flirty for comfort.

"All right, fine." His mouth fell, but his eyes twinkled and I knew he wasn't done. "Your contractor is coming by this morning, right? I thought it would be helpful to have me along while you show him what we talked about doing. If I can see where you are, it will be easier to explain things."

"That's a good idea."

"I know. Plus I get to see you. You look great, by the way. Especially going up the stairs." A grin tugged at his lips.

"A little advance warning would be nice so I can at least be dressed next time." I scowled but couldn't hold back my own laugh.

The doorbell rang, so I took Joel with me to answer it. Luke and Walt were both on the porch, so I introduced Luke to Joel and we began our tour of the house. I pointed out all the repairs Joel and I had written down on our first visit, and then we discussed the renovations we wanted to do.

Joel kept it "friendly" the whole time, but the longer we talked, the more I missed him. I tried to push the feeling away—we were talking drywall and two-by-fours, not love—but it only got stronger. I was almost relieved when we finished our walk-through and my screen flashed a low-battery warning.

I said goodbye to Joel and walked Walt and Luke to the door at the same time Annie came down the stairs in her pajamas. Good thing it had been another cool night because flannel wasn't what she usually slept in.

Luke tore off his hat and nodded to her. She raised her eyebrows and dipped her chin before retreating back upstairs. Luke cleared his throat and turned back to me.

"You can put your hat back on now." Walt's grin spanned his entire face, and Luke glared at him.

"Just being polite." He put his hat back on and pulled the bill low.

"Uh huh," Walt nodded, and his grin grew.

"Your sister looks like someone I used to know."

"She did have a TV show," I said, and confusion spread across his face. "You've seen *Up and Away*, right?"

My explanation only increased the crease in his forehead, and he shook his head slowly.

Walt broke into a laugh. "You didn't know she's a big-time Hollywood actress?"

Now it was Luke's turn to shake his head. "I don't watch much TV. Is it still on?"

This made Walt laugh harder. "You're a few years too late, buddy." He slapped Luke on the back and walked into the bathroom.

"You could get it on Netflix. It's pretty good, in my unbiased opinion." I held back my own laugh to keep him from feeling worse.

"Netflix?" he asked with a blank look in his eye.

"You don't know what Netflix is?" I blinked back my disbelief.

"I'm just kidding. I'm not that out of it." His lip twitched, the only indication he wasn't serious. "Tell me the name again, and I'll check it out."

"*Up and Away.*"

The toilet flushed, and Walt returned. We went on with the inspection of the house, but I couldn't get over the fact Luke didn't know who Annie was. I didn't know anyone who hadn't seen her show.

By the time we made it to the kitchen, Annie was sitting at the counter eating a bagel. I walked in behind Luke and watched his ears turn red as soon as he saw her.

"Sorry to catch you right out of bed." He took his hat off again and spun it in his hands.

"No biggie." She shrugged and took a bite of her bagel.

"Emily says you're an actress." Luke ground the words out of his throat with obvious effort. "We have a theater here in town. They put on some pretty good plays."

Annie stopped mid-chew and stared at Luke. "Are you asking me to *go* to a play or telling me I should be *in* one?"

Red spread from Luke's ears to his face. "Both, I guess," he mumbled.

"I'm more of a film actress than stage, but I'll check it out. Thanks." Her non-reply to Luke's invitation didn't go unnoticed. Seconds ticked by as everyone waited for her answer.

Finally, Luke put his hat back on and walked to the back door. "Okay then. I think we've covered everything. I'll get back to you with an estimate." He walked out the door without saying goodbye and before I could say thank you.

"That was rude," I said to Annie.

"I've known Luke a long time. I've never seen him look at anybody the way he just looked at you. You oughta give him a chance." Walt's friendly tone was underlined with a scolding.

"I just met him yesterday." Annie tugged at the ends of her hair, a sure sign of her embarrassment.

"You could have at least told him, 'Thanks, but no thanks.'" I softened my own scolding. She was embarrassed enough, but I didn't want to see a repeat of what she'd done today.

"I'm sorry. I didn't know how to tell him no." She picked up her bagel then set it back down and licked cream cheese off her thumb.

"Then tell him yes, for crying out loud. There aren't too many fellas around here, and you won't find one better than Luke, I'll tell you that much." Walt kept a smile on his face, but his disappointment for his friend came through loud and clear.

"I'll keep that in mind," Annie said through clenched teeth.

"You girls need anything else?" Walt rubbed his chin, and I couldn't tell if he wanted to say more or wanted to make up for saying too much.

"No. Thanks for everything, Walt." I scrambled to open the door for him and waved goodbye.

"It's still freezing," Annie said. For the first time, I noticed she had a hoodie on under a sweatshirt, and it looked like she'd layered up on pants too.

"Yeah, it's almost as cold in here as you were to Luke."

"What was I supposed to say? That was so awkward. *He's* so awkward."

"He's a nice guy. You could give him a chance." I took a bite of the bagel she'd set down.

She answered by rolling her eyes and pushing the rest of the bagel toward me.

"You're not in Hollywood anymore, Annie." I picked up her bagel and left.

Chapter 20

I WAITED A DAY BEFORE I couldn't wait to talk to Joel any longer. As a friend, of course. His phone rang and rang, but right before it went to voice mail, a woman answered. I looked at the number to make sure I had it right.

"Emily? It's Becca," the woman said before I could respond. "Joel stepped out for a minute so I answered his phone for him."

"Oh, is he coming back?" I could barely get the words out, my mouth had gone so dry. I knew it was a bad idea to call him, but I'd let my feelings get in the way of my head and had done it anyway.

"We're at Rachel's and he ran over to the guesthouse, so he should be right back. It's so funny you called because we were just talking about the ranch. I'm going to send you some more plans tomorrow."

She kept talking, but I couldn't hear her over the ringing in my ears. Five days I'd been gone, and already Joel was hanging out with Becca, talking about *my* ranch. Five. Days. I shouldn't have been hurt since I was the one who'd told him to see other people. I thought I could handle it. Nope. Not at all.

"Here he is now," I heard her say, followed by, "It's Emily."

"Hi!" Joel sounded breathless. Or nervous. I couldn't tell which.

"Are you seeing Becca again?" I burst out then sank onto my bed, hoping to soften the blow of his answer.

"No. . . . It's complicated."

"Is she going to be okay with you coming to see me?" I asked in sharp jabs.

"I don't know. Do I need her permission?" He spoke slowly, but his words were as pointed as mine.

"If you're dating her."

"I'm not seeing Becca." He measured each word carefully. "We have a long history, and we're friends. Like you wanted the two of us to be."

He had me there, but I couldn't think about him and Becca without getting jealous, and I hated that feeling. It made more sense to cut things off before I got hurt.

"I can't just be friends," I said finally. "It's too hard." I tugged at the knotted yarn on the tied quilt on my bed. It had seen better days. So had I, for that matter.

"Good. Then we're on the same page. I'm still coming." His relief only made what I had to say harder.

"No," I said, shaking my head. "I need to—"

"Don't say what you're going to say." His words tumbled out and took my heart with them, causing a rock slide of emotions.

"I have to."

"*You're* the one I can't stop thinking about. *You're* the one I want to be with. You need to know that. I don't care if you want to hear it or not."

I gritted my teeth and pushed back the lump rising in my throat. "I wish I didn't like her so much. It would be easier to hate her. She's perfect for you."

"I don't believe in perfect. That's why I'm willing to take a chance on us." He didn't hold back his hurt, and I was stunned into silence.

"Don't make this harder." I let go of the yarn and dropped my head into my hands.

"It's not me who's making this hard, Emily. I've had the missionaries over; I'm trying to read the Book of Mormon."

"Are you doing it for me or for yourself?"

"I'm doing it because of you. Will that work for now?"

My first instinct was to say yes, but I shook my head no. "I wish I could say it would. You've got to feel it for yourself though."

"It feels familiar. The words, I mean. But I have a lot of questions that I don't know can be answered."

"You have to ask."

"Who? Eighteen-year-old boys?"

"Try God."

He took a deep breath. "Isn't it enough to live a good life for the sake of living a good life?"

"It is, Joel. Just not for me. I can't give up what I know is true." I pressed my eyes closed, pushing the memory of his face out of my head.

"I'm not asking you to give up anything."

"I know, but I'm asking you to give up everything. That's why I don't see how this can work." I waited for his reply while formulating my next defensive move.

"Okay. I've gotta go," he said, cutting off every argument I had ready for him. "I won't plan on this weekend." He hung up before I had a chance to say anything.

I dropped my phone and lay back on my bed staring at the popcorn ceilings—one more thing that had to be fixed. *What am I doing?* I had a guy I was crazy about begging me to give him a chance, and I'd told him no.

It's not what's right, I argued to myself.

It feels like it is, my heart replied.

Returned missionary. Temple marriage. Stick to the plan.

This went on for a while, my heart trying to win over my head. But I'd spent my life doing the smart thing, the right thing. My heart never stood a chance.

*   *   *

A knock at my bedroom door put an end to the tug-of-war between my emotions and my brain.

"Luke just pulled up." Annie stuck her head in my door, giving me a look with a lot more meaning behind it than the words she'd said.

"Sorry. I'll be down as soon as I get dressed." I folded back the warm duvet and swung my legs off the bed.

"I'll be in my room." She started to close the door, but I stopped her.

"You can't stay there all day," I said, realizing as soon as the words left my mouth that she could, actually, stay in her room all day. She had mastered that skill.

The doorbell rang as she turned to leave.

"Can you at least answer that before you disappear?"

She looked over her shoulder and eyed the threadbare flannels and bright orange sweatshirt I was wearing. "Fine," she mumbled and shut my door with a loud bang.

Five minutes later she was a new woman. Her voice bounced off the ceiling as I walked down the stairs. It went up and down like notes on sheet music, with her tinkling laugh providing the orchestra.

I wondered what had caused her sudden change in mood until I saw the man at the bottom of the stairs. His tight T-shirt hugged his shoulders and biceps in a way that perfectly explained Annie's one-eighty. Even if it hadn't, his face would.

Deep brown eyes peered out of a face so perfectly chiseled it belonged in a museum. His meticulously manscaped beard stubble surrounded a dangerous smile. He had to be almost a foot taller than Annie, and she wasn't short.

My sister was a goner. She'd left Hollywood, but Hollywood had found her. She was so spellbound, she didn't even notice Luke standing nearby, looking as much a wallflower as the new guy looked magazine-cover ready. The defeat on Luke's face didn't help either.

"Hi, I'm Drew." He stuck out his hand, and Annie's eyes widened even more, as though Drew were the first person to master a greeting by handshake.

"Emily Carter." I stepped around Annie and offered my hand, realizing Drew was the photographer Luke had found to document the ranch's transformation.

"Thanks for giving me this opportunity." He talked to me, but his eyes darted back to Annie.

"Thanks for not charging me what you could have." I waved him in and walked toward one of the leather sofas in the great room.

"Photography is a hobby, not my profession." He followed me with Annie and Luke in tow. "I can't believe you're Annie Carter."

"What *is* your profession?" Annie blushed and changed the subject as we all sat down.

"Nothing at the moment. I'm at the University of Utah. My aunt wants me to go into the property management business with her—I'm working for her for the summer—so I'm majoring in business. But photography is my real love." He held up his camera as proof then changed the subject back to Annie. "So what's it like being the sister of a famous movie star?" His eyes flicked to mine but then stayed glued to her.

"I'm not that famous. I've done a lot more television than movies." She grinned from ear to ear. Humility was not her strongest trait.

"I've seen everything you've been in. I still can't believe I'm standing in the same room with the girl I crushed on all through high school." His little-boy excitement was endearing, especially to Annie. She giggled, tucked her hair behind her ear, and ran her fingers down a lock of it.

"We probably better get to work and let these ladies get on with their day," Luke said to Drew then cleared his throat and looked to me for help I couldn't offer.

"Right." Drew nodded without taking his eyes off Annie. There were so many sparks flying between them, I could have roasted a marshmallow. "Where are we starting?"

"Kitchen," Luke answered with a sternness that got Drew's full attention.

"I'll see you around," Drew said to Annie before following Luke to the kitchen.

"I'm sure you will," Annie said under her breath with a huskiness I was relieved Drew couldn't hear.

"Down, girl," I said.

"Oh. My. Gosh. Can you believe that?" She grabbed my hands, her eyes wide with excitement.

"That? That what?"

"That." She pointed her chin toward the kitchen. "Lives here! Who knew Utah could grow boys who look like . . ."

"Like what?"

"That!" She let go of my hands and pointed toward the door Drew had gone through.

"Whoa, there. Settle down now. You don't know anything about him except his name and the fact he liked your show when he was seventeen." I was happy to see a light in her eye I hadn't seen for a long time, but I couldn't help feeling sorry for Luke.

"I don't need to know anything else. I *felt* the connection between us. That's all that really matters." Her whole body was wound into a tight ball ready to explode. "I have to get dressed. I can't believe he saw me like this!" Brushing me aside, she ran up the stairs.

"Remember, he's here to work!" I yelled after her.

If she heard me, she didn't acknowledge it. I couldn't help but smile. Annie's excitement was always contagious, and it had been too long since she'd had enough of it to infect anyone else.

I ignored the snag in my heart threatening to unravel. I wouldn't think about Joel, and if something happened with Drew and Annie—which, if Annie had anything to do with it, was 100 percent likely—I would be happy for her.

I tiptoed around the concerns I had about her impulsiveness and her vulnerability. I had to believe Drew was a good guy if five minutes with him brought back my old Annie.

Chapter 21

"JOEL'S COMING NEXT WEEKEND, RIGHT?" Bryce asked the next morning while shoveling cereal into his mouth. "I found a perfect fishing spot. I told him I'd teach him how."

I dropped my spoonful of yogurt back into my bowl and looked at Bryce. I hadn't considered how excited he was about Joel's visit when I'd uninvited him. I'd been questioning my decision all night, and Bryce's hopeful eyes didn't help.

"I don't think he can, buddy." I dropped my eyes to keep from seeing the disappointment in his and stirred my yogurt.

"Can he come another weekend?" he asked, his voice cracking. Bryce had been more excited than anyone to move to the ranch, but after a week of being homebound while we unpacked, cleaned, and planned for construction, my gregarious brother was bored and lonely.

"I'll see what I can do, okay?" I faked a smile. As much as I hated to admit it, I wanted Joel to visit even more than Bryce did, but Bryce *needed* him to visit. Which meant I had to make that happen.

So I called him. He deserved an apology anyway, and Bryce's plea gave me the shove I needed to do the right thing.

"I'm sorry," I said as soon as he answered.

"Does that mean you still want me to come?"

"Yes, but no . . ."

"You're killing me with these mixed signals, Emily." He sighed.

"I'm sorry." My broken-record replies couldn't be any less annoying than my mixed signals. "I do want you to come, but mostly for Bryce. He misses you." I wouldn't say *I miss you*. I'd told him he should be with Becca, and I had to stick to that.

"What about you?"

"I don't want to lose our friendship. Can we keep that? It's all I can offer right now." I closed my eyes and rubbed my temple waiting for his answer.

"You'll always have that. I wish you wanted more, but I'm not going to push you." The frustration was gone from his voice, and he sounded almost happy. Or at least relieved. I hoped he was faking it because it was the opposite of what I felt.

"Thank you." I opened my eyes and stared up at the ceiling. "Do you still want to come visit?"

"Yes, but I think I'll wait. If my excuse to come out can't be to see you, then I'll do it to see how the remodel is coming along. I don't need to be there for the demolition part. Why don't you let me know when you're past the nails-and-studs point and you have walls again."

"Of course. That gives me an excuse to call you again, right?" I asked lightly, blinking back the tears threatening to fall.

"You don't need an excuse. I always like hearing from friends." The way he emphasized friends didn't help with the tears.

*   *   *

A month passed of almost daily texts and weekly calls from Joel—mostly about the ranch renovation—but no visit. As Bryce made new friends, he quit asking when Joel was coming, but I didn't stop wondering if—and hoping—he would.

Fortunately, the ranch kept me too busy to spend all my time missing Joel. Construction was moving quickly but not without some inconvenience—like the giant tarp-covered opening that used to be a wall. Within a week it would be the huge picture window and sliding glass doors Joel had suggested. Once the window and doors were in, we'd have unbroken views of the grounds, from the stream to the horses grazing in the pasture, all the way to the mountains surrounding us. But at the moment, the gaping hole let in all the hot air from outside, which made it too expensive to run the air conditioner and impossible to cool down anywhere.

One morning I pushed the plastic aside and stepped outside to find Luke and his crew hard at work.

"Hey, it's looking good!" I yelled over the cacophony of nail guns and saws.

Startled, Luke looked up from the board he was cutting. In the time it took for his saw to stop buzzing, the look on his face went from excitement to disappointment as he struggled to cover his feelings with a smile. "Hi. Yeah, it's moving along."

Despite all of Annie's brush-offs, Luke's crush had only gotten worse. Obviously, I wasn't the sister he was hoping to see. He took his gloves off to shake my hand, something he did every time he saw me, but the formality of it still surprised me.

"We're on track for November." He put his hands on his hips and scanned the house from top to bottom, squinting in the sunlight. The plastic moved, and Annie stuck her head out.

"Oh, hey." She barely glanced at Luke and me. Her face matched Luke's in the disappointment department when she saw Drew wasn't outside.

"Drew's not here yet. If that's who you're looking for." Luke's lip twitched into a pained smile.

"So, he's working today then?"

"Supposed to be."

Drew came every day to photograph our progress so I could update our website. Every day it took him a little longer to "get all the shots" he needed, many of which seemed to be of Annie. Her mood lightened with him around though, so I decided to be grateful for that—and the fact I wasn't paying him by the hour.

"Oh, okay." She tried to brush off his answer, but she couldn't stop her smile. Still, she did make an effort to be polite. "I can't believe how fast everything is coming together."

"Well, I'm trying." Luke ran his arm across his brow. "I watched your show, finally, and that movie you were in."

"You did? What did you think?" Annie pushed the plastic out of the way and stepped outside, looking directly at Luke for the first time.

"I thought you were great. It was crazy to watch you but see you as somebody totally different."

"I'm glad you liked it."

He hadn't exactly said that. The movie she'd had a leading role in was quirky enough that people either loved it, hated it, or thought it was the stupidest show ever. I'd put Luke in the third camp, but he was so twitter-pated with Annie there was no way he'd ever say it. "I liked the soundtrack. It's almost as good as you." He followed his comment with an awkward wink that made Annie scrunch her nose.

"Are you into music?" I asked to ease the awkwardness.

"Oh yeah. I love all the blues stuff they used."

"You do?" Annie didn't hide her surprise.

"Elmore James and Muddy Waters? They're the reason I learned slide guitar."

"You play slide guitar?" Annie didn't have to fake interest in what he had to say now.

"Yeah. I'm in a blues band. Actually, it's kind of eclectic. We mix blues, jazz, and folk. Sometimes we even throw in a little bluegrass when I feel like playing fiddle."

"Have you heard of the Stringdusters?"

"Yeah." Luke grinned wide.

"I heard they're coming to town."

"Yeah." His smile deepened. "My band is opening for them."

That left Annie speechless, which had happened maybe one other time in her entire life.

"Would you like to come?" Luke's eyes lit up like a little boy's who'd discovered his treasure map might actually be real.

"You have a band?" Annie asked, still shocked.

"Yeah." Luke laughed. "The concert's tonight at Park City Live. If you two want to come, I can get you into the VIP mezzanine."

"That sounds fun, but—" Before I could finish my thought, Annie grabbed my arm and pulled me close.

"We'd love to. What time?" she said, bouncing on her tiptoes.

"Nine. I'll leave your names at the door."

"Awesome," Annie said.

I nodded and watched Luke's face, trying to determine if he had really wanted to invite me or if he did it just to get Annie to go. Either way, he seemed happy enough Annie had said yes, even if I'd be tagging along.

The plastic tarp rustled again, and this time Drew stepped through.

"Sorry I'm late, boss." He didn't sound sorry. In fact, as soon as he saw Annie, he looked even less sorry. "Hey, beautiful." He appraised her in the same way Luke had the house.

"Hi." She moved closer to him. Really close. I guess she didn't find his greeting as cheesy as I did.

"The windows are going in today, so maybe you should shoot out here. Then tomorrow you can do an after picture," I suggested.

Drew tore his eyes away from Annie. "Great idea," he said after a pause and a nod of his head. Drew walked twenty feet away, and Annie followed.

He set his camera case down then pulled equipment out, handing lenses to Annie to hold.

"Thanks for the invite," I said to Luke while I watched Drew and Annie.

"Oh, yeah, no problem." Luke tore his eyes away from the spot where Annie had been standing and picked up a hammer.

"You just scored some serious points with her. She loves blues guitar. The Stringdusters have been one of her favorites since they were included on her movie soundtrack."

"Looks like Drew's another favorite." Luke tugged the brim of his hat down then pushed it back up.

"What's his story anyway?" I asked as much out of curiosity as a desire to make Luke feel less embarrassed of his feelings for Annie—something anyone with half a brain could see.

"I don't know him that well, but I know his aunt." Luke shook his head. "She's got a lot of money, and he'll get it all, but she's got some high expectations for him. As far as she's concerned, photography is a hobby, not a career."

"So what happens if he decides he wants to be a photographer?"

"She won't like it," Luke answered. "She expects him to learn the business from the bottom up."

"Like handyman stuff?" I asked, still watching Drew and my sister. I didn't want to make it too obvious I was watching, but when they stood close enough to kiss, I couldn't look away.

"I don't know how he's fitting any work in with all his picture-taking." Luke followed my gaze but quickly looked away and grabbed a piece of wood.

"Yeah. He's the first designer-jean-wearing handyman I've ever met." I shot my gaze to the ground as their lips met.

"Yep. I think he's hoping it's going to be a quick climb to the top." He marked the wood and set it on the table saw, then made a quick cut.

"What do you think?" I asked when the saw stopped.

"You really want to know?"

I nodded. I trusted Luke's opinion, and I didn't like the worry niggling me every time Annie and Drew were together.

"I think he's a nice guy who, by the looks of it, has had things too easy. His aunt's a great lady who's had to work hard for everything she's got. I don't think she's going to get the same kind of work ethic out of him." Luke set the wood down and grabbed another piece.

"Will he still get her money?" I'd known a lot of wealthy kids in LA who felt entitled to what their parents had earned. I hoped Drew wasn't as bad as them.

"She doesn't have any other family, but I think he may be overestimating his aunt's generosity. She'll give it away all day long to people who haven't had the same opportunities she's had. But Drew's got a lot more than she did at his age, and he's going have to prove he deserves it." His voice lowered, and he finished his thought just as Drew and Annie walked back over.

"I'll see you tonight, Luke," Annie said, following Drew inside.

I walked behind them as the whir of the saw started again. Annie laughed and grabbed the hand Drew held out to her. I'd have to talk to her later about that kiss, but in the meantime, I loved hearing her laugh again.

Chapter 22

My phone rang as I pulled into a parking spot half a mile away from Luke's concert venue. Annie and I were already running late, and we were in for a fast walk in heels if we were going to make it on time. But it was Joel, so I had to take it.

"Hi!" I answered and climbed out of the car, ignoring Annie as she pointed to the time on her phone. I'd waited through her forty-five wardrobe changes before she finally settled on jeans and a basic black T-shirt. She could wait a few minutes while I talked to Joel.

"Hey. What's up?"

No matter how many times I reminded myself Joel was only a friend, my heart never listened. The sound of his voice always made it beat faster. "Annie and I are headed to a concert."

Annie grabbed my hand and pulled, forcing me to speed walk with her.

"That sounds fun. How'd you get Annie out of the house?" His voice echoed, reminding me how far away he was.

"Luke's band is opening for another group she likes, so he invited us to come. Actually, she's been going out a lot lately. Plus, she's working. I hardly ever get to see her."

Annie glared at me, but when I mouthed Joel's name, her brow smoothed and she went back to pulling me down the street.

"That's good to hear. I'm glad she's feeling better."

Of course he was, because he was a friend. A good friend. "Thanks. What are you up to?" I yanked my hand out of Annie's and slowed down. We were almost there, and I didn't want to end my conversation with Joel.

"Well, I've got Becca with me—"

"Hi, Emily!" Becca interrupted, and I realized he had me on speaker. With his ex- (maybe not anymore) girlfriend.

"Hi," I answered, not even trying to match her enthusiasm.

"Joel has been keeping me updated on how everything is going, and I can't wait to see it." Becca kept talking, and the world started spinning.

"Becca wants to come with me when I visit." Joel's words came out slowly, carefully.

Everything stopped. Except for Annie, who left me behind.

"I hope that's okay," Becca added while I tried to process what Joel had said.

"Of course," I answered automatically. "We'd love to have both of you." I forced myself to start walking again. The sooner I got to the club, the sooner I would have an excuse to hang up. I just had to make it before I said something stupid.

"When can we come? I'm dying to see all the changes we talked about." Becca's bouncy voice left me deflated. I knew she didn't mean to, but she'd stolen all the excitement I'd felt when I answered Joel's call, and now she was taunting me with it.

"Next month is probably best." The club was still half a block away, but the loud music pouring out of it gave me the reason I needed to hang up. "I'm here, so I'd better go. I'll give you a call in a couple days to work out details." I held the phone away from my ear and yelled into it, hoping the background noise would sound louder than it actually was.

"Great! Looking forward to it!" Even from an arm's length away, Becca's excited voice grated in my ears.

"Okay, bye!" I thought I heard Joel say something before I hung up, but I brushed it off as wishful thinking on my part.

I gave the doorman my name, and he pointed me toward the VIP section at the same time Luke's band came on the stage. People were stacked shoulder to shoulder, and all I wanted to do was go home, pull the covers over my head, and scream. Or cry. Maybe both.

I pushed my way through the crowd, and Luke played the first few chords of his song. Apparently a lot of people already knew it because their clapping got louder. And for good reason. Luke knew his way around a guitar. I stopped and watched as his playing created an energy that swept over the whole crowd and chased thoughts of Joel and Becca out of my head—or at least to the back of it.

Even Annie was on her feet, jumping up and down. I smiled and squeezed around the cheering fans until I made it to the mezzanine Luke had reserved for us.

"This is really good. *He's* really good!" Annie yelled over the sound of Luke's steel guitar once I reached her.

"Who knew?" I yelled back.

"Right?" She let out a cheer and clapped louder than anyone else in the audience as the song ended.

Luke nodded to the crowd as the lead singer stepped to the mic. "Thank you all for comin' out. Let's give another hand to the band." He turned to the band and introduced each one. Luke got the loudest applause and answered it with a short riff on his guitar and a giant smile.

They played a few more songs before the lights went out and they left the stage, but the cheering didn't stop. A few minutes later, Luke hustled down the stage stairs and glanced up to the mezzanine. Annie waved, and he wound his way through the high-fiving crowd and up the steps until he got to our table.

"That was awesome!" Annie said, and Luke's grin widened.

"Thanks. I'm glad you liked it."

He twisted the cap off a bottle of water and took a long drink.

"You were amazing up there. You're like a different person!" Annie's words spilled out unfiltered.

"Annie!" I smacked her arm, but Luke laughed.

"That's why I like being on stage. I can be someone else for a few hours—not that I don't like who I am," he added quickly. "But it's nice to wear a different hat sometimes."

"No, I get it. That's how I feel on set. It's like playing pretend. You put on a different persona, but you don't have to stay that person forever." Annie nodded, smiling wide in a way she never had before with Luke.

"Exactly. I don't want to be up there every night, but when I am, it's the same kind of rush I got as a kid when I was making up a game or building something new."

Their conversation continued, veering toward stories of stage fright and forgetting song lines at the worst times. They forgot about me, but I didn't mind. Seeing Annie recognize Luke's merits was better than being included. Her eyes sparkled and her hands waved the more animated she got.

Suddenly Luke's face dropped, and seconds later I understood why when Drew walked up behind Annie.

"Hey, did I miss the show?" he asked Luke as he draped his arm around Annie's shoulders.

"Hi!" Her face beamed. "You missed Luke's band. They were incredible! The Stringdusters are going on soon."

"Shoot. Sorry, man. I really wanted to see your set." His words sounded genuine, but I doubted his sincerity.

"Speaking of, I better get back," Luke said.

"Are you going back on?" Annie asked, momentarily tearing her gaze away from Drew.

"No, I have to pack up my stuff." His face brightened with her attention.

"Darn, I wanted to hear you play again. Will you let me know when your next concert is?"

Before Luke could answer, Drew said something and Annie turned her back to Luke. Luke waited, but with Annie's attention monopolized by Drew, he didn't have a reason to stay. He tapped the table twice then walked away at the same time Annie turned to finally get his answer.

"Can I get you ladies something to drink? Martini? Piña colada?" Drew asked, and we laughed. He knew we were Mormon—at least I assumed he did—so he had to be joking.

"I'll have another Coke," Annie said.

"Diet for me," I said, holding up my empty cup.

"You got it."

Annie watched him disappear through the crowd of people around the bar before turning back to me. She buzzed with enough excitement to make her as dangerous as a live wire.

"You were kind of rude to Luke."

"What?" She blanched, and the buzzing stopped.

"You were rude."

"When?" She sat up straight and leaned away from me.

"Just now."

"What are you talking about?" She narrowed her eyes at me, and the dimple in her cheek disappeared.

"Luke invited you to come tonight, not you and Drew. As soon as Drew walked in, it was like Luke didn't exist anymore." My voice rose as the music started again, which made me sound angrier than I felt.

"Okay, thanks, Mom." Annie's words stung, and if I hadn't been angry before, I was now.

"Did you invite him or did Luke?"

"I told the guy at the door to add him to Luke's guest list," she said, less defensive than she had been. "He said he wanted to come, and since he and Luke are friends, I didn't think Luke would mind."

"Knowing each other doesn't make them friends," I said more gently.

"You're right. I'm sorry."

I opened my mouth to say more but shut it when I saw Drew gripping three clear plastic cups. Two obviously held Coke, but the third had an amber liquid the color of beer. I shouldn't have been surprised—we were the only people in the crowd not drinking, after all—but judging by Annie's gaping mouth, I wasn't the only one surprised.

Drew set our drinks on the table before taking a swig of his. He set it back down with an *ahh*. "How'd he do? Was he less uptight than he is at work?" His smile made his question sound less critical than it was.

"He was really good," Annie answered first. "Nothing like he usually is. The crowd went crazy for him."

"You're kidding me. I would have loved to see that. It's hard to believe." Drew took another long drink.

"He's legit. He can play, and he practically upstaged the lead singer," I jumped in, feeling protective of Luke.

"I believe you." Drew held his hands up in surrender. "I'm just saying it doesn't sound like the Luke I know."

All I could look at was the cup he held up in his hand. It bothered me how much I was bothered by it. "Maybe you don't know Luke very well," I said more to the cup than to him.

"That's true. I'm not saying he doesn't have it in him. I just haven't seen it, but Luke's a good guy." Drew's mouth stretched into a boyish grin that normally would have swept away my annoyance. But Luke and I had both been brushed aside that night. The anger I couldn't direct at Becca found a perfect substitute in Drew.

"A better guy than you . . ." I was tempted to leave it there, but I couldn't, so I added "realize" at the last second.

"Come on; let's dance." Drew set his beer down on the table and grabbed Annie's hand. They wound their way to the dance floor, where Drew held her tight but not too tight, and I breathed a little easier.

When the Stringdusters came on stage, Annie and Drew made their way back up to the mezzanine, still holding hands. Luke followed close behind, disappointment etched on his face.

I tried to talk to him once or twice during the show, but all the animation he'd had on stage was gone with his hope of winning Annie. I felt bad for him, but I also liked that Annie was her old self when she was with Drew, even if I didn't like his choice of beverage.

Luke counted the number of drinks Drew had even more carefully than I did. When the show ended the first thing Luke said to him was, "You okay to drive?"

Drew stood up, and for a second I thought he was angry. But then he spoke, his voice as carefree as usual. "Probably not. It's been a while since I've had that much to drink." He dug in his pockets and pulled out his keys. "Will you see me home, m'lady?" he asked and handed the keys to Annie.

"I can drive you." Luke didn't hide his anger.

"I've got it." Annie took the keys, and I couldn't tell if her annoyance was at Drew or Luke. "Emily can follow me."

Luke looked Drew up and down. "Be careful." He turned to leave, and Drew saluted his back.

"I'm not even buzzed, but it's better to be safe than sorry," he said once Luke was down the stairs. "Plus, my driver's pretty hot." He winked, and I rolled my eyes.

"Don't get too comfortable with me being your driver. Next time you decide to have one too many beers, you're on your own," Annie said without a hint of teasing.

A slow smile spread across his face, and he gave her the same salute he'd given Luke but without the sarcasm. "Got it."

She linked her arm through his and led him down the stairs and out the door. I followed, proud of Annie for saying something to Drew but also worried. He said he didn't drink often, but once was one time too many for me. I hoped it would be for her too.

I drove behind them and waited while they kissed goodbye, growing more uncomfortable as the minutes ticked by and their goodbye got longer. The smell of Drew's beer breath lingered in my nostrils, and I wondered how Annie could stand to be even closer to it.

When she finally got in the car, I blurted out the question that had been burning in my brain since Drew put the beer to his lips. "You're okay with what happened tonight?"

"What do you mean?" She was still all smiles.

"Drew drinking?"

"He's never done that before. I don't think he'll do it again." She shrugged then looked at her fingernails instead of at me before chewing the tip of her pinky nail.

"Did he say that, or are you just assuming he won't?" I pulled out of the parking lot and headed for the ranch, waiting for her reply. When she didn't say anything, I asked the question that had been on my mind for a while. "Is he Mormon?"

"I don't know." She knew. I could tell. "Does he need to be?" she challenged.

"That's up to you. Judging by your good-bye though, you'd better decide if finding someone who's Mormon is important to you before things get any more serious with Drew."

"Joel's not Mormon. Dad wasn't either, before he met Mom." Her voice rose, which meant reasoning with her wouldn't work, but I tried anyway.

"That's why I'm not seeing Joel anymore, and Dad's probably not the best example of a convert."

"Well, that's a stupid reason to give up someone who's perfect for you, and Dad's the best example of a man I can think of. I don't care that he didn't go to church every Sunday. That's not how *I* judge people." She reached over and turned up the radio, effectively ending our conversation.

Chapter 23

Joel called the next day. I let it go to voice mail, but a text quickly followed. *Please don't ignore me.*

So I called.

"Hi." He answered on the first ring.

"Hi." I forced the word out, but I couldn't put any other letters together to make more words.

"I'm sorry about yesterday. Becca wanted to call, and I couldn't talk her out of it."

I took a deep, silent breath. "There's nothing to be sorry about." Even though he couldn't see me, I plastered on a smile. It was easier to talk with my game face on. "Are you seeing each other again?" I asked, impressing myself with how cheerful I sounded. Just like Joel was any other friend.

"Kind of." There was a question in his voice. "We're taking things slow."

"That's great. She's great." My face hurt.

"Yeah. I wanted to make sure that wasn't weird for you yesterday. I meant to tell you first. . . ."

"No worries." *No worries? When had I ever said "no worries"?* "I'm the one who said you should get back together with her, remember?" That had been a better idea in theory than reality.

"I wouldn't say we're 'back together'; we're just seeing each other." He sounded defensive, which didn't make sense. If anyone deserved to feel hurt, it was me.

"What's the difference?" I shot back, letting my true feelings slip through the façade.

"The difference is, I'm still . . ."

I held my breath and waited for him to finish.

"I'm not ready to commit."

"Okay." I was back to fighting for words.

"So you'll let us know when you're ready for us to come out?" he asked, breaking the silence.

"Yeah. I'll text you." I couldn't hear his voice and not want him back, so I said good-bye, knowing our conversations would only be by text, about the ranch, and not every day from that point on.

If my conversation with Joel hadn't already ruined my day by nine a.m., Annie decided to get in on the game by giving me the silent treatment. I thought she'd be over our fight by the time she got home from work, but when she barely looked at me, I knew I had to apologize whether I was wrong or not. The girl could hold a grudge.

*   *   *

I knocked on Annie's door early the next morning before she could leave. I didn't wait for her to answer but went in and sat on the end of her bed. I endured the glares that quickly turned to normal eye contact as I apologized.

"If you like him, date him, but be careful," I added as I moved closer to hug her. "I don't want to see you get hurt."

"Love is not about being careful. When you decide to let yourself fall for someone, you'll see what I mean." She hugged me back and pecked my cheek. All was forgiven, but somehow I felt worse. I bit my tongue as I released her. There were so many times I wanted to set Annie straight, but I'd learned to wait for the right moment. When she was high on love— whether it was with a boy or a part—it was not that moment.

*   *   *

Over the next few weeks, Annie's happiness helped keep my spirits up and all of our minds off the one-year anniversary of the accident. Not that we could ever forget it, but it did feel like we'd cleared a major hurdle once the date passed, even though we all still missed Mom and Dad as much as we ever had. I'd hoped to wake up the day after the one-year mark and not miss them anymore. That was stupid.

I thought things would get easier the longer I went without seeing or talking to Joel too, but it only got harder. I missed him so much more than I had anticipated. Even staying busy didn't keep my thoughts from drifting back to him and what could have been. Seeing Annie with Drew in some way let me live vicariously through her. She had courage I didn't have.

My lack of courage also had me dreading when construction would be at a point that Becca could come back to start the design side of things. I was grateful Luke had been able to keep our plans on schedule, but the day I had to call Becca came too soon. We'd kept in contact via e-mail, and she'd mentioned she and Joel were back together. I didn't know if her definition was different from Joel's, but reading the words had been hard enough. Hearing her talk about him would be even harder.

Except part of me wanted to hear everything about him—what he was doing, how his business was going, what he was feeling—even if it meant I'd have to feel all the emotions I'd been trying to bury. Another part of me only wanted to hear he felt as lonely as I did and things weren't working out with Becca. I hated that part of myself. I wanted him to be happy— that's why I'd broken things off—but his happiness meant that he'd been able to move on, and his feelings weren't as strong as mine. That hurt.

I dialed Becca's number in late September when I couldn't put it off any longer.

"Hi, Emily! It's so good to hear from you!"

Again I wished she was someone I could dislike, even hate.

"Have you looked at the pictures I've sent you?" she asked.

"I have. Everything looks great. I'm excited to see the samples and put it all together."

We talked for a while, going over her ideas about how to incorporate materials we'd saved into the new design. I loved that she was invested in my vision yet not afraid to point out what could be better. I felt guilty for not calling her sooner because every time I talked to her I got excited about what I was doing, which led to me feeling stupid for letting jealousy get in the way of what I wanted to accomplish.

"So you're ready for me to come out?" she asked when we'd gone over everything.

"Everything's framed and a few weeks out from being ready for fixtures, paint, and everything else. Do you want me to book you a flight?"

"If you don't mind, I'd like to bring Joel. He'll fly us; plus he's been so involved since the beginning, I think his input is really important."

Her question sucker punched me, and it took me a second to get my breath back. "Of course. We'd love to have both of you. I'll have two rooms ready." I prayed she wouldn't say they only needed one room.

"Okay," she said slowly. "I was going to ask for one, but he'd probably like two, so that's fine. I'm trying not to push him too hard."

"Oh." I breathed a sigh of relief, hoping it didn't sound too relief-y. "But things are going well? You're still seeing each other?" I asked, my need to know winning out over my fear of the answer.

"Things are going great. I think he feels the same way, but he still wants to take things slow. Really slow. I guess I owe him that." Her voice pled for encouragement.

I wanted to give it to her, but I was too relieved by her words to find any of my own. "Taking things slow" was easier to hear than, "We'll only need one room."

Chapter 24

Two weeks later they arrived, and I was looking into eyes whose color reminded me of the ocean I'd left behind and the feelings I'd been trying to forget. I vacillated between holding out my hand and hugging Joel. Hugging was my first choice, but I was afraid I wouldn't let go, so I held my shaking hand out instead. He ignored it, giving me a quick squeeze before Becca wrapped me in a tighter one. An unfamiliar smell of soap and sandalwood cologne lingered behind him, and I wondered if he wore it for Becca.

"Joel!" Bryce's shout traveled across the great room, reaching Joel milliseconds before its owner did. Bryce threw his arms around Joel in a way that made my throat catch. He'd stopped hugging Annie and me months ago, declaring, "Only girls hug." Waves of guilt pounded me as I listened to him spill all the details of his life in a few minutes that I'd been trying for months to pull out of him: friends he'd made, what he liked best about living on the ranch, what he thought about school. Dad was the one person Bryce had never hesitated to tell everything. He had that same kind of connection with Joel, and I took that away from him right when he needed it most. My heart wasn't the only casualty of my breakup with Joel.

"Wow. I didn't know they knew each other so well." Becca watched the two of them, smiling but with an undercurrent of annoyance I guessed she felt from being shut out.

"Joel spent a lot of time at our house while he was doing the kitchen remodel. He took Bryce under his wing. He could tell Bryce was lost without our dad."

"Oh." She visibly relaxed. "I'd forgotten about your parents. I'm so sorry." She placed a comforting hand on my back, but I bristled at her touch. After all her talk about our almost being family, how did she forget something as huge as my parents' accident?

"Joel has a way of connecting with people who have lost loved ones," she continued, not noticing my irritation. "He was so devastated when he lost his brother. He still is, really."

"I'm gonna show Joel the horses!" Bryce interrupted.

"Can I come too?" Becca asked.

Bryce's face crumpled before he remembered his manners and forced out a "Sure."

"You'd better change your shoes first," I said, pointing to her sandals.

"No problem. I bought a pair of boots just for the trip!" She walked to the suitcase she'd left in the entryway, laid it on the ground, and unzipped it. "Here we go!" She pulled out the fanciest pair of cowboy boots I'd ever seen, brown leather with a cream vine winding to the top and intricate stitching on the toe. They were beautiful. And they were about to take a trip through a pasture covered in horse poop.

"What do you think?" She kicked off one flip-flop, slipped on a boot, and held up her leg.

"They're perfect," I fibbed then glanced at Joel. I was surprised to see him grin before Bryce pulled him out the door.

"How long has it been since Joel's brother died?" I asked once Becca had both boots on and we were following the boys at a distance.

"Five years now," Becca answered. She walked slowly, and I didn't know if it was because her brand new boots hurt or if she was allowing Bryce alone time with Joel. I gave her the benefit of the doubt and went with the second reason, touched by her consideration. Bryce clearly wanted Joel to himself. In a house full of women, he was starved for some male companionship. When Luke was around, he was pretty good about letting Bryce tag along, but the more Drew showed up, the less Luke did, letting his crew handle the work. And Drew only had time for Annie.

"The past few months seem to have been easier for him," Becca continued. "I don't know if it's just time or something else, but he hasn't mentioned David—his brother—for a while. In fact, the only time Joel's mentioned him is when he told me what the missionaries from your church said about life after death."

"He's still seeing the missionaries?" I stopped short and stared at her.

"You knew about that?" Her eyes narrowed. For the first time, I realized she had no idea Joel and I had been more than friends.

"He mentioned it to me once." I waved my hand in a lame attempt to brush aside my obvious shock and the fact I knew Joel a lot better than Becca thought I did. I continued our walk, hoping we could get back to the easy conversation we were having before.

"Did you set him up with them?" She stayed rooted to her spot, so I planted myself in front of her again. If she wanted to know how Joel met the missionaries, I'd tell her.

"He met them when he was with me one day and invited them over. So technically I didn't set him up, but he probably wouldn't have met them if it hadn't been for me." Five minutes before, the sun's rays had provided a sprinkling of warmth. Now they beat down on me, adding to the heat searing through my body.

Becca looked toward the boys, licked her lips, then lasered in on me. "Is there something more than friendship between you and Joel?"

"There was . . ." I met her gaze. "Before I moved, while you were still broken up." I had nothing to be embarrassed about. I'd given him up so she could have him, after all. "We're just friends now."

"Did you sleep with him?"

"No!" That question embarrassed me. "I'm Mormon. We don't do that before we're married."

Her shoulders relaxed, and she took a deep breath. Apparently that answer had been more convincing than my others. She began walking again, and I followed.

"That's a huge relief. He's been so different since we got back together. I thought we could just pick up where we left off, but we haven't. I've wondered if he dated anyone else while we were apart—I've even wondered if he still is. I mean, I'm sure he's not. . . ."

"We spent a lot of time together, but we weren't really anything more than friends. I don't think he was over you." Not entirely true if I believed everything Joel had said about his feelings for me. But she didn't need to know about the emotional connection Joel and I had, and by her definition of dating, Joel and I were only friends since there was no physical relationship between us. At least not beyond a few kisses. There was no point in causing problems by telling her the whole truth, especially when there was no possibility of Joel and I getting back together.

We followed the trail to the pasture where the horses were grazing. Becca hadn't answered my question about Joel and the missionaries, and I couldn't ask her again. I had assumed Joel quit taking the discussions once we broke up. The possibility that he hadn't, that he was still studying the gospel, had stirred up an emotional tornado in my chest. Seeing Joel with Bryce already had me questioning if I'd made the right decision when I broke up with him. This new piece of the puzzle made things even more confusing.

If I'd been okay with Joel being perfect in every way except the whole religion thing, would we be planning a wedding? Would Bryce and I both have the man we needed in our lives? I tried to brush those thoughts aside, telling myself even if things had worked out, it wouldn't necessarily mean Joel would have left his life and business in LA for small town Utah. That really was pure fantasy on my part.

But it was a hard fantasy to let go of as it played out in front of my eyes. Add to that the fantasy of him getting baptized, and there was no part of me that didn't think letting him go was the dumbest thing I'd ever done. And that made me angry. I'd done the "right" thing. I'd followed the plan I was supposed to. So why did it feel like I'd been wrong?

"Seeing him with your brother almost makes me want to have kids." Becca's words brought me back to the present.

"You don't want kids?" I couldn't imagine Joel not being a father. Anyone who saw him with Bryce would see Joel was meant to be a dad.

"It's not that I'm set against having them, I've just never really *wanted* them, you know?"

"Not really." I shook my head. "I'd love to have kids someday."

"Really? That surprises me. You seem so driven. I'd think you'd want to put all of your energy into this place. I predict it's going to be huge once it's finished." She eyed me closely, and I could see what she was thinking. *I thought you were different from other Mormon girls.*

I'd dealt with that kind of assumption a lot in grad school. People were always surprised when I said I planned on putting my career on hold once I became a mother. Of course, I'd ended up putting aside my career for other reasons, and none of my other carefully laid plans had actually panned out yet. Living on an old ranch had never been in my plans, and the only sound I heard day in and day out was the pounding of hammers, not the pitter-patter of little feet.

"Well, it's not something I have to worry about any time soon, so hopefully when it does happen, this place will already be up and running." I sounded more confident in my future motherhood prospects than I felt. Truth be told, my confidence in the vision I'd always had for myself was pretty shaky at the moment. Especially with Joel here.

"I'm not good at balancing, and I love my career. I don't think I could give a kid the kind of attention a mother should if it meant taking focus away from my job." She bent over and slid through the lodge-pole fence, following me into the pasture.

Tall grass that the horses hadn't eaten grew around the fence post, and I pulled a handful of it to take to them. Bryce and Joel had done the same and were already luring the horses from the far corners of the pasture with it. Or at least Bryce was. Joel hung back, looking far less excited than Bryce about the thousand-pound animals ambling toward him.

"You're sure we're safe?" Joel said loudly when Becca and I were still twenty feet away.

"Just keep your voice down, and you'll be fine," I answered then laughed as his eyes widened and he clamped his mouth shut.

"Does Joel know how you feel?" I asked Becca in a much quieter voice as Bryce talked Joel into holding out his hand to let the horse eat from it.

"Oh, yeah. It's part of the reason we broke up the first time. But I'm leaving the possibility of kids on the table this time. I guess if he really wants to be a dad, I could have a baby." She lifted her shoulder in a slow, unconvincing shrug.

"He's really great with Bryce," I said weakly, torn between my jealousy of her and my desire for Joel's happiness. I liked Becca a lot. But the more I talked to her, the more I became convinced she wasn't the right person for Joel. And the more convinced I became that I was.

Chapter 25

BECCA WANTED TO SEE THE surrounding area, so we planned a picnic on horseback for the next day. LaRell packed a lunch for us, and Walt agreed to lead our excursion. He talked Luke into joining us with his horses so we would have enough for everyone. He was waiting for some materials that were on back order so work was at a standstill anyway. Annie wanted to go too, and since Drew, who'd gone back to the U, was visiting for the weekend, they both came.

Bryce was a natural with the horses, but I hadn't ridden them yet. Pet them, yes, ridden them, no. I wasn't necessarily *afraid* of them, but I sure wasn't excited about riding on them. But I figured I'd have to get over that if I were going to be a legit dude ranch boss or whatever they're called (one more thing to figure out). The ride would give me the opportunity to check out some of the trails behind our property that guests could use and also see how greenies would handle it. It also gave me un-work-related time to spend with Joel. Not that I'd have the chance to be alone with him, but it was something.

Walt, Luke, and Bryce caught the horses and saddled them while the rest of us watched. Joel offered assistance, but Walt took one look at him and proclaimed he'd be "more of a hindrance than a help." Drew, who I knew had plenty of experience with horses, sat on the fence with his arm slung over Annie's shoulders. He'd barely contacted Annie in the month since he'd returned to school, so his easy affection with her annoyed me.

"We're ready to go!" Walt yelled and waved us over to the saddled horses.

"Come on, scaredy cat. You'll be fine." Becca slipped her hand into Joel's and pulled him toward the horses.

"They're pretty tame, right?" he asked me over his shoulder.

"Oh, yeah. You'll be fine," I said automatically, concentrating hard on not noticing his hand in Becca's.

"You've ridden them?" His eyes pled for assurance.

"Well, no. But Bryce and Annie have."

His face fell.

"Come on; what's Bryce? Six?" Becca nudged him forward.

"Ten," I interrupted as Walt handed me the reins to my horse.

"If a ten-year-old can do it, you can." Her encouragement wasn't increasing Joel's confidence.

"A horse is less complicated than a plane," Annie said. "You'll be fine." She nuzzled her cheek against her favorite horse, Pepper. "Plus they're a lot softer, and they love you," she added, baby-talking to Pepper, who snorted in agreement.

"You're a pilot?" Luke asked as he helped Joel onto a horse that looked a short ride away from the glue factory.

Joel nodded and clutched the reins Luke handed him. Luke moved Joel's hands down the reins, showing him how to grip them loosely, then positioned Joel's feet in the stirrups, all while talking to him about his plane. The more Luke talked, the more Joel relaxed until he almost looked comfortable.

"We ready to go?" Drew asked while leading his more spirited horse in tight circles.

"Not yet," Luke said through gritted teeth as he helped Annie onto her horse.

After some instructions, Walt pointed the horses toward the trail at the back of our property that climbed the mountain, skirting the ski resort. I'd wanted to hike the trail, but in the four months since I'd moved to Park City, I'd been too busy to come anywhere near it. As we left the pasture and rode single file through the tall pines, we instinctively lowered our voices. The trees blocked the sounds from the road, and all we could hear were birds and horses. The pine needles rustled in the breeze, and the cawing of crows was followed by the more melodic robins' songs. The weight I'd been shouldering since Mom and Dad died felt lighter, and I sat up straighter, enjoying the rhythmic sway of my horse and the soft tap of its hooves.

"See? This is nice, right?" Becca's voice behind me interrupted my meditation.

"It is," Joel answered quietly, and I cocked my ear to listen for his voice again.

Instead I heard Becca's as she chattered about the trees, asking what kind they were, did they always change colors like this in the fall, what kinds of birds were singing, what animals lived there, and on and on. It wasn't annoying, but it wasn't peaceful. At one point she even took a phone call.

"I didn't think we could get reception up here," Luke mumbled.

We rode to a meadow filled with wildflowers where we stopped the horses and put down blankets to sit on. Walt unloaded the picnic basket from the pack mule and handed the food to Annie.

"Mmm, smells like chicken," she said, opening the basket. She set it down and started pulling out containers, napkins, and plates.

"This is lovely," Becca said, picking up a plate.

"Everything is eco-friendly. This is one of the ideas we want to test as an excursion we offer, horseback riding and a picnic with farm-fresh food. You're our guinea pigs," I said as I dished potato salad on plates.

"I love it so far, even before the food," she answered.

"LaRell's cooking won't disappoint," Walt bragged.

Annie sat down and stretched out her legs, tipping her head back to soak up the sun. "The sun feels so good."

Drew plopped down next to her and laid his head in her lap. She smiled down at him and ran her hands through his hair. I glanced at Luke, who walked away to make sure the horses were secure.

Becca sat down next to Joel and handed him a plate. She took a bite of her fried chicken and closed her eyes with satisfaction. "Mmm, you've got to try this." She tore off a piece of her chicken and put it in Joel's mouth.

I decided I'd go check the horses with Luke.

He was a short distance away, but far enough that we could talk without being heard.

"Can I help you?" I asked.

He ran his hand along his horse's neck. "No, they're all right. I just don't feel like eating right now."

"Me neither."

He stopped and looked at me then looked back at Joel. "That's your guy?"

"What gave it away?"

"Your face looks like I feel." He tugged on the strap holding the saddle on his horse. "You can help me check the cinches."

"Okay. Should I know what those are?" I followed him to the next horse, where he tugged the saddle-holding strap again.

"You should if you're going to own horses and take people for rides on them." He pointed to the strap he'd pulled tighter and rebuckled. "This is a cinch."

"Got it, but to be clear, I'm not the one who'll be leading the horse rides."

I followed him to the next horse, and he showed me how tight the cinch should be to keep the saddle on and the horse comfortable. We checked each cinch. None of them needed to be tightened, but it did give us some time to get our game faces on.

"We can't avoid them forever, and I'm hungry. You ready?" I asked when we reached the last horse.

He nodded, and we walked back to the blankets and into a tense conversation. I stepped over Drew's outstretched legs to reach the chicken and potato salad. Even though he still had his head in Annie's lap, he was at the heart of the conversation.

"I don't see what the big deal is with having a beer every now and then. I don't need anyone telling me how to live my life. I'm man enough to know when to stop and how to handle my alcohol." Drew's comments were clearly directed at Walt, who looked angrier than I'd ever seen him. Everyone else was very focused on their food. Even Bryce could tell nothing good was going to come out of this disagreement.

"That's fine, but you're lucky. Not everyone is. The only way to find out if you're going to have a problem with it is to try it. If you don't want the problem, then it's better not to try it." Walt spoke slower than usual, his anger simmering at a low boil. He didn't get angry easily, and I wondered what else had been said.

"The problem isn't alcohol; it's telling people they can't have it. That makes them want it. Then if they try it, they don't know how to control themselves." Drew popped a grape in his mouth with the same confidence he did and said everything. Annie's forehead creased as she considered what Drew had said before she slowly nodded.

"That's stupid."

In one collective move, everyone's head turned toward Joel. We looked like a row of open-mouthed emoticons.

"I didn't grow up with any Mormon rules. My parents had wine with every meal, and I've never seen them drunk. But my brother drank himself to death." He stood up and brushed off his pants. "Telling someone to stay away from something because it has the potential to be dangerous doesn't seem like such a bad idea to me."

Drew's mouth opened and closed as he struggled to find something to say. "I'm just saying, people should make their own decisions and not be told what to do by some religion."

Joel shrugged. "There are worse things in the world." He helped Becca up and brushed some dirt off the seat of her pants.

"Is everybody ready to go?" Luke asked. He spoke softly, breaking the tension that had been building.

"Yes! This is boring." Bryce sent an accusing glance Drew's way before walking swiftly to his horse.

I'd only taken a few bites of the food on my plate, but I'd lost my appetite. I scraped what was left into the garbage bag and began packing up the lunch. Annie and Joel stayed to help while the others went with Luke to get on the horses.

"Sorry. I should have kept my mouth shut," Joel said to Annie.

"It's fine." She shrugged and smiled. "Drew isn't shy about expressing his opinion, but he doesn't mean anything by it. He likes everyone."

I wanted to echo Joel's "that's stupid" comment, but he spoke before I could.

"It doesn't bother you when he's critical of what you believe?" Joel stuck the potato salad back in the cooler, and we both waited for Annie's answer. I hoped she wouldn't disappoint me.

"No. I see his point, even if I don't agree with him. It's not worth getting in a fight with him. I've got plenty of time to help him change his mind." She dropped the dirty plates in the basket and walked away, leaving me too stunned by her naïveté to say anything.

"What do you think about that guy?" Joel asked as we watched Drew help Annie mount her horse.

"I like him. Just not for my sister."

"Yeah. She's out of her depth if she thinks she can get a guy like that to change his mind about anything." Joel picked up the cooler and basket and headed for the pack horse. I folded the blankets and followed. Joel had put into words the worry I'd felt every time Annie and Drew were together. She thought she could tweak him just enough to make him perfect; he thought he was perfect the way he was.

*   *   *

For most of his visit, Joel and I didn't have many opportunities to talk, mostly because he went to great lengths to avoid being alone with me.

Becca didn't make things any easier. Ever since our conversation about Joel and me dating, she had been a lot more possessive. Even if he had wanted to talk to me, she didn't leave him alone long enough to try. I didn't blame him for avoiding me, but it hurt. If he still had feelings for me, he wouldn't avoid me. The question about whether he was still investigating the Church also bothered me night and day. I didn't want him to leave before I had the chance to ask him.

I finally got my chance on the day he and Becca were scheduled to leave. I got up after another restless night of sleep. I didn't bother changing out of my pjs but did take the time to pull my hair into a ponytail. Becca had suggested paint colors, and I still hadn't decided which ones I liked.

I opened my blinds to see rays of sunlight breaking over the mountain, bringing out shades of blue in its barren top. I wondered if those rays would do the same to the shades of gray that we'd put up. But when I went downstairs, I saw that the sun wouldn't hit the paint-swatched wall for a while. I could wait, or I could put more paint on the opposite wall. I chose the second option and popped open the cans with my favorite shades. I painted wide stripes of each color on the sun-dappled wall then laid planks of the wood flooring next to them.

"I like the gray one."

I jumped at the sound of Joel's voice. There may have been a squeak too. I'd been so absorbed in what I was doing I hadn't heard him come down the stairs from the guest rooms. Once I realized it was him, we both laughed.

"Sorry," he said and moved closer to me.

"You should be. You scared the heck out of me."

"The heck?"

I rolled my eyes. "It's a Utah thing. What are you doing here?"

"I had some inspiration last night about what to do with the posts Luke saved from the old porch. I wanted to check them out to see if they're long enough for what I'm thinking. What are you doing?"

"Trying to choose a color for the walls." I blew hair out of my eyes as I looked down to see paint running down the brush to my fingers. My pajamas hadn't been spared either.

"For the wall or for yourself?" He smiled.

"Funny."

"You look good in gray." His eyebrows arched, and I stared at the familiar scar that divided his right brow. I fought the urge to run my finger across it like I had before.

"Thanks, but which one?"

"They're different?"

I raised my eyebrow. "Don't play dumb. Help me out here. I have to choose one before Becca leaves."

He took a step back, and the easiness between us disappeared. "I'd probably better let her help you with it. I'm just the builder; she's the one with the eye for color." All the teasing was gone from his voice.

"Yeah, okay." My mouth tasted like cotton, dry and coarse. The words I wanted to get out were stuck. For half a second Becca had been a separate entity, not a part of Joel. Not the girl who had taken my place. Or had I taken hers and she was only reclaiming what "belonged" to her?

"I'm going to take a look at those beams. Good luck with the color." His professional tone cut deeper than his avoidance had. He walked to the back door, where the beams lay outside. As he reached for the knob, I found my voice.

"Joel?"

He turned around slowly but didn't let go of the doorknob.

"I know it's none of my business, but Becca mentioned something about you and the missionaries. Are they still teaching you?"

He let go of the handle, looked down, and took a deep breath. When he let the air out, he looked back at me, and I saw in his eyes what I used to see when he looked at me. "I tried to get rid of them when you . . . we . . ." He paused, looking for the right words, finally settling on "stopped talking," and I was relieved not to hear "broke up."

"But they keep showing up," he added. "Not even the same ones and not even in the same places. I just run into them, and I can't help myself—I start talking to them."

Now I was confused. "So you're not taking the discussions?"

"I don't know. They're not coming to my house to teach me, but every time I talk to them I learn something." He walked back to me.

"Like what?"

"I don't know." He shook his head. "Different things. I'm still reading the book you gave me."

"The Book of Mormon?" I knew he hadn't forgotten the name of it.

"Yes," he muttered like it hurt him to admit it. "Not all the time, but whenever I ask the elders questions I think will stump them, they give me a verse from it, and I have to look it up. I always end up reading more."

"Is that a bad thing?" I stepped closer to him, closer than I'd been in months.

"No." He shook his head. "And, yes." He gazed down at me. We were close enough to touch, and the irony wasn't lost on me that the thing that had driven us apart was now drawing us together.

"What do you mean?"

He took a deep breath. "Things were a lot less complicated before it. Before you. I was happy. At least I thought I was."

"You're not now?"

"It's harder." His gaze seared through me, adding meaning to the words he had spoken. He reached his hand toward mine, and my senses came alive with anticipation. Ever since he'd stepped off the plane, I'd dreamed of this moment. I'd almost given up hope it would happen, but as our hands touched I knew everything would be okay.

Until Becca poked her head through the kitchen door. "Hey, there you are!" she said, and we jumped apart. If she'd seen how close Joel and I were when she opened the door, she didn't show it. "I went out for a run. I didn't think you'd be up yet." She crossed the room and pecked Joel on the lips.

"Yeah, I had an idea about the beams and came down to check them out."

"I was looking at the paint." I pointed to the wall, as upset about Becca's interruption as I was about the color climbing up my cheeks.

"Oh, what did you decide?" Her words came out as more of a challenge than a question.

"Joel was just saying I should let you decide. You're the one with the eye for color." I forced the words past my pasted-on smile.

"The pearl gray has a rustic feel but would go well with the modern touches we've talked about." She touched a still wet swatch I assumed was the color she meant. Then she rubbed her fingers together to get the paint off.

"That's the swatch I like best." I should have complimented her ability to tell what shade of gray it was, but I couldn't say anything else.

"I told you she was good." Joel smiled at her with genuine admiration but flinched when she wrapped her arms around his waist.

"The color still looks great, even in the different light." She let go of Joel and circled the room, inspecting the matching swatches I'd put on each wall. "I think it's the one."

"Okay, let's order it then." I didn't really care what color we chose anymore. If Joel had to leave with Becca, I wanted it to be soon.

"I'll plan on coming back once the paint is done and the furniture has arrived, so we can place it." She walked back to Joel, wrapping both arms around him this time. "Don't worry. I won't make you come with me."

"I don't mind. I can come." He looked over her head at me.

"Whatever. It was enough of a fight to get you here this time. I'm not going through that again." She grinned at Joel then looked at me for back-up. That universal plea for sisterhood when talking about all the ways our men drive us crazy. Sadly, sisterly wasn't what I felt at that moment. More like empty.

"Either way, you're welcome to come back," I stammered. "I should get dressed." I pointed to the door as I walked to it, anxious to escape. I knew I was being rude, but I had to get out before I broke down.

Chapter 26

GOODBYE WAS THE ONLY THING Joel said to me before leaving. I had the answer I'd been looking for, but it had raised so many other questions that left me feeling more confused than I'd been before. I knew I needed to talk to him again, but I couldn't work up the courage to call him. So when I got a text from him the next day, it was a huge relief. Sort of.

I want to finish our conversation, but I need time, it read. Which meant I could stop the Be Brave pep talks to myself, but it also meant waiting for him to call me.

Practicing patience, it turned out, wasn't any easier than building up courage. Two long weeks passed before he called.

"Hi!" I answered as soon as I saw his name pop up. I'd built up this moment for so long, I wouldn't let myself believe it could turn out any other way than how I'd imagined it.

"Hi," he answered in a careful tone that turned the bubbling excitement in my stomach to lead weights.

"How've you been?" I was on my way to pick up Bryce, but I pulled over and took Joel off speaker.

"Good." He paused. "I'm sorry it's taken so long to call."

"I'm not going to lie, it hasn't been easy." I wanted to keep things light because I sensed that's not the direction we were headed.

"I know. The last few weeks haven't been easy for me either." The silence that followed was anything but light. When I didn't respond, he went on. "I started taking the discussions."

"Really? That's great." A tiny bit of hope bubbled up.

"Becca's taking them with me."

And . . . *pop*! So much for hope.

"What does she think? What do you think?" My questions came out with the same effort it took to push a wagon without wheels. On a spiritual level, I wanted to be excited. Emotionally it didn't feel so good.

"I haven't figured it out yet, but I think I'm more into it than she is. I appreciate that she supports me and wants to be a part of it."

The meaning behind his words hit hard and fast, knocking the breath out of me. I realized fear had kept me from having faith. Faith in Joel and faith in God's plan. "You feel like I didn't support you, don't you?"

"You gave me the tools and the direction, but I would have liked to have you with me." He let out a heavy sigh. "We had something good, Emily, even if it didn't look the way you thought it should."

"I got scared, Joel. I'm sorry."

"It's okay."

"It's not. I can't tell you how much I regret it. If I could go back, I'd do things differently." I wanted to plead with him to give us another chance, but even from a thousand miles away I could tell it wouldn't work.

"I don't want you to regret anything. I don't know if I'll join the Church or not, but I don't regret the time I spent with you or the time I've spent learning about your religion. It's made me a better person." He paused, and I tried to hold on to the last scrap of hope I had. "But I'm happy with Becca, and that's where I need to be."

I swallowed hard. His words weren't totally unexpected, but I still had to fight back tears. "I understand. That's all I want for you—to be happy. Thank you for being honest with me."

We said good-bye quickly. There wasn't anything else to say. Then I tossed my phone onto the passenger seat and took deep breaths until the lump in my throat disappeared. Joel and I were really done. I couldn't change that, so why cry about it? I had one month until Becca came back to help with the finishing touches on the ranch. I would *not* be sad when she got there.

*   *   *

"It's not official yet, but Joel and I have a date on the calendar."

Those were the first words Becca said to me when she walked through my front door, pecking my cheek as she delivered the news.

"A date for what?" I asked before the reality of what she'd said hit me.

"Our wedding. He hasn't officially proposed yet, but I needed to get my calendar set for next year so we chose a date." She dropped her bags in the foyer and scanned every inch of the great room. "This looks amazing. Furniture is here tomorrow?"

How she jumped from her future engagement to my great room in a single bound, I'll never understand. I was still scraping my heart off the floor while she was talking about sofas and end tables. I'd spent a month preparing myself for the worst, and still it had taken me by surprise.

"Congratulations." I forced the word out and picked up her bags. "Everything is being delivered tomorrow."

"Like I said, it's not official, so keep it on the down low for now." She walked to the staircase and examined the timber railing. I followed.

"I'll show you what we've done with the rooms." I walked past her and climbed the stairs. My heart pounded but not from exertion. "Not official" sounded pretty official. I opened the door to her room and set her bags down then started the fire.

"This is exactly like I pictured it." She fingered the hand-stitched quilt at the foot of her bed and ran her hands over the crisp, white linens.

"I followed the plan we created." I loved the way everything had turned out too, but I didn't know how I'd be able to look at it every day and think that Joel's fiancée—his future wife—was the one who'd designed it all. Would it bother me less in a year? Two years? Becca had taken my vision and made it better for half of what it should have cost. The ranch had been transformed into the luxury resort Dad had dreamed of because of her—and all I wanted to do was forget her.

Or for her to forget Joel. That would have worked too.

"Do you want dinner here or should we go downtown?" I tucked away my resentment and put on a smile.

"Let's go out."

"Okay. I'll go change." I escaped her room, glad she'd been too distracted with unpacking to notice my face. I'm sure it didn't hide how little I wanted to be trapped at a restaurant listening to her wedding plans.

I headed to Annie's room in our wing of the ranch. I needed backup if I was going to make it through dinner, even if it meant finding somewhere for Bryce to go. I needed my sister. I knocked on her door and waited for an answer.

When I heard rustling inside, I poked my head in her room. The overhead lights were off, but a light came from the bed, and as my eyes adjusted to the dark, I could see Annie holding her phone.

"What's going on?" I asked.

"Nothing," she answered without putting her phone down.

"You want to go to dinner?"

I'd been so wrapped up in getting the ranch ready to open, I'd barely talked to Annie for weeks. If I stopped to think about it, when she wasn't at work, she'd been spending a lot of time in her room.

"I don't think so."

I flipped on the light, and she dropped her head into her knees that were pulled up to her chest. All I could see was the messy knot of hair at the top of her head.

"What are you doing?" she peeked over her knees.

"What are *you* doing in bed at five o'clock?" That was never a good sign with Annie.

She sat up and tossed her phone to the foot of the bed. "Waiting for stupid Drew to text me back."

"What's going on with Drew?" I crossed the room and sat down on her bed, tucking my legs underneath me.

"It takes him forever to return my calls or texts. He's totally into me whenever he's here, and then once he's gone, I don't even exist." Tears started to form in her eyes.

"He must be busy. He hasn't returned my calls or texts either, and I really need some updated photos now that the exterior is done." Part of me was relieved things were cooling down with Annie and Drew, but I also needed him to finish the job he'd started for me.

"I called his aunt to make sure he's okay. All she said is he's probably busy with school." She wiped her eyes and picked up her phone again.

"Forget Drew. I need you to come to dinner with me and Becca." I wiggled her big toe and smiled, pushing back my own pain.

"Becca is here?"

"Yeah. She wants to go out, and I want you to come."

She dipped her chin and stared at me. "Really?" She pointed her eyes toward the mess on her head. "I'm not going out like this."

"Then get ready. We'll wait for you." I jumped off the bed, grabbed her hand, and pulled. "Come on. Keeping busy will get your mind off him."

"Fine." She went limp and let me pull her off the bed. When I had her standing up, I threw open her closet. What I saw made me worry even more.

Annie was disorganized in every aspect of her life except her closet. It was a thing of beauty. She had everything organized by season and color, with shirts on the top rack and the coordinating pants, shorts, skorts, and skirts on the bottom. Her accessories were hung in organizers, not buried in a jewelry box like mine. Getting dressed for her was a work of art.

Except when she was depressed. Then her closet reflected her state of mind—scattered and dark.

That's what it looked like now. There were more clothes piled on the floor than on hangers. Tops and bottoms were tossed on top of or trapped under mismatched shoes. Even necklaces and earrings were lying on shelves instead of hanging in their special organizer. I stared at the mess until she nudged me out of the way, rifled through what was left on hangers, then picked up a T-shirt from the closet floor.

"How serious are you and Drew anyway? I mean, I know you've spent a lot of time together, but are you just having fun or are you making long-term plans?" I asked while I watched her. We hadn't talked about their relationship. In fact, lately she hadn't brought him around much, even though he'd been back on a lot of weekends.

"We haven't talked about getting married or anything, but he told me he loves me." She spoke slowly and pulled a pair of jeans from a hanger. "Is this too casual?" she asked, holding them up with the T-shirt.

I shook my head, hiding my shock. "He said he loves you? That's kind of big."

"That's what I thought. And then suddenly, nothing." She peeled off the top she had on, which I realized was a pajama top.

"Do you want to shower first?" I didn't want to push, but clearly that hadn't happened today.

"I guess." She lifted her shoulder with resignation.

"Okay. Knock on my door when you're ready. But hurry!"

I walked to my room, mulling over everything Annie had told me. She hadn't fought me too hard about going out, but she'd obviously been in bed most of the day. That was always a sign that she was off her meds or that she was slipping into a depressive episode even on them. I'd have to ask her, but it would have to be carefully. I didn't want to push her away.

An hour later the three of us were sitting down to dinner at my favorite Mexican place. Becca had already delivered the good news to Annie about her unofficial engagement to Joel and was talking about the design ideas she had for the wedding. Every time she said Joel's name, Annie eyed me warily from the other side of the table, looking for a reaction I made sure not to give her. *Smile and nod, smile and nod,* I told myself over and over.

"I'm sorry. I'm being rude talking all about myself." She pushed her menu away and leaned closer to Annie. "I'm just so excited. But tell me what's going on with you and Drew."

"There's not much to tell. He's back at school, so we don't get many chances to be together." Annie glanced up from her menu only long enough to answer Becca.

"Well, I could tell he was crazy about you. Things will work out."

"Thanks." Annie's lip curved into the closest thing to a smile that I'd seen for days. As much as I hated what Becca had to say about Drew, I loved that she got Annie to smile.

How could I not like Becca? How could Joel not like Becca? She was thoughtful. She was fun, smart, cute—no, gorgeous—successful. Of course he'd love her. I was practically in love with her.

Our waiter set a margarita in front of Becca then took our food order. As soon as he left, Becca took sip of her drink and jumped to the next topic of conversation, one I'd been hoping to avoid, even as I felt guilty for that thought.

"Can I ask you some questions about your church?"

"Of course. What do you want to know?" I took a sip of water but set the glass down when I couldn't hold it still. Mormon questions meant she and Joel were still taking the discussions. I should have been happy about it, but instead it hurt.

"Well, Joel keeps talking about it, and he's taking those lesson things from the missionaries, so I've been sitting in on them."

"Do his parents know?" I interrupted. That's something I hadn't asked him but had wondered about since we'd talked.

She shook her head. "No, and they won't like it if they find out. I can't figure out why he keeps studying Mormonism. It's like he can't stop, and he keeps wanting me to listen to the elder guys too."

"So what do you want to know?" Annie asked with excitement. Her church attendance may have been spotty—especially since she'd been dating Drew—but she never hesitated when it came to telling people about her beliefs.

"I don't know. I guess I want to know what he sees in it. No offense or anything, but if I didn't know you two and a few other Mormons, I'd honestly think he was being brainwashed." She laughed and took a longer sip of her drink, licking salt off her lips when she finished.

"You wouldn't be the first person to say that," I said.

"So what is it about this church? I look at you two and what you've been through and can't understand how you even still believe in God. My parents got divorced, and I stopped believing. You lose both your parents, and you still do the whole religion thing. What kept you from giving it all up? What kept your family together? My sister and I barely speak since the divorce, but you two are closer than any sisters I know."

"God did," Annie answered before I could. "We know our parents are with Him, and we know we can be too."

I was floored by her answer, especially since our parents had never been sealed in the temple. Sure Dad had been baptized, but he'd never been committed. Frankly, I'd questioned Annie's commitment more than once. She'd picked up from Dad's example the idea that she could believe but still be casual in the practice of those beliefs.

"You don't think God caused the plane wreck? Because I know a lot of Christians who would say it was God's will. I don't get that. Why would God do that or any of the other terrible things that happen?" Becca's hands flew as she talked.

"I don't think He causes terrible things to happen, but He does allow them to happen so that we can grow and learn. He loves us, but He knows that for us to live with Him again, we have to become better than what we are." Annie's answer couldn't have been better.

"That's what Joel keeps talking about. He says he feels God's love the more he studies Mormonism. I don't know." She shook her head. "I don't really feel like we need anything different. I'm happy the way things are, so I don't get why he's putting everything at risk."

"Would you break up with Joel if he converted?" I asked.

"No," she responded without hesitation. "I made the mistake of letting him go once. I'm not doing it again."

I felt Annie's eyes on me, but I couldn't meet them. The waiter rescued me by setting our appetizer in front of us and giving me an excuse to not respond. I took my napkin off the table and spread it carefully in my lap then directed all of my attention to the chips and queso dip in front of us.

"So do you think you'd get baptized if he did?" Annie asked.

Becca pursed her lips and thought about the question. "I'd support him, but I doubt I'd join. I look at you two, and I see all the good things about your religion. I just don't know if I could live it. I barely know Judaism. To jump from that to believing in Jesus and not drinking alcohol . . . that's huge. And is it true you don't drink coffee either?" She threw the last question in as an afterthought, but the panic in her voice left no doubt it was a big one.

"Yep." I nodded.

"Ohhh that could definitely be a deal breaker." She took a long sip of her drink as she let that reality sink in.

"Don't let that keep you from listening to the missionaries." I swallowed hard. I couldn't let my own feelings about Joel keep me from encouraging her. "You may find what you learn—and feel—is better than coffee. Or anything else you think you'd have to give up. It doesn't always look easy to be Mormon, but what we know makes life easier. I can't imagine going through what we did without our belief in Jesus and a Heavenly Father who loves us."

Becca nodded, and for the first time since I'd met her, she was quiet. Her whole body was still, like someone had unplugged her, and the energy that normally rolled off her in waves stopped. "That's really good to know." She nodded, staring at her glass.

A few quiet minutes passed before our waiter reappeared, cleared the appetizer plate, and set our dinners in front of us. We talked in spurts as we ate but not about Joel or the gospel. We were all still thinking about our discussion though. I could tell by the way Annie smiled and looked more at ease—as though her answers had been more for her than for Becca—and in the way Becca listened instead of talked, even though what we said wasn't nearly as important.

By the time we got home, I had to be alone to think. I said good night to Becca and Annie, snuck into Bryce's room to kiss his forehead—something he'd never let me do if he were awake—then went to my room and turned on the bath. I sank into the deep tub as it filled, then put a cold washcloth over my eyes. I pressed it hard, trying to keep the tears back.

It didn't work.

Chapter 27

OVER THE NEXT FOUR DAYS, Becca and I worked nonstop to get all the furniture arranged in the great room and the guest bedrooms. Annie had finished shooting the first season of her show, so she helped a little, but she was so distracted that I finally put her in charge of keeping Bryce occupied when he got home from school. She still hadn't heard from Drew, but I was too busy trying to keep our heads above water to worry about her broken heart.

After Becca left, Luke came over for our final walk-through. Annie popped out of her room to say hello but then disappeared again.

"What's going on with her?" Luke asked as her door closed.

"What do you mean?" I pointed to a ding in the wall that needed to be touched up, and he took a picture of it before writing it down in his notepad.

"She doesn't seem like herself. I haven't seen her smile for weeks."

"She's upset that Drew hasn't called or texted. He's basically fallen off the face of the earth, which, honestly, doesn't bother me. She'll get over it, I'm sure."

Luke knelt down to look at a nick in the baseboard, wrote it down, then followed me to the next room. When I glanced over my shoulder at him, worry lined his face. We stopped at the next spot that needed a touch-up, and he finally spoke. "I'm not so sure. I hate to say it, but they seemed pretty into each other." He tugged at his hat, and I waited for the words I could tell he wanted to say. "I know she's had some problems." He paused. "With depression. Is this thing with Drew going to set her back?"

"I don't know. I hope not."

"Let me know if I can help." He flipped through the papers on his clipboard and stuck the pencil behind his ear without looking at me.

I was touched by Luke's concern and relieved I didn't have to carry the entire burden of worrying about Annie by myself, especially since I'd been ignoring the problem. Not that I didn't care; I just had too many other things to worry about. Worries that could be fixed in a day with paint or nails or glue. They were easier to think about than Annie and didn't scare me the way another possible "episode" did.

We finished our walk-through and said good-bye. With most of the work done, we wouldn't be seeing Luke as much, leaving fewer opportunities for Annie to see what a good guy he was. He hadn't asked her out again since the concert, but I guessed his feelings for her had only grown.

He proved me right when he came by the next day for no other reason than to give Annie tickets for a concert. He knocked on the back door before walking into the kitchen and setting the tickets in front of Annie's cereal bowl. "I thought you and Emily might like to see this band. I've played with them before, and they're great."

"Yeah, I've heard of them. Thanks," she said, staring at them. "Are you sure you don't want them?" She handed them back to him, but he waved his hands no.

"I'm not up for it, but you two go enjoy it. I'll look after Bryce if you need me to." He wouldn't look directly at her, but when she smiled he rubbed the back of his neck.

"That's sweet. Thanks. What do you think, Emily?"

"Definitely." I looked at the tickets. I'd never heard of the band, but if it got Annie's mind off Drew, I was in.

"The concert's in Salt Lake. Maybe we could go by Drew's, just to make sure he's okay." Now she was genuinely excited. Luke's face fell, but she didn't notice.

"Okay, well, have fun. I better get going." Luke put on his hat and adjusted the brim to hide his face.

"Thanks again." Annie stood up and threw her arms around him. Luke put one arm around her waist and returned her squeeze with a tentative hug. When she let go, he nodded, cleared his throat, and left.

"Are you really sure you want to see Drew?" I asked as soon as Luke shut the door.

"Why wouldn't I?"

"If he's not returning your calls or texts, how do you know he wants to see you?" I asked as gently as I could.

"You don't tell someone you love her one day and then never want to see or talk to her again. Something had to have happened, and I want to know what." Her words were quick and determined, shutting down any argument I could come up with. She'd made up her mind, and I couldn't talk her out of her plan, no matter how stupid I thought it was.

"Okay, I just don't want you to get hurt." I laid a gentle hand on her shoulder, which she promptly shrugged off.

"You don't understand what we have because you've never been in love. I know how he feels about me. I'm not going to think the worst just because you are." She turned around and walked up the stairs, taking two at a time.

The weird thing about Annie was she could stay in bed for days because she couldn't find one good reason to get out then be totally optimistic about the most unrealistic ideas ever. I hoped this wasn't one of those times. There were a lot of things I didn't like about her relationship with Drew, but I really didn't want her to be hurt. Not now, especially. I couldn't give her the attention and care she'd need and open our resort at the same time.

*   *   *

On Saturday Annie and I drove to Salt Lake. The plan was to stop by Drew's before the concert, but I made her swear not to make us miss the show before I'd get in the car. I secretly hoped we'd get caught in traffic and be forced to skip Drew's, but Salt Lake doesn't know how to do traffic the way LA does.

"Do you want me to wait here?" I asked after I pulled into Drew's apartment building.

"No, I'm sure he'd like to see you too," she answered in a shaky voice, looking up at the high rise. He lived in a pretty swanky place for a college student, which was weird. I had assumed he lived in a frat closer to campus.

When we got to the apartment, Annie knocked on the door and stepped back.

"It's Saturday; there's a good chance he won't be here," I said when a minute passed with no answer.

"I think I hear someone." She held her ear to the door and knocked again. It opened almost as soon as she pulled her hand back. A tall blonde woman with long hair that covered more than her shorts and tank top did answered the door.

"Hi. I think maybe I have the wrong apartment. Does Drew Willis live here?" Annie stammered, looking the lady up and down.

"Who?"

"Drew Willis." Annie's confidence was fading by the second.

"Let me ask. I don't actually live here. Chase!" she called over her shoulder.

"What!" a deep voice yelled.

"Do you have a roommate named Drew?" she yelled back.

A man came around the corner. "Who's asking?"

Miss Blonde Thang opened the door wide so a guy with wet hair wearing only basketball shorts could see us. He sucked in his gut and smiled at us, which didn't make the blonde happy at all. She huffed and stormed into the hallway. Seconds later the opening riff for TMZ floated through the air.

"Hi! I'm Annie. Drew's a friend of mine." Annie raised her hand but dropped it as he looked her up and down.

"Oh, dude! I recognize you. You're in that *Far and Away* show. Drew mentioned something about hanging out with you in Park City." He opened the door all the way and waved us in. "That's so tight."

"*Up and Away*," I said, irritated.

"Yeah, is he here?" Annie asked. I'd seen a flash of annoyance at the words "hanging out," but it quickly changed to relief as Annie realized she had the right place.

"No, he bailed on me." He led us into the kitchen, where he grabbed an energy drink from the fridge.

Annie's face fell. "Do you know when he's going to be back?"

He cracked open the can and took a drink. "He's not coming back. Didn't he tell you?"

"We haven't talked for a while," Annie stammered, red splotches creeping from her neck to her cheeks.

"His aunt totally cut him off when she found out he dropped out of school. I covered his rent for a while, but my parents weren't really cool with that. They made me kick him out. I haven't seen him in a month."

"How long ago did he drop out?" I asked.

"Like a year ago, but the old lady just found out. I quit trying to find him when I figured out he wasn't paying me back. If you find him, tell him Chase wants his money."

The more he talked, the more Annie's face drained of the red color until, by the time he finished, she looked chalky. "I will," she whispered.

"You're welcome to hang for a while if you want."

"No, that's okay. We've got a concert to get to," I answered for both of us, even though his question had been directed at Annie, who had hurried to the door before I finished talking.

As soon as the door shut behind us, she sprinted for the elevator and punched the down button over and over until the doors finally opened. We stepped in, and the moment they shut, she burst into tears. "I knew he was in trouble! No wonder he won't answer my calls or texts. He probably thinks I won't want to see him anymore if he doesn't have money."

I blinked back my surprise, stunned beyond words. I thought she'd be upset that he'd lied to her about being at the U. I doubted that was his only lie either. How could it be? It was a huge one, and people who were okay telling one big lie were usually okay telling any kind of lie. But Annie wasn't seeing that. "Annie, it sounds like the trouble he's in, he's created. Did you hear that guy say Drew's been lying to his aunt for a year? He lied to us about still being in school too, remember?"

The elevator doors opened, and two more people stepped in, so Annie didn't respond until we got to the car. By then I figured she was giving me the silent treatment for even suggesting Drew might be responsible for his own problems.

In reality, it took her that long to come up with another justification for his behavior. "How could he tell his aunt the truth? She promised him a job and all her money but then attached all kinds of strings to it. He can't be a photographer like he really wants; he has to work crap jobs and go to college. What's the point of getting an education if all you're doing is cleaning stuff up and taking orders from other people? It doesn't take a college degree to plunge toilets." Her words were sharp and urgent, like she had to convince herself as much as anybody that Drew had good reasons for lying.

"Maybe not, but it would come in handy if he's going to be running his aunt's entire business." I started the car, wanting to get far away from what just happened.

"Why? She doesn't have any kind of degree. I don't think she even went to college."

I didn't know anything about Drew's aunt except what Luke had told me, so I kept my opinion—that she had life experience Drew didn't have—to myself. There was one question I wasn't going to let go though. "Even if all that is true, why did he lie to us?" I glanced at her long enough to see her squirm then turned my focus back to navigating our way to the concert venue.

"I don't know. Maybe he was worried if we knew, we'd tell Luke, and then it would get back to his aunt." She stuck her thumbnail in her mouth and chewed, a clear sign she was a lot less certain about this answer than her others.

"Maybe."

We stayed silent until I was a block from our concert. Then Annie spoke. "I'm not in the mood. Let's go home." She turned up the radio and stared out the window.

I didn't bother arguing. I changed course and headed toward the freeway. I had a lot more to say about Drew and his lies, but now wasn't the time. Annie wasn't the type of girl who'd usually put up with that, which made me wonder just how deep she'd gotten herself with him. If she could find excuses for his behavior, was she doing the same for herself?

Chapter 28

THE RANCH OFFICIALLY OPENED THE second week of November, but we threw a grand opening Halloween party the week before. We invited anyone within a hundred-mile radius involved in the travel industry and told them to dress as their favorite cowboy or cowgirl. I went as Annie Oakley, Annie went as Jessie from *Toy Story*, and Bryce dressed as Billy the Kid, refusing to be Woody and barely tolerating Annie's "Brycie the Kid" taunts, pointing out that since he was the "man of the house" he shouldn't be called Brycie anymore.

Truthfully, it was a little hard to tell who was who, but we had a full house. We served samples of the plum-glazed ribs, sage-fried chicken, and straight-out-of-the-orchard peach cobbler—all cooked by LaRell—so our party guests could get a taste of what we would be feeding any guests they sent our way. Luke's band played, and Annie took pictures to post to our website since Drew was still MIA. I knew she still missed him, but she put on a brave face. I did the same when a huge basket of fruit and gourmet cheeses arrived with a card attached signed by Joel and Becca. I had invited both of them, but I'd been secretly praying Joel would surprise me by showing up alone with an armful of roses. But a basket of fruit and cheese was good too. . . .

All in all the night was a success, and even though we were only booked for the next two weeks, the positive responses from our guests gave me hope we'd be booked solid through the winter in no time.

"I think Mom and Dad would be proud of you," Annie said after our last guest and the help had gone. We flopped down in the leather chairs in the great room. Bryce was spread out on one of the couches gently snoring, his face smashed in the seat cushions and his arm flopped over the edge.

Tears sprang to my eyes as much from weariness as genuine gratefulness that she had said exactly what I needed to hear.

"They'd be proud of *us*. They *are* proud of us. I couldn't have done any of this without you." I pressed my fingers into my eyes to stop any other tears that might try to escape.

"Yeah, I think they are." Annie laid her head back and sighed. "I think they'd be proud of my show too."

"I know they would. I can't wait to see it."

"Thanks."

"Luke did a good job tonight," I said to change the subject from Mom and Dad. Luke had been keeping Annie occupied over the past few weeks since she'd tried to see Drew. He'd invited her to a couple of the shows he and his band played in Park City and Provo. I was surprised she'd gone but didn't want to scare her away from him by asking too many questions. But the time seemed right to get some info out of her.

"Yeah, his band is always good."

I waited, hoping for more.

Nothing.

"How were his other shows?" I asked finally.

"They were good. He's actually kinda fun to hang out with."

"So he's growing on you?" I tried to play casual, but she saw through me.

"Slow down there, Flash. We're friends; that's it." She gave me a stern look, and I held my hands up in surrender.

"I wasn't saying you were more than that." I hesitated, but I had to ask, "Have you heard from Drew?"

She shook her head. "I know I will though."

The thing with Annie is that when she wants something, she doesn't give up. She'd pursued her dream of being an actress from the time she was five years old, begging Mom for acting classes for the next three years before Mom caved. She'd auditioned and been rejected plenty of times without ever losing her certainty that she would get a part, even when the rest of us had no hope. Not that we doubted her talent, we were all just more realistic about the competition she faced. She'd proved us wrong then and a hundred times since.

She was pursuing Drew with the same doggedness, but I hoped this time she was wrong. Ever since our conversation with his roommate, I'd prayed she wouldn't hear from him again. Her blind faith in the rightness of what—or whom, in this case—she wanted had the potential to turn out bad. Really bad. But I wasn't going to point that out and risk having her ignore me again.

"What should we do about our sleeping outlaw over there?" I asked.

"I'm too tired to move him." She curled up in the chair and closed her eyes.

"Me too. I'm too tired to move myself." Unfortunately my brown, twill, fringed skirt and matching shirt weren't as comfy as my flannel pajamas; otherwise I would have fallen asleep in the chair. Annie's heavy breathing told me she was about to.

"Let's crash down here," she mumbled.

"Okay. I'll get some blankets."

I forced myself out of the chair and up the stairs to change and grab some blankets. By the time I came back downstairs, Annie was on the other side of the couch from Bryce and snoring softly. I laid a blanket over her and another over Bryce then lay down on the couch across from them. For the first time since my parents' accident, my chest didn't feel like a gaping hole that couldn't be filled. The hole was still there, but a little less empty. I smiled and closed my eyes before whispering, "Love you, Mom. Love you, Dad."

*   *   *

The ranch was packed with guests on Thanksgiving Day when my phone rang and Joel's name popped up. I stared at it, my heart pounding. I wanted to answer it, but fear clenched my heart. What if he'd only dialed my number on accident? What if it was just Becca calling from his phone? Both of those seemed more likely than Joel calling for the reason I wanted him to: to tell me he loved me and wanted to try again.

I waited to answer until the last second, right before it went to voice mail. I told myself it would be better to hear what he had to say by message rather than in person. But I couldn't resist. "Hello," I said. There was a brief silence, and I thought maybe I hadn't answered soon enough.

"Emily?" His voice caught, and he cleared his throat.

"Yeah. Hi, Joel."

"Hi. How are you?"

"Good. How are you?" I sat down on the edge of the bed, my knees too shaky to hold me anymore.

"Great. I mean, good. It's nice to hear your voice again."

"Yeah, you too. How are things?" I stayed calm, but inside I was hyperventilating. I squeezed my hand between my knees, trying to control the shaking in it and my legs.

"Things are good. I'm doing well." He was stalling. Whatever he had called to tell me couldn't be good, and I clenched my eyes shut waiting for the blow.

"I hope it's okay I called. I've been wondering how you're doing . . . with the opening and the holidays and everything."

"Oh." I opened my eyes and relaxed.

"I know how hard holidays are when someone's missing." The tenderness in his voice caught me off guard and let loose the emotions I'd been bottling all day. Or all year. Okay, maybe I'd done a lifetime's worth of bottling. I'd found every way not to feel the loss of my parents that day, but his words gave me a release. I wouldn't cry in front of my sister and brother, but I could cry to Joel across a phone line and a thousand miles.

I could, but I wouldn't. Instead, I swallowed hard a few times and got control of myself. "Thanks. I appreciate you calling. It's been a hard day. I probably would have been a mess if we hadn't been so busy." I could be honest with him, but no one needed to see—or hear—me break down.

"I doubt it. I can't picture you ever being a mess, no matter how bad things might be."

I let out a jagged sigh as Joel talked and hoped he didn't notice it. If he knew how close to the total breakdown brink I was, he probably wouldn't have called. Actually, he would have. That's what made our conversation so hard.

"How's Bryce?" he asked. Of course.

"He's doing okay. Last Thanksgiving was definitely a lot harder. Walt and Luke have been great about keeping him busy." I talked fast and a lot, giving Joel all the boring details about how Bryce spent his time. As hard as it was to talk to him, I didn't want the conversation to end.

"I'm glad to hear that. He's a good kid."

"Have you seen Jason? How is he?" A twinge of guilt flared up in my chest. If I was going to have a relationship with my half-brother, I'd have to put in most of the effort. I knew that, and I'd been determined to stay in touch with him, but I hadn't. Other than a text he'd sent inviting us for Thanksgiving, we hadn't spoken since the move.

"He came to my parents' for dinner," Joel answered. "He seems fine. It's hard to tell with him. Are you coming out for the wedding?"

"We're planning on it. I can't believe they chose Valentine's Day." Jason had sent a save-the-date card months ago, but the ranch renovation had taken up most of my brain space, and I'd put the wedding out of my head.

"They chose it based on the Jewish calendar. Plus, Jason liked the idea of consolidating two celebrations into one so he doesn't have to try to remember them both." Joel laughed. "And you know Rachel loves to multitask, so he didn't have to work too hard to get her on board."

"Those two were made for each other." I shook my head, amazed at how unlike my dad Jason was. Then I realized my conversation with Joel had veered toward wedding stuff. White-hot fear ran through me as I wondered if he was leading into his own wedding announcement. I didn't really want to know if the answer was yes, but I also had to face the inevitable. "How about you and Becca? Any official plans yet?" I bit the bullet and asked. I couldn't use the word *wedding* though.

There was a long silence. "We've talked about it. There may be some complications though."

"What kind of complications?" I asked slowly. *Complications that involved me? Complications that would break off their engagement?*

"Nothing. It's nothing. Weddings are just . . . they're a lot of work. But everything is fine." His words rushed out like a kid late for curfew. He obviously had more to say but kept it to himself. Which was better for both of us. I loved talking to him again, but letting him go had been too hard and falling back into easy conversation with him only made me want him back.

"Well, thanks for calling. It means a lot that you remembered me." That's all I could say. A familiar lump formed at the back of my throat, holding back all the other things I wanted to tell him.

"I remember you all the time, Emily." The words came out with a deep breath, as much out of his control as his need for air. Before I could respond, he added, "I better go."

"I haven't forgotten you either, Joel," I rushed to say, but he'd already hung up. "I wish I could," I whispered to no one.

Chapter 29

CHRISTMAS PASSED, AND NEW YEAR'S came with a sigh of relief that we'd made it through another holiday without Mom and Dad. We did our best to celebrate, but the emptiness was still too big to ignore.

The day after New Year's, the phone rang at the worst possible time: the dinner hour. We were booked again, and I was helping LaRell serve our guests the steaming-hot chicken potpies she'd spent the afternoon making from scratch. Normally I wouldn't have picked it up, but Joel's name popped up, and I didn't want to miss a call from him.

"I'm sorry. I've got to get this," I said to LaRell and set the tray down I was balancing one-handed while attempting to answer my phone.

"Hello?"

"Are you watching TMZ?" Joel asked, skipping the greeting.

"What? Why would I be watching TMZ?"

"Becca's watching. There's a story about Annie coming up."

My stomach dropped. "What kind of story? Is it bad?" I rushed out of the kitchen to the stairs leading to my room.

"It's TMZ, Emily."

That's all he had to say. Really, he didn't even need to say that. I avoided TMZ for the same reason I avoided babies in saggy diapers: they were both full of the same thing.

"I don't even know if it's on right now," I said as I climbed the stairs two at a time.

"Is Annie home?" Joel asked.

"No, she's on a promo shoot for her new show." I flipped on the TV and scrolled through the guide until I found TMZ. "Got it."

"The story's on now," Joel said. I could hear his TV in the background, which meant I was getting Harvey Levin and crew in stereo.

Mormon Girl Gone Wild! flashed across my TV, and the sick feeling in my stomach moved to my throat. Harvey leaned over the cubicle partition waiting for his lackeys to feed him the garbage splayed across their computer screens.

"So, remember how Annie Carter walked off the set of *Boomtown* because it was too 'risqué'?" a spikey-haired guy asked, making air quotes when he said *risqué*. Harvey nodded and grinned his wide Hannibal Lechter smile, his too-white teeth gleaming out of his too-tan face.

"Well, I've got some photos of her that make *Boomtown* look like *Sesame Street*." Spikey Hair's lip curled into a mean grin.

"Seriously? Show me what you've got." Harvey leaned farther over the partition, and Spike (or whatever his name was) turned the computer toward him. My TV screen filled with pictures of Annie. Blood rushed to my face as I saw them, and I had to sit down on the edge of my bed.

"Whoa! Where'd you get that?" Harvey's smile spread, reminding me of an oil spill.

"Snapchat."

"Oh, snap!" Harvey exclaimed to placating laughter. "How'd you keep it from disappearing?"

"You just gotta have the right app. A viewer sent it in and said a friend sent it to her."

It was of a photo of Annie. It looked like a professional photo, but it didn't look like anything she'd ever choose to have taken. She wasn't naked, but she had a lot of skin showing, and her pose was definitely suggestive.

The group of "reporters" commented back and forth a few more times about it, but one sentence really caught my attention: "Apparently there are more like this." *Repelling* is the only way to describe the smile that slithered across the reporter's face before he and Harvey moved on to their next victim, brushing aside Annie and her reputation in less time than it took for them to ruin it.

"Oh, this is bad." I put my head between my knees. If this story was on TMZ, by tomorrow it would be everywhere. And there would be more pictures coming out. The press had ignored Annie for almost a year, but now that she'd messed up they'd be all over her.

"Did you know about these?" Joel asked. I still had my phone pressed to my ear, but I'd almost forgotten Joel was on the other end.

I shook my head even though Joel couldn't see me. "I had no idea."

"They're not that bad." Becca's voice came from the background, and a sick feeling washed over me again.

"I've seen worse, but what was she thinking?" Joel's gentle voice cushioned some of the blow from the pictures, but my head spun.

"I don't know . . . because she's eighteen. Because she lost her parents and her career in a matter of weeks. Because she feels as lost as the rest of us without Mom and Dad, but the stupid things she does don't get to stay private the way ours do. I don't know, Joel. There're a million reasons."

"Do you think her boyfriend had anything to do with these? The photographer guy?" he asked.

"I don't know who else she'd send pictures like that to. He's probably the one who took them in the first place." Bile rose in my throat, and I came close to gagging.

"What are you going to do?" Joel asked.

"I don't know." Panic rose in my chest. I had figured out how to handle my parents' deaths, how to open a business, how to mother a ten-year-old boy, but this? I had no idea.

"What can I—we—do to help?"

What I wanted was for him to hold me and tell me there wasn't a "we" that involved Becca, but that wasn't any more possible than the second thing I wanted to request—ring Harvey Levin's neck. "I really don't know, Joel. I don't even know what I should do." The only clear thought in my head was that I had left LaRell alone downstairs to take care of our guests, and I needed to get back there.

"My dad knows a lot of people in the industry. If Annie can prepare a statement, I can have him pull some strings to get it in print media right away. You know how to do the social media part. Get her message out fast so she can regain control over her image." As Joel ticked off his suggestions, I sat up and things became clearer.

"You're right. If we can get her words out and keep her out of the public for a few days, this will pass." I turned the TV off and tossed the remote to the side. It would be a while before I'd be able to turn it on again without picturing Harry Levin and his Voldemort face.

"I'll get a hold of my dad. You can fix this."

I didn't know if I could fix anything, but his encouragement at least made me feel like I had a chance. "Thanks, Joel."

I heard Becca's voice again. I couldn't tell what she was saying, but the confidence Joel's words had given me slipped away.

"Becca will update you after I've talked to my dad. She sends her love," Joel said in a more distant than consoling voice.

"Tell her thank you. And thank you for your help." I paused for half a second. "I miss you." I didn't care if Becca heard me or not, and I didn't care how desperate I sounded. He had to know how I felt. I didn't miss him as a friend. I missed him as the person I wanted to share everything with, especially the hard stuff.

I hung up before he could say anything then pressed my face into my hands. It didn't matter how much I wanted Joel right by my side, he couldn't be. But at least he was doing what he could. If that was all I could have from him, I'd take it.

Annie wouldn't be home for a few hours, and I wasn't going to tell her what happened over the phone. I hoped she wouldn't hear about it before then, but I seriously doubted that possibility. Not with the way she checked Twitter and Instagram. My only hope was that her shoot would keep her off social media until she got home. Then I could break the news to her.

I walked slowly downstairs, practicing the smile I'd have to keep plastered on my face as LaRell and I served the guests. My emotions bounced between anger and sympathy. I couldn't believe she had done something so stupid, but I also felt responsible. I was her only parent now, and what kind of job was I doing? I'd been so wrapped up in the ranch that I'd left her alone at her most vulnerable. I ignored my instincts about Drew because he kept her happy and out of the way. I couldn't help feeling how disappointed my parents would be in me.

I expected Annie home by the time LaRell and I finished serving and cleaning up dinner, but she didn't show up. I read to Bryce and tucked him in, and she still didn't show up. I gave myself another hour before I started to panic. I'd sent her a couple texts, to which she hadn't replied, so I picked up my phone to dial her number. The moment I hit Call, she walked in the door. Her tear-streaked face told me everything.

I jumped off the couch and ran to wrap her in my arms. Every bit of anger vanished when she buried her head in my shoulder and let out a jagged cry.

"Come on; I'm going to start you a bath." I led her up the stairs with my arm wrapped around her and her head leaning on my shoulder. I didn't say anything—I doubted Annie could answer my questions, and she definitely didn't need a lecture. I led her into her room and set her on her bed while I started the tub and poured in half a jar of lavender bath salts. The earthy smell rose with the steam from the hot water. I took a deep breath, closed my eyes, and hoped it would have the same soothing effect on Annie.

"I don't want to take my clothes off," Annie said from the other room.

"You can't stay in them forever, and it's easier to take them off *before* you get in a bath than after you get out." My attempt at a joke fell flat. I walked out of the bathroom to see her curled up on the bed with her hood pulled over her face.

She let out a sigh that sounded somewhere between a huff and a laugh. "I'll just stay right here like this. Then I never have to look anybody in the face again."

I took two steps to the bed and pulled her hood back. "You have to look me in the face, and you don't need to be embarrassed to do it. Go get in the tub, and we can talk after, if you want to. Or we can wait until tomorrow. Or you don't have to talk about it ever if that works for you, but I'm here for you no matter what."

She burst into tears again and pushed herself up. "Why would he do this to me?"

"Drew?"

She nodded. "He said he loved me."

"I'm sure he did." I helped her up and peeled her jacket off before leading her into the bathroom.

"Then why would he do this?"

I'd meant I was sure he *told* her he loved her. Whether he actually did love her, I doubted. But now wasn't the time to tell her that. "Desperate people do desperate things, even if it hurts the people they love," I said, as she sat down on the toilet and tugged on her boots until they came off. I stepped out of the bathroom and started to close the door.

"Don't leave me!" she protested.

"I'm just going to change into my pj's while you're in the tub. I'll be right out here when you're done."

She thought for a second and then nodded. I pulled the door closed then went to my room. I had no idea what I was going to say to her, but as I thought back over the past few months and some of her behaviors, it occurred to me that she had probably gone off her meds. She hadn't just been happy since she'd started dating Drew, she'd been manic. This photo thing could easily send her back into a hard-core depression.

I hurried to change so she wouldn't be alone too long. When I got back to her room, Annie was still in the tub, but I didn't hear any crying, which I took as a good sign. I sorted through her dresser drawers, looking for her favorite pajamas until I finally found them stuffed under jeans and tank tops. I forced myself to resist the urge to organize the clothes the way she kept them when she was in a better state of mind.

Instead I brushed some cracker crumbs off the rumpled sheets on her unmade bed and crawled in. I pulled the covers up to my chin. I'd poured so many bath salts into the tub that the lavender smell crept into the bedroom, tempting me to close my eyes.

"Are you okay in there?" I asked as my eyelids drooped.

"Yeah. This was a good idea. I may be in here for a while," she answered. "Like maybe forever."

"Okay, well, I'll be out here whenever you're done." Whether I'd still be awake or not was another question. Facing this beast in the morning was looking like a better plan the longer Annie stayed in the tub.

My eyes drifted closed, and the next thing I knew I was running through the dark, trying to find a whimpering animal. I knew opening my eyes would make it easier to find, but no matter how hard I tried, they wouldn't stay open. In my mind, saving the animal would somehow save my parents too. I groped my way through the dark, forcing my eyes open. Suddenly they were open. It wasn't as dark anymore, but I still didn't know where I was and the whimpering sound hadn't gone away. I blinked until I was fully awake and realized I was in Annie's bed. The crying in my dream was her.

I turned over to face her back and rubbed it, her shoulders trembling under my hands.

"I'm so stupid," she wept.

"Tell me what happened." I pulled her close and held her tight.

"Drew offered to take new headshots for me. He's been so encouraging, telling me I shouldn't give up on my Hollywood career. I mean, my experience here has been great, but I miss what I had before. And Drew's never stopped believing in me."

I took a deep breath, waiting for the moment I knew the story would turn from praising Drew to the truth about what he'd done to her.

"So he took me to his friend's studio in Salt Lake who's photographed a lot of models. We did the headshots, but then Drew suggested I should do something more artistic. His friend had all these props he's used for magazine shoots, and Drew had some great ideas. He thought we could get the shots in a magazine or something, and it would help us both with our careers. I'd be back in the public eye, and he'd get some recognition too." She hiccupped, and her shoulders began to shake.

"Why didn't you tell me about this sooner?" I could guess how that photo shoot turned out. I'd seen the evidence splattered all over the TV only a few hours before.

"I don't know. When we were doing the shoot, I didn't think it was that big of a deal. Drew kept saying I looked beautiful, and the pictures would show everyone I was legit—that they should take me seriously." She stopped and sniffed. I handed her a tissue from the box on the bedside table.

"As soon as I saw the pictures, I realized how suggestive they were. I told Drew I didn't want to use them, and he promised he'd get rid of them." She sniffed again, and I handed her the whole box of tissues.

"Did you tell him he could keep any for himself?"

She waited a long time before she answered. "Only a few he loved— he'd worked so hard."

"Annie . . ."

"You don't know what it's like to be an artist, Emily," she interrupted. The irritation in my voice must have clued her into the lecture on the tip of my tongue. "Asking him to destroy all those photos would be like asking me to erase all the film from my shoots."

"Is that what he told you?" I couldn't hide my anger anymore, but I was as angry with myself as I was with her. She wasn't stupid, but she had done something really stupid. And I'd been even stupider for not seeing through Drew from the beginning, for not trusting my instincts.

Annie sat up. I could feel her glaring at me in the dark. "Do you think I don't know how bad I've messed up? I don't need you getting all judgmental."

"I'm sorry. You're right." I sat up too, wrapped my arm around her, and squeezed until she dropped her head on my shoulder. I switched my anger at her to my parents. They were the ones who'd left me alone to deal with this. And I was angry with God. And with everyone on the planet.

But what I felt toward Drew went beyond anger. So far beyond anger that I didn't even know the word for it. He'd manipulated an eighteen-year-old girl grieving the death of her parents into doing something she knew was wrong and then humiliated her publicly for doing it.

"Lie back down, and let me tuck you in." I couldn't let Annie see what I was feeling. She needed comfort, not judgment. I let go of her and climbed out of bed to better help her lie down, then I tucked the blankets around her like Mom used to do to us when we were little.

"Will you stay here with me?" she asked as I was about to leave.

"Of course." I climbed under the covers and held her until she cried herself to sleep. Then I held her more because I couldn't sleep. I had to protect her.

Gray light peeked through Annie's blinds before I finally fell asleep, and my rest didn't last long. I awoke with a start before the sun topped the mountains.

"I've got to get downstairs," I said, then realized Annie was still asleep. I wanted to stay with her, but I had guests to feed and take care of. I slid quietly out of the bed and headed to my own room to get dressed.

As much as she needed me, Annie's crisis would have to wait until after breakfast. The only problem I could solve at the moment was that of hunger. But knowing I could solve *that* problem gave me some motivation to think about the bigger problem of Annie and her pictures. It may not be as easy to solve, but I could do it. And I would.

Right after breakfast.

Chapter 30

I KNEW LARELL HAD SEEN the pictures the minute I came downstairs and she wouldn't meet my eye. I doubted she and Walt watched TMZ, which also meant the news had spread. I waited to ask her until we had served everyone and had a few minutes alone in the kitchen.

"How did you find out?" I asked.

"Find out about what?" She still wouldn't look at me.

"The pictures. Of Annie."

She sighed. "My granddaughter asked me about them. She saw them on Instagram. Her Mia Maid teacher just used Annie as an example of standing up for what you believe, no matter what the cost. She's confused."

I groaned. How many other Young Women leaders had told the story of Annie choosing her standards over her job? Would they be using her as an example of hypocrisy now? Or as a warning? The ramifications of her indiscretion went way beyond our family. But she didn't deserve to lose all of her credibility over one bad choice. Especially when so many of those same girls who'd be judging her had cast her aside when they'd outgrown her Disney sitcoms and PG-rated movies.

"I'm sorry, LaRell. She made a stupid mistake—"

I was about to say, "But it wasn't her fault," but didn't have a chance. I heard a gasp behind me and turned around to see Annie frozen with her mouth hanging open and her eyes full of hurt. Before I could say anything, she about-faced and ran up the stairs. I looked back at LaRell, wondering if she'd seen Annie come in. She shook her head no.

"You don't need to apologize for her. She's a good girl who got caught in a bad situation. This will pass, but she's in for a rough ride. Walt's already chased off some paparazzi or whatever you call them." She wiped her hands on her apron and smiled sadly. "I'll take care of the guests. You'd better go check on her."

I nodded and slipped my apron off. "I'll be back soon."

I walked slowly upstairs, considering what to say to Annie but still not sure when I knocked on her door.

"Go away," she answered.

I tried the handle, but it was locked. "Come on. Let me in, Annie."

"No. I don't want to talk to you or anyone else," she yelled back with such force I let go of the handle and stepped back from the door.

I turned to leave but not before anger bubbled to the surface. She couldn't hide from the situation she'd created the moment she chose to keep dating Drew despite the fact he didn't live by the same standards she did. If Mom and Dad were still alive, they might let her hide from the consequences, but I couldn't. They'd parented her for seventeen years. I'd done it for sixteen months. I didn't have the parental chops or time to coddle her through this.

I turned back around and tried the handle again. Still locked. I pressed my forehead to the door, getting my mouth as close to it as possible so she wouldn't miss anything. "I love you, Annie, but you can't stay in there forever. I love you even though you did something stupid. I love you even though you're going to do more stupid things in your life because everyone does stupid things."

"You don't!" The door flew open, and I nearly toppled into her.

"Yes, I do. You think I don't wake up every morning wondering how stupid this idea was? Running a dude ranch in Utah? Something I know nothing about! But I pull myself out of bed and do it anyway because you can't hide from your messes." My heart beat faster than my words could come out.

Annie stared at me, her mouth twitching with indecision. "Yeah, well, good for you. You always handle things better than I can, and your 'mess' is nothing like mine." She slammed the door and locked it before I could stop her.

I leaned my head back against the door and searched for words. They came to me suddenly, but they weren't mine. "The trick is to keep your eye on the beauty and not what has to be cleaned up." I paused, hoping for a response. "Try to find the beauty, Annie. That's all I'm asking."

I didn't wait for an answer I already knew wasn't coming. I went back downstairs to the kitchen, where LaRell was washing the dishes.

Bryce was at the counter shoving pancakes in his mouth. "What are we doing today?" he asked with his mouth full.

His brown eyes—the same as Mom's—held so much hope and expectation. I didn't want to disappoint him, but I didn't know how not to. I had to deal with the Annie problem, even though I had no idea how to do that either, and I had to tell him something about what was going on. If media started calling or showing up, it would be impossible to keep Annie's pictures a secret. Even if the media stayed away, it would still be impossible to keep those photos a secret.

"I don't know, buddy. I think Annie needs some cheering up. Do you want to make that your project?"

"What's wrong with Annie?" His brow wrinkled.

LaRell slid the last of the pancakes onto his plate then glanced at me, almost as anxious about how to answer Bryce's question as I was.

"Drew did something kind of mean, and she's embarrassed about it."

"Why would she be embarrassed about something Drew did?" He sat up straighter, and the crease in his brow deepened, but with anger instead of concern.

I bit my lip, buying time while I figured out what to say. LaRell went back to washing dishes, leaving me to sort out my words by myself. "He had a picture of Annie that he shouldn't have had, and now it's in the news," I explained, watching his reaction carefully.

"Like a picture of her without makeup?"

I shook my head. "More embarrassing than that."

He blinked a few times while he considered what would embarrass a girl. I hoped we could leave it at that, but then his eyes widened. "Like a sexting picture?" he whispered.

"Do you know what that is?"

He nodded. "Mom and Dad told me about it when we talked about bad pictures and . . . other stuff." His ears went red, and his eyes darted to the floor. "Did she do pornography?"

"No." I shook my head hard. "Drew took some pictures of her that were inappropriate but not pornography. He told her he wouldn't show them to anybody, but he didn't keep his promise."

He breathed hard in and out and kept his eyes on the floor. Then his chin began to quiver, and he rubbed his eye with the palm of his hand. "Why would Drew do that? Joel wouldn't do something like that. Luke wouldn't either."

"I don't know. That makes this even harder, doesn't it?" I rubbed his back to console him, wishing again that Joel were here to help me.

He nodded and sniffed. I was about to hug him, but suddenly, he lifted his head with a jerk, and a smile spread across his face. "I know who can cheer her up!" He stuck his finger in the air in such a stereotypical I-have-an-idea pose that I couldn't help but smile.

"Who?"

"Luke!"

"I'm not sure," I said slowly, not wanting to burst his bubble. It wasn't a bad idea, but I doubted Annie would be very excited to see anyone.

"I'll call him. I know he likes hanging out with Annie, and he always knows fun stuff to do." He jumped off the barstool before I could stop him and rushed to the phone. The water shut off, and out of the corner of my eye I saw LaRell leave to go into the dining room. It would be time to start lunch prep soon.

"I don't think she really wants to see anybody." I walked over to take the phone from him. A knock at the back door stopped me. Without waiting to be let in, the very man we'd been talking about hurried through the door.

"Luke!" Bryce ran to him and held his hand up for a high five.

Luke returned it and forced a smile that couldn't hide his worry.

"We were about to call you," Bryce said excitedly then lowered his voice. "Did you hear about Annie?" The concern in his voice was genuine, even if his understanding was limited. A little boy trying to be the protector his sister needed.

Luke looked to me before answering Bryce, and I lifted my shoulder. I didn't know how to talk about this with Bryce any more than he did.

He turned back to Bryce and nodded. "I did. What should we do?"

"We need to cheer her up," Bryce answered.

"Where is she?" Luke asked.

"She's in her room. I don't think she'll see anyone though," I answered for Bryce.

"Maybe we could take her to a movie or something," Bryce suggested hopefully.

"I don't think that's going to do it, buddy. Why don't you get dressed and brainstorm some more ideas for us while Luke and I talk," I said.

Bryce answered with a scowl made better by Luke ruffling his hair.

"I promise I'll stick around until we get something figured out."

Bryce nodded and dragged his feet to the stairs.

"You might try praying," I said.

"Fine," he mumbled and walked upstairs.

"How did you find out?" I asked once Bryce was out of earshot.

"It's everywhere. There are news vans at the end of the drive. Walt's locked the gate and threatened to hog-tie anyone who steps one toe across your property line. His words, not mine."

I walked to the kitchen table and sat down. Luke followed.

"Do you think she'd talk to me?" He took his hat off and ran his hands through his hair.

I considered his question before shaking my head. "I wish she would."

"Did Drew have something to do with this?"

"He took the pictures, so probably." I recounted the story Annie told me. "There's no other way the media could have gotten them. We don't know if he sold them or what happened."

"I'd really like to teach him a lesson or two about respecting women." Luke curled his hand into a fist and pounded it a couple times on the table. The muscles in his clenched jaw bulged.

"I think Annie could use a lesson or two in respecting herself. She's forgotten what she's worth." I picked at something sticky on the table and kept my eyes down. I'd had hours to think, and while my heart still broke for Annie, she'd have to take responsibility for what she'd done. She had to apologize to fans, like LaRell's granddaughter, who looked to her as an example.

"It's easy to forget who you are when you lose the people meant to remind you of it," he said, and I knew he spoke from experience. "Don't be too hard on her."

At that moment Bryce came bounding back into the room. Luke wiped the worry off his face and turned his attention to my brother. "Are you ready to make a plan?" he asked.

"Yeah. I went in her room to give her a hug and tell her you're here, but she just cried more."

"That was nice," I said and attempted a smile to comfort him.

"How about we take a walk out to the horses and talk things over?" Luke patted Bryce on the back and ushered him toward the door.

"Okay, lemme put my boots on." Bryce's spirits were on the way up with just a little encouragement from Luke, and I was grateful. With Bryce occupied and my guests taken care of until lunch, I could focus on Annie.

I started by making her a hot bowl of oatmeal topped with brown sugar, raisins, bananas, and a touch of honey. I took it upstairs on a tray and went into her room without knocking. I flipped on the lights, set the tray on a table, and opened the blinds to let in some natural light. Fortunately, it was a sunny day, and the smattering of snow we'd had the day before would soon be melted. Annie needed some sun.

"Time for breakfast!" I said and pulled back the covers she'd buried herself under.

"I don't want to eat." She tried to pull the covers back over her head, but I yanked them to the bottom of the bed. This had the added bonus of forcing her to sit up to reach for them. I sat down on top of them before she had a chance to hide again.

"What are you doing? It's freezing!" She wrapped her arms around her legs and shivered.

"I let you have time to cry, but now it's time to face the beast."

"That's easy for you to say. The whole world isn't looking at you naked this morning."

"No, but you know what? The whole world isn't interested in me. And the whole world won't be interested in you either by next week. Ninety-nine point nine percent of the people who've seen those pictures will have forgotten about them. It's that point one percent you've got to worry about." My words were harsher than I intended, but I had to get her out of bed before she slipped down a dark hole of depression. She needed some tough love.

"Is that supposed to make me feel better?" She glared at me, but anger was good. Anger was another emotion besides sad.

"No. The only thing that will help that is to own your mistake and move on."

"Are you telling me to repent?"

"If you need to, then yes." Her question had surprised me, but my answer didn't.

"My life is over, and you came to tell me to repent? That's very helpful." She glared at me before dropping her head onto her knees.

I wasn't sure that sarcasm really counted as an emotion, but I was happy to call it one if it meant we were up to two other feelings besides sad.

"I wish I could let you stay in bed and be sad until you weren't anymore or until this all disappeared, but I can't. Neither one of us has that luxury with Bryce and this ranch to take care of." I scooted closer to her. "The other thing is, we have to do damage control, fast."

"That's what my agent is for—if I even still have one. Remember the 'high moral standards' part of my contract?" She tightened her grip around her legs. "I'm probably fired."

"Then you have to handle it yourself. You've got to explain what happened to all the little Mormon girls who look up to you."

At this, her lip quivered. I scooted all the way to her and wrapped her in my arms.

"I messed up so bad. I don't know how I can ever face anyone again. Especially them. I look like the biggest hypocrite ever," she said, moving her head to my shoulder.

"You won't. This is fixable. You can choose to apologize and be an example of overcoming mistakes. You can be an example of being careful where we go and who we trust. There are so many girls who may feel like they've made mistakes too huge to ever overcome. You can prove them wrong."

"Yeah, they can always look to me and say, 'At least I didn't do anything as stupid as that.'" She raised her head, a sad smile tugging at her lips.

"Exactly." I smiled back.

She replied with a hiccup laugh. "What am I supposed to do?"

"You've got to release a statement. We can start with Facebook and Instagram, even Twitter. Explain the situation and apologize specifically to all those girls who have looked up to you as an example. Tell them you want to earn their trust again." I'd thought through the situation enough over the past twelve hours, and I had a lot of ideas about what she should say. "And Joel said his dad could help us get it in some big publications."

"I should tell them not to follow my example, right?" Her voice was still sad, but there was an undercurrent of hope in it.

"Tell them to learn from your mistake."

She nodded and wiped her eyes. "I'm sorry, Em."

"I know you are. That's why this is going to be okay." I rubbed her back then stood up to leave.

"Will you look at it after I write it? Before I release it?" She let go of her legs and crossed them.

"Of course."

"Thanks." She held out her arms, and I bent down to let her hug me. She held me tight and with all the strength I knew she'd need to get through the next few weeks.

Chapter 31

I LEFT ANNIE'S ROOM LIGHTER. She had a hard road ahead, but we could handle it together. We'd already faced harder. But the first thing I had to face was my guests. No doubt they'd heard or seen the news, so I'd have to do damage control there. Plus, I needed to figure out a way to keep the press away from them. Most of them were headed to the mountain for the day, and Walt was already working on getting them there without being followed. We didn't want them being hounded for information about Annie.

Once I'd talked to the guests, promising them a free night's stay plus dinner at Park City's nicest restaurant for respecting Annie's privacy, and Walt had spirited them away, I coaxed Annie out of her room. She even got dressed.

Good thing too. We hadn't been in the kitchen more than five minutes when Luke and Bryce walked in. Luke's eyes popped with surprise—the good kind—when he saw her.

"We were just coming to get you!" Bryce exclaimed. "We have a surprise."

"I don't think I'm up for any surprises." Annie shrank from Luke's gaze. She tried to step away from Bryce, but he grabbed her hand and had her halfway to the door before she knew what was happening.

"You've gotta see this. You're gonna love it," he said. She hazarded a glance at Luke, who gave her a slight nod and an even slighter smile. He seemed less sure of success than Bryce did, but he followed behind anyway.

Bryce flung open the door, letting in a burst of cold air but also the view of what he wanted Annie to see. She gasped with surprise and stepped outside. I ran to see what it was, grabbing her Wellies next to the door as I did. We almost collided when I stepped out the door at the same time she was hopping from one already frozen foot to the other. I handed her the boots and looked past her smiling face to see the source of her happiness.

Two horses stood saddled and bridled, tied to the fence at the edge of the lawn. One was Pepper, Annie's favorite. She'd cut her leg pretty badly in November, and then it had become infected. The vet had told Walt that, due to her age, Pepper might have to be put down, and she probably wouldn't ever be able to be ridden again.

"She's got a saddle on," Annie said to Luke, who still stood in the kitchen leaning against the counter. His face broke into a smile wider than the Grand Canyon.

"Luke has been taking care of her for you." Bryce bounced around Annie, unable to contain himself. Annie shivered, I couldn't tell whether from cold or excitement.

"You have?" she said to Luke over her shoulder.

"Yeah, Walt and I did." He nodded, then shrugged.

"Why?"

"I knew you loved her." He almost dismissed his gift with another shrug but then stopped himself.

"You did that for me?" Annie asked with surprise, like it had finally dawned on her how much Luke cared about her.

Bryce grabbed her hand again and pulled her out the door toward Pepper. "They didn't even tell me. I was so surprised when Luke showed me her leg was better and said we could saddle her. He says you get to ride first." I grabbed coats off the hooks next to the door and jogged to catch up with Bryce and Annie with Luke following behind.

"Can I really ride her?" Annie asked Luke when he caught up.

"That's what she's here for." He brushed past me to hold the stirrup for Annie. She stuck her foot in, and he helped boost her onto Pepper. Once Annie had settled into the saddle, I handed her the coat I'd grabbed and put the other one on myself. Annie slipped it on then leaned down to pat Pepper, wrapping her arms around the horse's neck and nuzzling her.

"How does she feel? Are the stirrups okay?" Luke circled Pepper, checking and rechecking every strap and buckle, anything to avoid looking directly at Annie.

Annie sat back up, stood in the stirrups, sat back down, and wriggled back and forth. "Everything is perfect." She took a deep breath and scanned the horizon like she was seeing it for the first time. "Thank you. This is exactly what I needed," she said to Luke as he handed her the reins.

He nodded and patted Pepper's neck, then zipped his jacket and tucked his chin inside it—but not before I saw his smile.

"Are you going to be warm enough?" he asked Annie as he stepped into a stirrup and swung his leg over the back of the other horse, aptly named Salt.

"Let me grab a hat and scarf for you," I said, but Annie had Pepper turned and ready to go before I even finished the sentence. She edged the horse around the fence then kicked her into a trot toward the trail.

Salt lifted his legs and swung his head, anxious to follow. Luke reined him in long enough to say, "I won't keep her out long," then kicked once and galloped to catch Annie. Bryce and I watched them ride side by side up the trail and around a bend until we couldn't see them anymore.

"I hope he takes me next," Bryce said as I laid a hand on his neck and turned him toward the house. The cold drove us to walk quickly.

Bryce talked nonstop. I nodded and pretended to listen as he told me all about Pepper and everything Luke had told him about nursing her back to health and getting her ready to ride again.

"I think he likes Annie."

Bryce's announcement got my attention. "Who?"

"Luke, duh."

I stopped with my hand on the doorknob and looked at him, trying not to laugh. "You see a lot more than you let on, don't you?"

"I'm not dumb." He pushed past me and went inside.

"Good because now that Annie's gone, I'm going to need your help."

He groaned and went limp but didn't protest when I pointed him to the fridge and started listing the ingredients I needed him to get. He may have even let a smile slip.

Chapter 32

ANNIE CAME INSIDE AN HOUR later, her cheeks bright from the cold and her mouth set in a determined line.

"I know what to say. Luke helped me sort it out." Annie slipped off her boots and hung her coat on the hook, barely noticing when it slipped to the ground. Without picking it up, she walked past me and up the stairs.

"Can I go for a ride now?" Bryce asked before Luke even made it through the door.

"What did you say to her?" I pulled Bryce toward me before he dragged Luke back outside.

"Nothing much. I just gave her some ideas for her statement." He kept his coat buttoned up and his chin tucked into it so only his bright red nose and blue eyes showed. "She'll show it to you when she's done."

"Can I ride Pepper now, *please*?" Bryce begged.

"Well, whatever you did, thank you. I wasn't sure I'd ever get her out of her room," I said as Bryce wriggled out of my grasp and sat down on the bench to pull on his boots.

"I didn't do much besides listen. She figured it out herself by talking through it." He tried to play down his help, but a pleased smile kept tugging at his lips. He looked around, unsure of what else to say until his eyes landed on the door. Moving quickly to it, he waved Bryce over.

"Let's go before those horses think they're done for the day."

Before I could help Bryce zip his coat, they were gone. I shut the door behind them and sat down at the kitchen table. The lack of sleep had caught up with me, so I rested my arms on the table and laid my head on them. It had been a rough day, and I'd done a decent job of keeping things together. I wanted to call Joel and tell him, but he'd made it clear Becca would call me. He may have been willing to help me, but he obviously wanted to keep his distance.

I'd cleared a lot of obstacles over the past year, but the one thing I hadn't conquered was my feelings for Joel. For the next hour, I let myself get swallowed up in thoughts of him and hopes that he'd be the one to call.

Finally I pushed my feelings aside and sat up straight when I heard Annie's footsteps on the stairs.

"It's ready," she announced when she came in.

"That was fast."

"Luke and I had it all worked out. I just had to type it up." She held up a piece of paper fresh from the printer.

"Can I read it?"

She shook her head. "I want to practice saying it before I put it on YouTube." She lowered the paper and her eyes to it, then threw her shoulders back and read.

"A few months ago I allowed someone to take pictures of me that I shouldn't have. What were supposed to be artistic photographs turned out to be much more provocative than I'd intended. I asked him not to make the pictures public but allowed him to keep the originals. I showed a lack of judgment in trusting anybody with them and a lack of respect for myself and my fans by taking them at all. I want to apologize to all those who have supported me in my career and looked to me as a role model. In a moment of weakness, I lowered my standards. I will carry regret and bear the consequences of that decision for the rest of my life. If you can no longer trust me as a role model, I hope you will learn from my example and not repeat my mistake."

I thought she was done, but she took a deep breath and continued in a voice that was no longer apologetic but conveyed all the hurt and anger she'd been feeling since the night before.

"However, the people who published these photos have violated my privacy, and they have violated me personally. Whatever anyone's thoughts on my behavior not being in line with my personal beliefs, no one has a right to look at my body without my permission. People may call me a hypocrite, but to look at or share these photos is to commit a sex crime. If any finger-pointing needs to be done, why don't we start with the criminals who treat privacy as a privilege public figures don't deserve, rather than a right everyone is entitled to? When we stop believing everyone has this right, we lose our own claims to it. And do we really want privacy to be as fleeting as fame?"

Annie lowered the paper and met my eyes, looking for approval.

"Whoa. You went all J. Law on them." I grinned. "It was awesome, but you know there's going to be backlash, right? It's going to drive some people to look who may not have known about them."

"I know." She nodded. "But I think I still need to do it, don't you?"

I thought about it for a minute before I nodded back. I didn't want anyone else looking at her, but I also didn't want her to be a victim. She had to stand up for herself.

"Thanks." She breathed a sigh of relief. "I took responsibility, right? It doesn't sound like I think what I did was okay? I want that message to get across too, but I'm not the only guilty party here. I'd say what people did to me is a lot worse. It's not okay."

"You're right, it's not." I pushed a chair out for her to sit down, and she did. Then I chose my next words carefully. "You say 'people' like you don't know who did it. It's obviously Drew."

She blinked a few times before she took her phone out of her back pocket and handed it to me. I read the message on the screen in front of me. Drew's name was at the top.

I didn't do this to you. I promise.

"When did you get this?" I handed the phone back to her. Even seeing Drew's name made me want to punch something.

"This morning."

"And you believe him?" I didn't.

"I called him after I got it. He answered this time." She set the phone on the table and sat down next to me.

"What did he say?"

"He thinks his roommate did it. Drew showed him his portfolio. He forgot he'd put the pictures of me in it. He thinks his roommate Snapchatted them to someone else who leaked them to TMZ." She spun her phone in a slow circle, not looking at me.

"That's his excuse? You're not really going to let him off that easy, are you?" I reached across the table and put my hand on top of her phone.

"I'm not letting him off. I'm just saying he's not the one who put the photos out there."

"But it's his fault they got out!"

"No, it's my fault for letting him take them in the first place." She pulled her phone from underneath my hand and put it in her lap.

"So where is he? Did he mention that? Or why he's ignored you for months? I hope you're not going to let all that go too." I thought the one benefit of this fiasco would be that she'd never want to see Drew again.

"I'm not letting anything go. Give me a little credit. He ran up a lot of debt on the credit card his aunt gave him for the business. She found out and blew up. She cut him off until he could pay her back, and he was too embarrassed to tell me." She crossed her arms and glued her eyes to mine.

"But he wasn't the one who sold the pictures?" I stared at her in disbelief.

"He's done a lot of stupid things, but I don't think he did that. Why would he text me to tell me he hadn't?"

"So we wouldn't sue him." That seemed pretty obvious to me.

"Don't be condescending. You don't know him like I do." She glared at me, but there was uncertainty in it.

I pursed my lips to keep from blurting anything else out. It wouldn't do any good to make her mad. She'd run to him if I pushed too hard.

"I'm sorry. I just don't want to see you any more hurt." I reached my hand across the table toward her.

She hesitated but then took it. "I know," she said; then we sat in silence for a few minutes. "I don't want to get back together with him, but it was nice to hear his voice again."

I nodded, not wanting to talk about Drew anymore. "Let's get this statement out." I let go of her and stood up. "The sooner we do it, the better."

"You're right." She pushed herself up. "My agent has called about a thousand times—I'm pretty sure to fire me—but I'll see what she can do. If not, it's up to us."

"Luckily you have a sister who knows a little bit about media." That got a smile out of her, and I touched her arm to keep her from leaving. "If you get any more calls from Drew, will you think twice before taking them?"

She looked at my hand then at me and nodded. "I can't promise I won't talk to him at all."

"Okay." I dropped my hand and walked out of the room. My emotions were so conflicted I couldn't think any straighter than she was. How could she write a statement that was not only clearheaded about her mistake but also about how she'd been victimized and then turn around and run right back to the guy who'd caused it all? I could deal with whatever backlash came from her statement. I had no idea how to deal with her inability to use logic when it came to love.

Chapter 33

BECCA CALLED THE NEXT DAY to tell me that not only were some of the Hollywood trade magazines going to print Annie's statement, but it would be read on *Entertainment Tonight*. I thanked her and swallowed my disappointment that she'd been the one to call instead of Joel.

Annie's agent released her statement on every social and digital media outlet possible. Then she fired her. She hated to do it, but a contract's a contract, and Annie had broken hers. The status of her show was also up in the air as the producers tried to figure out if they could push back the release date or if they'd have to cancel it all together since it was being broadcast by BYUtv. She seemed to take it pretty well, but the day after, when noon came and went and she hadn't come out of her room, I got worried.

I went upstairs and knocked on her door. She didn't answer, but it wasn't locked, so I went in. Annie was sitting cross-legged on her bed, still in her ratty flannel bottoms and T-shirt with a blanket wrapped around her shoulders. Her laptop was propped open on the bed, and her phone was next to it. The glow from both screens was the only light in the room. It reflected off her face, and even from across the room, I could see her mouth turned down in defeat.

"What are you doing?" I asked, walking toward the bed. As I got closer, I could see she'd been crying.

"Just a little light reading." She palmed tears out of her eyes and turned the laptop to me. I sat down next to her and looked at the multiple windows she had open with a different news source in each one. "Sorry, Not Sorry," read one, and "Annie Carter Wants Hackers Uncovered!" read another.

"What is this?" I asked and scrolled through the article with the least offensive title, "Annie Carter Not Proud." It was on the *LDS Life* site, which had basically reprinted Annie's statement.

"This isn't bad." I didn't understand why she looked so upset. Then she scrolled past the article and got to the comments section. I read the first one.

I used to look up to Annie Carter, but she's totally let me down. She shouldn't blame anyone else for those pictures getting out because it's her fault for taking them in the first place. She's embarrassed the whole Mormon Church, and she deserves to be embarrassed herself.

Irritating? Yes. But not bad enough for tears. I went to the next one.

Annie Carter should take responsibility for herself. If she's okay with one guy seeing her nude pics, what's the big deal about other guys seeing them?

"They weren't nude pictures," I said to the screen. Like a rubbernecker driving past a car wreck, I couldn't look away.

Annie Carter may be more modest compared to 99% of Hollywood, but that doesn't make her modest by Church standards. Her clothes have always been too revealing, and it was only a matter of time before she went from being "walking porn" to actual porn.

That one was a hard punch to the gut, and I had to catch my breath. I read it over again, not willing to believe anyone could be that judgmental. The words and their effect didn't change. I went to the next comment hoping to find something positive to rinse out the bitterness in my mouth.

Thank you, Annie, for admitting your mistake and for sticking up for yourself. I'm still a huge fan of yours and admire you even more now. Everyone messes up. It's nice to know you're human too!

"This one is nice," I said, reading it to her. "Did you see it?"

She nodded. "It's the only one like that. The rest are as bad as the 'nude pics' one. Or worse."

I looked at the comment count. Fifty-six. Not a crazy amount, but it hadn't even been twenty-four hours since she released her statement.

"They're trolls. Why are you even reading these?" I closed the site.

"I thought I could at least count on Mormons to be nice to me. We're all in this together, right? Why do they have to tear me down when I've already got the rest of the world doing that?" She held her hands out for her laptop, but I wouldn't give it to her.

"Just because they're commenting on *LDS Life* doesn't mean they're Mormon. Even if they are, they're still trolls who have nothing better to do with their lives than make other people feel as worthless as they do." I clicked on People.com to see the article and comments there. I didn't want to read anymore, but I had to in order to understand what Annie was facing.

The article quoted her statement along with giving some background on the Church's stance on modesty. *In light of the Mormon Church's belief that women should wear shorts to the knees and keep their shoulders covered, Annie Carter is in a position where she must defend her right to take inappropriate pictures and not have them publicized, but also apologize for doing so. . . .*

"I guess they sort of got that right." I mumbled and scrolled down to the comments. I could feel her eyes on me, waiting for my reaction as I read.

So after all her grandstanding about her high morals and how she won't do anything to compromise them, Miss Goody-Two Shoes turns out to be as "evil" as the rest of us? Doesn't surprise me. Any time someone climbs onto a high horse, they'll eventually get thrown off. Now maybe she can earn some legitimate fame by proving what she can do instead of harping about what she won't do.

I raised my eyebrows and glanced through the next ten comments. They weren't much different from the first; they just varied in degrees of nastiness. The more I read, the more my whole body burned until I was sweating with anger.

The last window she had open was TMZ. I wanted to look at that site like I wanted to climb into a tub full of rattlesnakes, but I had to. I didn't bother reading the story and went straight to the comments. The first one simply said, *invite friends next time morman gurlz gone wild!* Most of the other comments weren't any better. Some were so crude they made me sicker than I already was. Most had so many spelling mistakes I could barely read them.

"Why are doing this to yourself?" I slammed the laptop shut and pushed it aside. "You said what you had to, now walk away. Let it go. If people don't want to forgive, that's their problem, not yours. The only one who needs to forgive you now is you. And God, but that's between you and Him."

She closed her eyes and nodded but then opened them again and spoke slowly. "I get what you're saying, but your career isn't based on whether or not people like you. If you do something stupid, it's not going to destroy everything you've worked for your whole life. My life is pretty much over because of one dumb decision."

"Your life isn't over," I shot back. Fear seized me as I thought about how close she'd been to suicide not too many months before. I couldn't write off her words as being overdramatic anymore.

"It feels like it. All I've ever wanted to do is act, and now I never want to show my face in public again."

"Give it time. This will pass, and you have to remember what kind of people comment on these sites. It's not the people who support and love you. You've got to leave your room to find them—you've got to go back out in public. That's where your fans are, not on these stupid gossip sites." I reached out to touch her, but when she moved just out of my reach I dropped my hand back into my lap.

"I wouldn't call *LDS Life* a gossip site." She climbed back under the covers and pulled them up to her chin.

"No, but I wouldn't call people who say mean things online very Christlike either. You have to be willing to forgive them, even if they aren't willing to do the same for you. At least you have the ability to recognize and own up to your mistakes. They don't even see that they're casting stones. Like the Pharisees in that story." I rubbed her back through her bedspread.

"Isn't that the one about the woman taken in adultery? Is that who you're comparing me to?" The tremor in her voice was a cross between a cry and a laugh, and I couldn't tell which she was holding back. Either way, I'd made a huge blunder.

"No! That's not what I meant at all!" My foot was lodged too far in my mouth to make any sense.

"I know." She exhaled, and so did I. "I'm teasing you. It is a pretty good comparison though. . . ."

"Only between the Internet trolls and Pharisees. I wasn't calling you an adulteress."

A sharp *ha* escaped. The corner of her mouth twitched into an almost smile that was gone in an instant.

"Come on, come out." I pulled gently on the covers, but she caught them before I got past her shoulder.

"I need a day. I'll be okay, but I need a day." She drew the covers up to her nose. "I love you for trying, Emily," she mumbled and closed her eyes.

I hesitated before deciding I'd done all I could for the time being. I had to trust she really was okay and let her handle her grief in the only way she knew how, no matter how terrified I was that she wouldn't come out of it.

But as soon as I stood up, she pulled the covers all the way over her head.

* * *

Days passed and Annie stayed put. When I couldn't coax her out to eat, I caved and took food to her. If I'd been sure depression was the only demon she was fighting, I would have let her get hungry enough to come out. But there was an anxiety component to this episode that I'd never seen before. I worried she would starve before she'd get over the fear she had of leaving the house and facing anybody other than Bryce and me.

Luke came by every day, but she wouldn't see or talk to him. One day after she refused to see him again, he dawdled in the kitchen, offering to help pack Bryce's lunch even though I'd already zipped the lunch pack closed.

"Do you know if she's getting the cheer-me-up things I've been texting her?" he asked me when Bryce ran upstairs to put the deodorant on I'd reminded him about at least ten times.

"The what?"

"These quote things I find to . . . encourage her, I guess." His face colored.

"Do you mean memes? You find memes for her? Where?"

"Pinterest," he said at the same time Bryce barged back through the door.

I leaned closer to him to make sure I'd heard right. "Pinterest? Like, you pin things?"

"Isn't that for girls?" Bryce asked and wrinkled his nose.

"No." Luke shook his head then recoiled as Bryce stepped closer. "Dude, what is that smell?" He craned his neck as far from my brother as he could. I tucked my nose into my shirt as a cloud of stink accosted me.

"Axe body spray. The ladies like it." Bryce's face broke into the proud grin of a man who'd spent a thousand dollars to win a five-hundred-dollar lottery.

"Ugh. This one doesn't. Go outside and air yourself out." I took both his shoulders and marched him toward the door, pushing him as far outside as I could.

"It's not even time for school yet!" he protested.

"I don't care. Run to the bus stop and back again if you need something to do." I tossed his coat and gloves out to him. "Hopefully you'll work up enough of a sweat to cover the stench of that body spray."

He scowled at me then took slow, grudging steps down the road. I went back inside but left the door open to air out the room.

"That's some powerful stuff," Luke said.

"No kidding. Good thing I'm making garlic bread for dinner. Hopefully that will cover up the smell." I expected him to laugh, but instead he nodded gravely and stuck his hands in his pockets.

"So I guess she hasn't told you if she's getting them?" he asked, and I remembered what we'd been talking about.

"She hasn't told me much of anything for the past week," I said, sorry that I couldn't give him a better answer. "That doesn't mean she's not getting them. She may not be responding, but I'm sure they're helping."

"I hope so. Will you tell me what else I can do? She doesn't deserve to be treated like this. Nobody does, but especially someone as sensitive as Annie. Someone like her who's willing to share everything . . ." He pressed his lips tight together and shook his head. "There aren't many people like that, and this kind of hurt is soul crushing."

I was taken aback by Luke's words. I'd always thought of Annie as emotional and overdramatic. I'd never thought of her sensitivity as a good thing. But, of course, that's what made her who she was. That's what made her special. It let her stand in front of a camera and become whatever part she was playing. She could feel what that character felt because she let herself feel everything.

"I wish I'd never recommended Drew to you. None of this would have happened." His jaw twitched with anger, but his eyes looked close to tears.

"It's not your fault, Luke. You didn't know what he was like. None of us did. And there's no guarantee Annie wouldn't have done the same kind of thing for someone else." For the first time, all the things she'd been going through became clear to me, and I knew why she'd done what she had.

"She has been lost since our parents died, and I've been more worried about supporting her financially than emotionally." I shook my head, angry at myself all over again. "I ignored every instinct I had telling me Drew was trouble because he kept her busy and made her happy. I didn't have to worry about filling that need for her as long as he was around. If anyone is to blame here, it's me."

"We're quite a pair, aren't we?" Luke said after a long pause. "Fighting over who's to blame instead of figuring out what to do next." He snorted then smiled.

"You're right. I just don't know what else to do."

"You'll figure it out. I've got something I'm working on too." He pulled his keys out of his pocket and tugged the brim of his hat down.

"Thanks, Luke. I really appreciate the friend you've been to her. To all of us." I gave him a hug that surprised me as much as him, and he returned it with a pat on my back.

Chapter 34

AFTER A WEEK, ANNIE STARTED emerging from her room for more than fifteen minutes at a time. Each day her hair looked a little less disheveled, her clothes a little less ratty, and her face a little less slept on. I took that as a good sign that she had stopped reading what people were saying about her and she was taking her meds again. I had finally asked her whether she was after I thought about her erratic behavior over the past few months. No surprise she said she hadn't been taking them.

On the morning she came down for early breakfast and actually helped prepare and serve it, I knew things would be okay. Not perfect, but we were on our way to all right.

"Welcome back to the land of the living," I said, giving her a one-armed squeeze while balancing plates on my other arm.

"Thanks. It's the only way I could get Luke to stop sending me his daily affirmations. I couldn't look at one more cat 'hanging in there' or read any more 'you are amazing' memes." She stuck the last dish in the dishwasher and pushed the door shut before collapsing onto a barstool.

"Whatever works," I said, laughing.

"Yeah, they did kind of help. I mean, he sent *a lot* of them, but it gave me something to read besides the negative stuff." She stretched her arm out and rested her head on it. Her hair spilled over the countertop, and I tried not to imagine the health department walking into my kitchen at that moment.

"How many did he send?"

"Like, one an hour or more. I think he probably sent me every feel-good meme he found on Pinterest. He's either secretly a fourteen-year-old girl or he hired one to do it for him."

I laughed again. "Or he really cares about you."

She nodded her head without lifting it, and I left it at that. I wiped down the counter around her, and she sat up so I could get the spot under her.

"He's just so much older than me," she said.

"There were thirteen years between Mom and Dad. That's more than between you and Luke. They did all right."

"Yeah . . ."

My phone rang, and I pulled it from my back pocket to check the screen. "It's Jason," I said.

The corner of her lip lifted in a snarl, and she stuck her tongue out. "He keeps trying to call me. Tell him I'm not here," she whispered as I picked up the phone.

"Where is Annie?" were the first words out of his mouth after I said hello.

"I'm fine, thanks for asking. How are you?" I answered.

"Hi, Emily. I'm fine." His irritation came through loud and clear even though his voice sounded muffled on speakerphone. "Can we talk about Annie now? She won't answer my calls and *People* is trying to get a hold of her."

"What people?"

"The magazine." His irritation flipped to exasperation. "They want to do an interview, but apparently she's not taking their calls either. They finally called the home phone, but I don't know how long ago. I never check the voice mail. It's always calls for you guys."

"I told you to change the number."

"That's not the point," he huffed. "Rachel happened to listen to the messages, and she heard the one from someone named Susan Sheldon."

"Susan Sheldon?" I echoed.

"From *People*?" Annie had laid her head back on the counter, but she perked back up when she heard the name.

I nodded, and she hopped off the barstool and grabbed my phone.

"Jason? What's going on?" she asked.

I could hear Jason but only his baritone, not the actual words he was saying.

"What did the message say?" Annie asked and nodded as he answered.

"An interview? The *cover*? I don't know." She glanced at me like an animal not sure if it was being cornered or rescued.

"What?" I asked.

"They want to do a full interview with me, Jason says. He's already talked to them." She turned her attention back to the phone as Jason's rumbly voice came through again.

"You did?" Pause. "You're sure?" Longer pause. She looked at me again, not quite as frightened but still unsure. I opened my arms and raised my palms, begging for her to tell me what was happening. "Thanks for looking out for me."

"WILL YOU PUT IT ON SPEAKER PLEASE SO I KNOW WHAT'S GOING ON?" I shouted. I hated being left in the dark.

"O-*kay*. Don't freak out." Annie set the phone down and pressed the speaker button.

"What's all this about, Jas?" I asked, leaning on my elbows over the phone.

"They want to hear her side of the story. Joel got Abe to pull some strings with people he knows to make it the cover. I called this Susan person before I called Annie. I wanted to make sure it wasn't going to be negative or expose her to any more criticism."

"Oh . . . Thanks." I had a hard time hiding my surprise. Jason had never fit the protective older brother stereotype. I didn't know if this sudden protectiveness was out of actual concern or guilt over tossing us out of our house. Either way, I'd take it.

"They've followed all the criticism she's gotten from people in the industry but also from other Mormons. They know Annie's agent fired her because of the pictures and her show's on hiatus. Susan said they're interested in the 'rock and a hard place' angle."

"Really? Or are they just saying that?" Annie asked Jason, but the question in her eyes was for me.

"They promised we could check it for accuracy before it's published, and they'd make the changes Annie wants, if there are any."

Annie's eyes widened to Japanese anime proportions. "Seriously? They never do that."

"When do they want the interview?" I asked.

"As soon as possible. You can do it while you're here for the wedding."

"That's a month away. Everyone will have moved on to some other story. Why can't we do it sooner? In a month we'll be dredging up this whole thing again when it's headed for the grave." I looked at Annie, who nodded. Photographers and news vans had slowly stopped showing up, which meant the story was dying.

"I thought that too," Jason said, surprising me again. "But Susan says they'll make it a 'Annie speaks out for the first time' thing. She said it worked for Jennifer Lawrence when she waited a month or so to talk about her nude pictures."

"I wasn't naked," Annie interrupted.

"I know, but that's not the point. Do you want to do it or not? I need to let her know."

Annie drummed her fingers on the countertop and stared at the ceiling. I stared at her, waiting for an answer, but not wanting to push.

"Okay," she finally said then turned to me. "You'll come with me to the interview, right?"

"Do you want me to make the arrangements?" Jason asked.

"No, I'll do it," Annie answered and paused. "Thanks for helping, Jason."

"Don't worry about it." He gave her the name and number of the woman from *People* and then hung up.

Annie stared at the phone, picked it up, dialed, then set it back down without pushing Call. Then she paced.

"Do you want me to do it?" I asked.

She shook her head and dialed again. This time she didn't hang up, and while she talked, I texted the other person we needed to thank. I wanted to call, but Joel's silence since the last time we talked kept me from dialing.

Instead I typed, *Is there anything you can't fix? Thanks for helping Annie. You're my hero.*

I checked my phone about a million times that night, waiting for a reply from Joel. When I finally got it, it was a simple *You're welcome.* Not getting a text at all would have been better than that. At least then I could have told myself he hadn't seen it instead of knowing he had and that he didn't have anything else to say.

Chapter 35

A MONTH LATER, BRYCE, ANNIE, and I were on our way to Los Angeles. My chest tightened as we pulled away from the ranch. I hadn't left the ranch for more than a few hours for at least six months. I'd seen new mothers freak out over leaving their babies for the first time, and I finally got why. I knew Walt and LaRell, with some help from Luke, would take good care of it, but still I hated to leave. It was home now.

And yet, as we circled above LA, my heart expanded. Even with its blanket of smog and the unending sprawl of houses and buildings, my city welcomed me back. It wasn't home anymore, but it still held my heart—it always would. Especially as long as Joel was a part of it.

"I miss the ocean," Annie said leaning over me to see out the window.

"Me too," I said.

"I miss it, but I like the ranch better. There's too many people here." Bryce sat back in his seat and picked up his comic book again.

"It will be nice to be in a place where the sun works. I'm over being fooled into thinking it's warm until I step outside," Annie said, still crowding me in order to see out the window.

"Jason and Rachel should have a nice day for their wedding tomorrow." I gently nudged Annie's arm off the armrest between us to get back some personal space. She took the hint and sat back in her seat.

"Is there going to be dancing? The invite said to come 'dance' at their wedding. Does that mean we just get up and dance, or are we supposed to have a routine? Can guests refuse to dance at a Jewish wedding? The last thing I want to do right now is dance." Her questions tumbled out with increasing anxiety. She'd asked them a hundred times over the past week, but I still didn't have any answers. I'd thought about asking Joel; I just couldn't work up the nerve to dial his number.

I squeezed Annie's hand. "I'm pretty sure we don't have to choreograph our own dance routines. At least, Rachel didn't say anything about it to me, and you've seen the minute-by-minute pre-, post-, and in-the-moment wedding instructions she's given us. I don't remember seeing 'rousing dance number' anywhere on those ten pages."

"Those are no joke." Annie's voice trembled. She had been excited when Rachel asked her to be a bridesmaid, but that was before the Snapchat scandal. Now the thought of being front and center in a room full of people who had possibly seen her pictures filled her with anxiety. She'd feel exposed all over again standing in front of them wondering who had laughed at her downfall. My stomach turned when I thought about it. When Annie told me that was the reason she didn't want to be a bridesmaid anymore, I hoped Rachel would feel the same way and let her off the hook. At the same time, if Rachel did ask Annie to not be a bridesmaid because of the pictures, it would crush her. It was a no-win situation.

To Jason's credit, when I asked him whether Annie should offer not to be part of the bridal party, he said no way. Bryce and I were taking the place of Dad and Jason's mom in the wedding procession, and he didn't want Annie left out. He said Rachel didn't either, but I wasn't sure I believed it.

The plane landed with a bump and taxied to the gate, but we stayed in our seats. A few people had recognized Annie at the Salt Lake airport, and even though they didn't say anything, their stares and smirks said it all. She tucked her hair under a baseball cap and put on big sunglasses as the other passengers walked past us. When the last one disembarked, we got up and retrieved our overhead luggage before making our way into the airport and down to baggage claim. Luckily, between the normal LAX crush of people and Annie's disguise, no one bothered us.

"I have to pick up the car. Will you be okay getting the bags?" I asked her as we stepped on the escalator leading into the baggage area teeming with people fighting for space at the carousels.

She shook her head no.

"Okay then. I guess we'll all go, and then come back for the bags." I wasn't quite sure how that would work, but it would have to.

"There are always photographers hanging out here waiting to get shots of celebrities. I don't want to take any chances," Annie murmured and moved closer to me.

I couldn't argue with that, but it didn't leave us enough time to get to the hotel and change before the rehearsal dinner. I took a deep breath and closed my eyes, trying not to freak out. When I opened my eyes to step off the escalator, I spotted the answer to my problem.

"Joel!" Bryce yelled and ran to him before I could process my surprise.

"What are you doing here?" I asked, returning the huge grin and hug he had for me.

"Jason told me you were getting in this afternoon, so I offered to come give you a hand," he said, slaying the fear that had threatened to paralyze me moments before.

"Thanks. You didn't have to do that." I tucked my hair behind my ears to keep from touching him again.

"I'm glad you did," Annie said while she embraced him. "It's good to see a friendly face."

He held her in a comforting hug that almost choked me up. The surprise of seeing him right when I needed someone was almost too much to take in. And to have him comfort my sister when she needed it brought back every feeling for him I'd been trying to forget.

"What do you need me to do?" he asked, pulling away from Annie.

"Can you stay with Bryce and pick up the bags while I get our rental car? Bryce, you know what the bags look like, right?" My words were choppy with the excitement I couldn't contain.

"I think so." He looked a lot less sure than I was comfortable with, but it would have to do. I couldn't leave Annie there.

"We'll figure it out," Joel said and led Bryce to the carousel I pointed to.

"Did you know he was going to be here?" Annie asked as soon as they were out of earshot.

I shook my head and walked to the rental car counter as fast as I could, hoping to outrun the questions I knew she wanted to ask. Questions I had too but couldn't answer.

"He saved us."

"I wouldn't go that far. It is really nice he's here though."

Annie shook her head. "It's more than that. It's an answer to a prayer."

We'd reached the front of the line for our rental car, and the person at the counter waved me forward. *An answer to a prayer?* What was that supposed to mean?

I didn't have a chance to ask her until we got to the hotel and Bryce was out of earshot.

"I've been feeling so worthless since all of this happened," she said as she slipped into her dress. "All the stuff people are saying—it's true. I brought this on myself; I'm a terrible example. I'm a total hypocrite." She sucked in her breath as she fought back tears. "I couldn't see how Heavenly Father could possibly love me. I haven't even been praying because why would He want to hear from me?"

"Annie—"

"Wait, let me finish." She took a deep breath and turned her back to me so I could zip her up. "I was so nervous this morning about coming back here. When I woke up, I didn't think I could even get in the car to go the airport, let alone get on an airplane. I finally broke down and prayed."

"What did you ask for?"

"A friendly face. Someone who wouldn't judge me or stare at me or worse."

"And that was Joel?" Part of me wished it hadn't been. It was hard enough not to love him already.

She nodded and turned around. "I really didn't think that prayer would be answered. I mean, it's not like I have a lot of friends here to begin with, and I didn't tell anyone I was coming. Joel wasn't even on my list of remote possibilities. But as soon as I saw him, I knew he was my answer, even if he wasn't there for me."

"He's been a good friend to us." It hurt to use the word *friend* to describe him. I wanted more.

"He is. I wish things had worked out between you two." She checked the mirror and wiped under her eyes.

"It was too complicated. He would have had to give up too much." I looked over her shoulder in the mirror to touch up my own makeup.

"I saw the way he looked at you at the airport." She handed me her eyeliner, an unspoken order to apply it.

"What do you mean the way he looked at me? He just smiled." I handed it back to her and shut my eyes, so she could do it for me.

"Do I have to wear a tie?" Bryce yelled from the bathroom.

"Yes!" we both yelled back.

"I mean, he looked like he'd give up everything and more for you." She stretched my eyelid, and I tried not to flinch as she drew the pencil across it.

"You're crazy," I whispered. My heart pounded too fast for me to say anything else.

The bathroom door slammed, and I jumped.

"You made me mess up," she said at the same time Bryce handed me his tie.

"I can't get this right." He screwed his face into a ball, challenging me to make him wear the tie.

"Help him while I finish my face. We need to hurry." I grabbed the eyeliner. I would have done a rush job, but if Annie was right about what Joel's eyes said when he looked at me, I wanted those eyes to like what they saw tonight.

Chapter 36

IF JOEL LIKED WHAT HE SAW, it was hard to tell. We barely made eye contact throughout the entire rehearsal and dinner. Instead, I got to watch him hold Becca's hand and her kiss him on the cheek. I looked away when she went for his lips. I wasn't a total masochist.

When I wasn't busy watching them, I spent my time imagining the perfect life they were going to have together. Joel would build them a house. They'd go to synagogue on Saturdays and eat dinner with his parents on Sundays. They'd have beautiful, chiseled-cheekboned kids—if Joel talked Becca into having them. Which he would, because who wouldn't want to have his babies?

By the time the dinner was over and we got back to the hotel, all I wanted to do was cover my face with a pillow and scream. Instead I let Bryce order a *Star Wars* movie—Jason was paying for the hotel, so why not?—and planned on suffering for another two hours through that. But Annie had other plans for my suffering.

Once Bryce was engrossed in the movie, and she and I were curled up in the bed we were sharing, she started in again on Joel's "I want you" looks.

"I don't know what you're talking about," I whispered so Bryce wouldn't hear. "He didn't look at me all night."

"Trust me. I watched him. The only time he didn't have eyes on you was when you were looking at him. It was ridiculous the way you two kept trying to steal glances at each other," she whispered back. We were close enough her toothpaste breath tickled my nose, and my cheeks burned with her words. Apparently I was more Inspector Clouseau than James Bond when it came to spying.

"Becca noticed too," she continued. "Why do you think she pulled him out of there so fast? Dinner was barely over before they left."

"You think they left because he was looking at me?" I noticed they'd left in a hurry, and I was surprised Becca hadn't at least said goodbye after the warm hello she'd given me.

"No. I think she made him leave because you two couldn't keep your eyes off *each other*." Annie's voice rose, and Bryce shushed us.

"You're talking crazy. I'm going to sleep." I rolled over, wrapping the pillow over my head.

She leaned against me and pulled the pillow away from ear. "You know I'm right." She laughed and dropped the pillow, then rolled over and put her ice cold feet on me.

"Stop it!" I moved my legs, but she kept chasing me with her feet until I was hanging off the edge. I gave her a good kick then pushed her back to her side of the bed.

"You should have told Jason to spring for a suite with more than two beds," she teased and stuck one foot on me.

"Stop it, or I'm kicking you to the sofa bed!"

"Only if you admit you're still in love with Joel."

"You totally are, Emily," Bryce said, keeping his eyes glued to screen.

"Shut up, both of you. He's engaged to Becca, not to me."

Annie's teasing was a good sign she was on the mend. Too bad it tore me apart.

"I didn't see a ring on her finger," she whispered a few minutes later.

"I saw his whole hand wrapped around all of her fingers. Let it go. I'm going to sleep." I yanked the extra pillow from underneath her head and pressed it against mine to block out anything else my siblings or the stupid Darth Vader had to say.

But the fact was, no one needed to point out Becca's ring-less finger. I noticed it as soon as I saw her.

Chapter 37

WE WOKE UP EARLY TO get ready for the wedding. Jason had given me a few guidelines about what Bryce and I had to do, but I'd never been to a Jewish wedding, so I wasn't sure what to expect. I knew there'd be a rabbi, and I assumed a glass would be broken, but that's it. Dad had never talked about his first marriage. Even though he had a good relationship with his former in-laws, they weren't happy when he married Mom, so the rest of us never got to know the grandparents Jason spent so much time with before they died.

The wedding was being held at Rachel's home. The Beverly Hills address gave me some idea of how nice it would be, but its size still blew me away. It wasn't a house; it was an estate.

"Whoa," Bryce gasped from the backseat.

"Are you kidding me?" Annie said as we drove through the gate. She craned her neck to see the grounds on my side of the car. I tried to keep my eyes on the road but almost hit the valet when I got distracted by the long line of roses bordering the driveway.

I handed my car keys for the rented Kia to the frightened valet, and we walked down the lantern-lined pathway to the backyard. Giant white tents were set up on either side of a rectangular pool with water spouting from its center in perfect high arcs. One tent looked ready for the ceremony while the other had tables and chairs I assumed were for the dinner and reception. Both were decorated with so many gardenias and lilies it felt like a nursery. A nursery with chandeliers, crystal goblets, and real silverware.

"I'm thinking I chose the wrong career in entertainment," Annie said, leaning close. "The law looks like it pays all right."

"No kidding."

It finally made sense why Joel's dad was so upset Joel went into construction instead of law. But at least his dad hadn't cut him off for doing it. Joel would still have an inheritance, and he still had his family. If he joined the Church, it would be a different story. He'd give up money and so much more.

If we had stayed together, would he have been willing to give up that much for me? The thought sent excited chills up my spine before I could stop them. Maybe the months of loneliness since I'd left LA made the thought of someone losing everything to love me more appealing than it should have been. I knew what it was like to lose parents. I wouldn't wish that on anyone.

As if my thoughts had conjured up his presence, Joel stepped through the open back door—which was a "back door" like Everest was a mountain. The whole glass wall slid open to create a seamless transition from inside to out.

He waved and walked toward us, holding out his fist for Bryce to pound when he reached us. I couldn't meet his eyes for fear everything I'd been thinking about him was written on my face. He made small talk with Annie, answering the questions and compliments she had about the house, while I kept my eyes on the caterers rushing around in the kitchen.

"Emily?"

"Yeah?" I forced myself to look at him.

"I said I'll show you where everyone else is." We followed him into the house. "The bridesmaids are all with Rachel, if you want to join them, Annie."

The look Annie gave me behind Joel's back told me she didn't, but I answered with a nod and a raised eyebrow. She shook her head and mouthed *no*, nearly colliding with a caterer as Joel led us through the kitchen.

"Jason is in the library with the rest of the guys, but things are getting a little crazy in there, so maybe you and Bryce would like to hang out in the theater room until we're ready. Unless you need to get ready . . ." He looked back at me. "But you look ready to me." He ran his hand over the scar on his eyebrow.

"Thanks. The theater room sounds great," I said.

"I know Becca will want to see you, but Rachel is kind of freaking out right now, so it's probably not the best time." He turned a corner, and we entered a foyer the size of a hotel lobby with a spiral staircase in the middle of it.

"I think I'll hang out with Bryce and Emily, if that's okay," Annie said. Her eyes followed the curve of the stairway to its top.

"Actually, I'm under orders from Rachel to make sure you're with the rest of the bridesmaids. She has some last-minute instructions or something." He grabbed the handrail and gave Annie an apologetic half smile. "Becca is with them. I told her to take care of you."

We climbed the stairs and turned right into what Joel called the "west wing" of the house. He was joking, but it wasn't far from the truth.

"Why does a house need wings?" Bryce asked.

"Good question, dude. Good question." Joel grinned and with it the air of tension that had been following us disappeared. "It's kind of silly for four people to have this much house, isn't it?"

"It'd be fun to play hide-and-seek in," Bryce answered and peeked in one of the bathrooms where he opened a cabinet door. "I could fit in here."

"Yeah, my brother and I had a nanny for a while who loved playing hide-and-seek with us. Except it always took her a really long time to find us, now that I think about it. We'd be under beds or in closets for hours. We got a new nanny after I told Mom I'd found a hiding spot so good Lupe couldn't find me all day." His brow creased, and he pursed his lips in exaggerated thought that made us all laugh.

"I didn't know you had a brother," Bryce said.

"Yeah. He died a few years ago." We stopped in front of a gold-framed family picture with a much younger Joel and Rachel and another boy who had Joel's same crooked smile but Rachel's brown eyes. "That's David there." Joel pointed to the teenage boy and stared at him with his head cocked to the side.

"I wish I had a brother," Bryce said.

"I wish I still did too," Joel answered softly.

"You do though because you'll be with him again." Bryce's little face suddenly looked grown up in all its seriousness. "It's like my mom and dad still being my mom and dad, even though they're . . . not alive anymore. They'll still be my parents in heaven."

Joel tore his eyes from the picture and looked down at Bryce with a softness around his eyes that quickened my pulse. "You know, that's not what I learned growing up, but I really like the idea of families being forever. Isn't that how you say it?"

"You never learned that? I thought everyone knew that. No wonder you're still so sad about your brother," Bryce answered.

Joel let out a soft laugh and smiled. "Aren't you still sad about your parents?"

"I miss them, but I know where they are so that's what I think about when I'm sad. I know they're watching over me, and that makes me happy. Except now I have to be extra good because they can see everything I'm doing, and I want them to be proud of me." Bryce's certainty surprised me. I had no idea the depth of his feelings. I was amazed by his maturity and touched by his innocence at the same time.

"You're a smart man, Bryce." Joel lightly gripped the back of Bryce's neck and shook him gently then led us down the hall. A cacophony of squeals and laughter pulled us toward Rachel's room. Joel knocked and opened the door, and Annie stepped in, giving me a cornered animal look as she did.

"Annie! Emily!" Becca saw us from across the room and rushed over to greet us with a hug. "It's so good to see you! We need to catch up later, Emily. Come with me, Annie, and I'll help you get ready."

She grabbed Annie's hand and led her to the group of bridesmaids gathered around Rachel, who was getting her makeup done. Annie hung back as Becca introduced her to the four other women, but as each one smiled at her, the fear on her face slowly relaxed to a low level of nervousness. Rachel stayed in her seat and held her hand out. A cloud of confusion brushed over Annie's face before she gave it the squeeze Rachel was waiting for.

"Should we go? It looks like she'll be okay," Joel said. Bryce was already tugging on his sleeve.

"Sure." I waved to Annie, but Rachel caught it and returned it with a wiggle of her fingertips. Fortunately, she missed the eye roll Annie sent me.

I backed out of the room and followed Joel back down the hallway in the direction we'd come from.

"The theater is on the other side of the house."

"You mean the *east* wing?" I fought a smile tugging at my lips.

"Yes, the *east* wing, if you're going to make me say it." He glowered at me, but he was fighting the same battle with his mouth I was with mine.

"You can't really have a west wing without an east. I mean, what would the neighbors think?" I ran my fingertips along the smooth walls.

He shook his head and laughed. "It's not my house, you know. I would have been fine with just one wing."

"A one-winged house is like a one-winged butterfly. It may still be beautiful, but you can't do much with it, right?" I teased.

This time he laughed loud enough that it echoed off the vaulted ceilings as we went back down the stairs into the two-story entryway. Joel's mom was at the bottom of the stairs giving directions to a line of people holding floral arrangements. Joel's laughter drew her eyes up, and her brow wrinkled with annoyance at Bryce, who was sliding on his belly down the banister. I yanked on his shirt to pull him off, but not before her mouth followed her eyes in a downward pull.

She waited for us at the bottom of the steps, looking as beautiful— and intimidating—as she had the night before when I'd met her. All three of us subconsciously slowed our descent.

"Hi, Mom." Joel kissed her on the cheek she held out for him. "I'm showing Emily and Bryce to the theater room to hang until we're ready."

"Nice to see you both again." Her face was unnaturally smooth—the result of a skilled plastic surgeon and regular Botox, I was sure. It relaxed into a smile that made me feel more at ease. "Things are pretty hectic here today."

"Can I help?" I asked.

She brushed me off with a wave of her hand and a *psh*. "Just relax for the rest of us." She turned her back to me, peppered Joel with questions and instructions, then turned to me again. "The theater room is down the hall and to the left of the kitchen. I'm sure my husband is hiding out in there, so tell him I sent you, and he needs to find something for you and Bryce to watch. He can show you how to work whatever video game or whatever movie you want. That's about all he's good for."

She gave me a gentle nudge on my way and sent Joel in the opposite direction. He mouthed an apology to me then reluctantly followed his mom back up the stairs. Bryce and I made our way through the caterer-crowded kitchen and down the hall. I knocked on the first door I saw, which turned out to be a bathroom; then I knocked on the next door.

When no one answered, I opened the door only to be blasted by a slew of cursing in stereo. "I think we found the theater room," I said to Bryce as I yanked the door closed. I didn't let go of the handle while I debated whether or not to interrupt whomever was in there or find somewhere else to hide out for the next two hours until the ceremony started.

I'd decided on the second when the door opened and I was face-to-face with Joel's dad. "Hi there." His tall, wiry body was the opposite of his wife's stout, petite body, and the light from the hallway glinted off his bald head.

"Hi," I answered. "Mrs. Rickman told us to hang out in here for a while." I shrank back, regressing ten years, while Bryce poked his head around Mr. Beckman to see the whole room.

"Cool . . ."

"Come on in." Mr. Rickman lifted his arm to let Bryce in while he opened the door all the way.

"Whoa . . ." Bryce walked open-mouthed and wide-eyed to the movie screen covering almost the entire width and length of the back wall. Unfortunately the paused picture on that giant screen was of an enormous Al Pacino holding a gun and surrounded by men lying in pools of blood.

"I'm watching *Scarface* if you want to join me." Mr. Beckman pointed a remote at the screen.

"Um, that's probably not okay for my brother." My words came out in fast-forward, trying to beat his finger to the play button.

"Oh, right." He lowered his remote-loaded hand, and our standoff was over.

"I think Mrs. Rickman wanted you to find something that he could watch or play," I added.

He waved me inside, not hiding his disappointment, and clicked a button on the remote. Al Pacino disappeared, releasing Bryce from the blood-soaked trance Al had him in.

"The movie catalog is in the notebook there on the table." Mr. Rickman said, pointing. He turned his attention back to me, staring at me with the identical steely blue eyes of his son but without the same kindness.

"So you're the girl who's trying to get my son baptized a Christian." His gaze had the same hold on me Scarface had had on Bryce thirty seconds before.

"What?!" I shook my head in a panic. "I've answered some of his questions, but I never asked him to get baptized."

His eyes narrowed. "Let's keep it that way. Becca's smart enough to walk away from all this missionary nonsense, and Joel will follow her lead if you and your church friends will stay out of his way."

Blood rushed to my face, leaving me dizzy. My cheeks had to be as bright as my accuser's red tie, which I couldn't take my eyes off. I didn't dare meet Mr. Rickman's glare. I knew the nervous tears attempting to escape would do just that if I had to look at him or say anything.

"Don't get me wrong." He laid a not-so-reassuring hand on my arm. "I like Mormons. I think they're good people. It's nothing against them; I'd be just as upset if he were interested in any other Christian church. Probably even more so. We're Jewish, and we're going to stay Jewish. My relatives did not die at Auschwitz so Joel could become a Christian. If he does, he does it without mine or his mother's blessing, and he won't be welcome in our home again."

I set my jaw and met his gaze. I was empathetic to his concerns, but he was accusing me of something I hadn't done, and the thought of him voluntarily severing his relationship with his son made me mad. "Mr. Rickman, I don't want to be disrespectful to you, especially in your home, but you're not going to threaten me. Joel's choices are his own, and so are yours. I hurt every single day, I miss my parents so much. If you want to cause your son that kind of pain, that's your choice. I purposely stayed out of anything to do with Joel and my church, but I'll stand by him no matter what he chooses, because that's what you do for the people you love." My words shot out like a rubber band without direction or control. The sound of Mario Kart only partially registered in my brain, keeping time with the pounding in my chest. I would have left, but the game reminded me Bryce was there. I only hoped he hadn't heard our conversation.

Mr. Rickman's jaw twitched as we stared each other down. Or up, in my case. After an eternity, he blinked and walked out of the room. I let my breath out, and with that release came the realization I had declared my love for Joel to his father.

Chapter 38

To say the rest of the day was awkward would be an epic understatement. The ceremony itself was beautiful, but every time I got near Mr. Rickman, I froze. I didn't regret standing up to him, but the looks he shot me made me want to duck for cover. And, I discovered, Jewish weddings aren't short. They are all-day affairs.

Having grown up with a Jewish brother, I thought I'd know more about what was happening, but Rachel and Joel's family seemed to be a lot more observant than Jason's. The only part of the ceremony that was familiar was the breaking of the glass. I'd seen that in a movie or two.

After Jason smashed the glass, he and Rachel disappeared. No one else seemed concerned about it, but I wasn't quite sure what to do. Everyone else was mingling, but Bryce, Annie, and I gravitated toward each other. We stood apart from everyone else waiting for the newlyweds to return, wondering if they would.

"So, can we go?" Annie whispered after half an hour of waiting.

"I don't think so. There are still a lot of things listed on this program." I flipped the program open and read through the events again. There were three hours of dinner and dancing planned. I glanced around the crowd, hoping people would be sitting down for dinner, but no one was. My eyes landed on Joel, who was weaving his way through the crowd to us.

"Hi," he said when he reached us. "You look confused."

"Is it over?" Bryce asked.

"No. It's the yichud."

"What's that? Is it dinner? I'm hungry." Bryce tugged at his tie, and I swatted his hand away before he could undo the knot. I was not tying that thing again.

"No, that's coming soon. Yichud is when the bride and groom spend their first few minutes as husband and wife together in a private room."

"Only a few minutes? For real? Because I'd love to eat soon." My stomach grumbled with my question.

"Cocktails last about an hour, then we'll dance the horah, then dinner." A waiter passed by with a tray of appetizers, and Joel stopped him. He took the whole tray and held it in front of Bryce who took five mini eggroll-looking things.

"Bryce!" I shook my head, but Joel pulled the tray back before Bryce could put any back.

"Eat up. We've got pictures right now. You'll need fortifications," he said to Bryce.

He was about to hand the tray back to the waiter, but I grabbed four of the eggrolls and handed two to Annie. Bryce had already stuffed two in his mouth, and his cheeks puffed out like the Pillsbury Doughboy. We followed Joel into the house, where a photographer and the rest of the wedding party were waiting for us.

The photographer directed us out front, where she took pictures of the whole wedding party, and then a family picture of the three of us and Jason, which felt a little awkward for everyone. Jason and Rachel had made us a part of their wedding, but I wondered if our picture would make it up on their family photo wall. The whole thing felt forced, and I was relieved when the photographer moved on to Rachel's family.

"You want to see if there are any appetizers left?" Joel asked me as soon as he was done with the family and wedding party pics. Since Becca was Rachel's woman of honor, she stayed behind to help Rachel while I followed Joel to the backyard. Annie took Bryce by the hand—much to his horror—and pulled him ahead of us, leaving Joel and me alone for the first time in months.

"Okay, what's the horah? Is that the chair dance?" I asked as we walked through the house instead of taking the path to the backyard.

"No, it's where we all hold hands and dance in a circle. We'll do the chair thing too." He slowed his walk, and I met his pace

"What do you call the thing they stood under during the ceremony? It was beautiful."

"A chuppah."

"I liked what the rabbi said, that it represented a home and was open on all sides to welcome guests."

"It goes back to Abraham and Sarah and the description of their tent being open to everyone. The covering on it is symbolic of God's presence over the covenant of marriage. It's a reminder that the institution of marriage has divine origins." He stopped us in the middle of the kitchen and pointed his chin toward the people milling around the pool. "I could use a break from the crowd. Do you want to hang inside for a while?"

I hesitated for half a second as Becca's face and Mr. Rickman's words flashed in my mind, but my heart wouldn't let me say no to a few minutes alone with Joel. They might be the last we'd ever have together.

"That sounds perfect."

He smiled and, in a few long strides, was at the fridge grabbing a bowl of grapes and a couple of Cokes. He pulled out a chair for me at the kitchen island then sat down next to me. The glass door had been shut, and the caterers were setting up the food in the tent, so we had the kitchen to ourselves even though we could still see the guests outside. The ice-cold can he handed me stung my hot palm.

"Okay, tell me more about these Jewish wedding traditions," I said, trying hard not to notice how our arms were almost touching. "Is that contract they signed really binding? Can Rachel take Jason to court if he doesn't provide clothing, food, and . . . the last thing?"

"Conjugal relations?" Jason's lip twitched as he held back a smile. "It's called a ketubah, and, no, she probably couldn't take him to court. It's more tradition than anything."

"I like the idea of a contract that protects the bride. I liked everything about the whole ceremony. It's really beautiful, the way they fasted together and how he put the veil on her. And the circling thing—I didn't really understand it, but I liked it."

"I can't remember why they do that. Something about seven days in a week. Not every Jewish couple includes that part, but Rachel wanted it." He popped a grape in his mouth and took a long sip of his Coke.

"I don't think there's anything like that in a temple sealing. Except for maybe the reminder that marriage is a covenant and comes from God." I sat back and slipped my feet out of my shoes to stretch my toes.

"You've never been to a Mormon wedding?"

"Not a temple one. Mormon weddings I've been to outside of the temple are usually pretty simple though." I shifted in my chair, and our arms bumped, making my skin prickle.

"And you want one in the temple?" His eyes bored into mine.

"I wouldn't have given you up if I didn't." The words had been sitting in my heart since we'd broken up, and it took a long time to get them to my tongue. But once they were out, the weight in my chest lifted, and I knew I'd made the right choice.

"I guess you and Becca will do a lot of the same things for your wedding," I said to change the subject and to remind myself he was engaged. I took a swig of my Coke to calm my nerves but then set it back down when he didn't answer right away.

"I'm still taking the missionary lessons, Emily." He glanced at me then down at my drink. "We may want the same things," he added softly.

The heavy glass door slid open before I had time to process what he'd said.

"Oh, I'm glad I found you two." Becca stepped inside with a smile plastered on her face that didn't match her words. "They're about to walk into the reception." She held her hand out to Joel, and her eyes darted to mine. The pain in them was like a knife to the soul. Joel and I hadn't done anything more than talk, but her face said she felt betrayed.

I followed Joel and Becca to the backyard just before Jason and Rachel emerged from their . . . whatever it was called. I found Annie and Bryce, and we cheered and clapped for our brother and his new wife. Then we held hands with strangers and danced in a circle cheering some more. We helped lift the chairs holding Jason and Rachel, we ate the kosher meal of salmon and the challah cut by the rabbi. We danced again, then danced some more. It was an all-around joyous celebration for everyone.

Except for me.

Joel's words and Becca's face spun in my head faster than I did in the horah, leaving me dizzy. I should have been happy he thought he wanted the same things as me. But I had hurt Becca, and there was only more hurt coming for everyone if he actually did join the Church. The more I thought about it and the faster we spun, the more my stomach churned.

Chapter 39

ANNIE HAD HER INTERVIEW WITH *People* first thing the next morning, and then we were flying home. I had to push all thoughts about Joel holding Becca as they danced out of my head. I couldn't think about how my conversation with Joel would have gone if Becca hadn't walked in. Even if we wanted the same things, he hadn't said he wanted them with me. I couldn't think about saying goodbye to him at the end of the night, wondering if it would be the last time I saw him.

I couldn't focus on any of that because all my attention needed to be on Annie and prepping her for what would probably be the most important interview she would ever do. I dropped Bryce off at an old friend's house then returned to the hotel to help Annie get ready.

"Don't let them put you in anything that even hints at sexy for the photo shoot," I told her when a knock at the door told us wardrobe and makeup had arrived.

Annie took a deep breath and closed her eyes. When she opened them again, she had a smile on her face, ready to greet them. They spent an hour doing her hair and making her even more beautiful. While they were working, I went through the wardrobe rack they'd brought, nixing anything that didn't scream MODEST. We finally settled on a red cap-sleeve dress with a full skirt that looked straight off the set of *Mad Men*.

Annie was stunning in it. It brought out the auburn in her hair and the blue in her eyes. The photographer spent about an hour posing her around the sitting area in our suite. The longer it went, the more comfortable Annie looked, like she was back in her element. By the time she sat down on the couch across from Susan Sheldon, I'd been reminded what a great actor she was. If I hadn't seen her on the verge of losing her breakfast that morning, I would have never known she was nervous.

"You have created an image for yourself as a good girl, and your career has thrived despite the pressure to change. What made you take those photos knowing it could destroy your reputation?" Susan asked as soon as Annie sat down across from her. "Was releasing those photos a calculated move for attention or to distance yourself from the image you'd created?"

Annie considered carefully before answering, and I held my breath. We knew she'd get a question like that, we just didn't think it would be the first one. We'd discussed ways for her to answer it, but she hadn't settled on anything this morning, and I was as curious about the answer as Susan was.

"Not many people know this, but I suffer from bipolar disorder." She stopped, expecting a reaction from Susan. I had one, but I stifled it. All of our discussions had been about how to explain without revealing her mental state at the time.

"I've always had mood swings, but I wasn't diagnosed as bipolar until recently. Last year when my parents died I fell into a deep depression. When I got fired from *Boomtown*, and then my agent let me go, it got worse. I went on medication, which helped, and I thought I was better."

She bit her lip and lowered her eyes. "To make a long story short, we moved to Utah, I met a guy, thought I was in love, and went off the meds. It was a dumb thing to do, and I wasn't thinking rationally when he convinced me to take those pictures. I was manic. I felt invincible and trusted someone I shouldn't have. I knew the pictures didn't represent who I am as soon as I saw them, but I let him keep them instead of destroying them. I didn't think he'd sell them."

"Are you saying it's not your fault?" Susan's brow creased with doubt.

"No, I take full responsibility for what I did. I knew it was wrong at the time, but I did it anyway. But had I been taking my meds, I would have been thinking more clearly. I don't know that I would have made the same decision."

Susan nodded, and Annie went on.

"I like to think I wouldn't have, but the truth is, this past year has been hard. I've been lost without my career and especially without my parents. I only bring up my diagnosis to give you an idea of my mental state at the time and because I feel a sense of responsibility to others who may be living with it. I'm not using it as an excuse for my behavior, but I'm also not going to be ashamed of it."

"You and this guy who took the pictures aren't together anymore?" Susan asked, skipping any kind of reply about Annie's courage in revealing her mental illness.

Annie shook her head.

"What did it feel like, after the year you've had, to be betrayed by someone you thought you could trust?" Susan held her recorder closer to Annie.

I rolled my eyes and shook my head so Annie would know she didn't have to answer the question. But she did anyway.

"It hurt. A lot. But I don't believe he meant for the pictures to get out. I'm really more hurt by the people who treated me like a thing instead of a person, clicking on every link to the pictures they were sent and passing it on to more people. That's what really hurts. I don't know why people think that a celebrity is less deserving of respect and privacy than anybody else."

Susan nodded and looked at her notepad. "How have these photos affected your membership in the Mormon Church?"

"Not at all. My bishop—that's the pastor of my congregation—and I discussed them, and he was very understanding and compassionate." Annie looked Susan straight in the eye, answering without hesitation.

"What about other Mormons and their negative online comments? Do you feel betrayed by them?" Susan scrunched her eyes and nodded, her empathy less than sincere.

"I do, but I also betrayed them. I've given a lot of talks to youth groups about sticking to their beliefs and the things we're taught at church. They have a right to be angry that I didn't do what I encouraged them to do. But I hope they'll follow the example of Christ and forgive. That's what I'm trying to do." Annie crossed her legs and sat back, completely at ease.

I stared at her as her words registered. I knew she believed what we'd been taught, but I'd never heard her actually say it. As much as I hated what she'd been through, the experience had helped her to gain some maturity and, more importantly, a testimony.

"So this really hasn't made you reconsider your commitment to Mormonism?" Susan asked.

Annie blinked with surprise. "It's my commitment to my faith that's gotten me through this last year. It doesn't really matter what a few people I don't know say about me online even if we do share the same religion.

It's that religion and the things my mom taught me that have given me the strength to go on when I lost everything."

She swallowed hard and fought back tears. "It's that religion that kept me grounded when I was ten years old and Disney was throwing money and fame my way, telling me I was going to be their biggest star. It's that religion that kept me grounded when all of that went away and my parents were killed, all within a matter of months. It was when I forgot about my commitment to Mormonism—and to Christ, really—that I lost my way."

Annie sat up straighter. I knew she hadn't planned to say all of that before. She was formulating her ideas as she went, but as she said them aloud, all the confidence she'd lost over the past year came pouring back.

"So, yeah, this experience has made me reconsider my commitment to Mormonism," she continued. "It's made me decide to recommit to it, no matter what the consequences are for my career. I can't lose anything more important than what I've already lost, but if I lose my faith, I've lost everything."

Susan asked a few more questions, trying to bait Annie into saying something negative about the Church and its members "shaming her instead of blaming the people who published and shared the pictures." Annie responded the same each time, saying what she had done was as wrong as what those people had done, and she wasn't going to point fingers at them without taking responsibility for herself.

The interview ended with Susan promising to send over the final copy of her article as soon as it was done. She looked pleased with the way it had gone, but Annie looked even more pleased. As Annie shut the door behind Susan, she took a deep breath with her eyes closed then opened them again and smiled.

"Did I do okay?"

I pulled her into an embrace before I answered her. "You were amazing."

"It felt good. I didn't even know what I was going to say most of the time, but then the words just came out, and they were perfect."

"They were. You should be proud of yourself." I let her go and stepped back to see my sister lighter and brighter than she'd been for a year.

"We should celebrate! Let's go to Sprinkles! I deserve a giant cupcake." Her eyes inflated into bubbles of excitement I hated to burst.

"You do, and we should, but we have a brother to pick up and a flight to catch."

"Jason is ready to run from Rachel already?" She unzipped her dress and walked into the bathroom.

"Ha ha. Very funny. The other brother, Sassy Pants," I said through the closed door. My heart was full, even the tiny part of it that ached for Joel. My sister was healthy and happy. She had been knocked down over and over, but she was so much stronger than I realized, and her strength lifted me.

"I have to be honest, some of the things you said really surprised me." I pulled open the dresser drawer where I'd put all of my clothes and took out a neatly folded pile to transfer to my suitcase. "I've never heard you talk about the Church like that."

"What do you mean? I've spoken at a bunch of firesides." She came out of the bathroom dressed in the clothes she had on before the interview and handed me the borrowed dress.

"Yeah, but those were about sticking to your standards when you face temptation. I've never heard you talk about the Church as what's kept you grounded or about your faith being so important. It was really cool. I hope Susan will keep all of it." I hung up the dress and wheeled the rack into the hallway for the wardrobe people to pick up.

"Thank Luke for that. I think he's starting to rub off on me. That or his million uplifting memes have me brainwashed." Annie stuck her foot underneath the bridesmaid dress she'd dropped on the floor and kicked it up into her arms. I handed her a hanger, but she wadded up the dress and stuck it in her suitcase.

"There's a lot to thank Luke for. He's a good guy."

"Yeah, he is." She kicked up the other clothes piled on the floor, but with less success.

"Still just friends?" I pushed her out of the way and had her clothes all picked up in less than thirty seconds. "Fold them; don't just stuff," I said, handing them to her.

"Maybe." She shrugged, her mouth pulling into a reluctant grin. I wasn't sure if it was because of Luke or because she'd tricked me into packing for her. If it *was* because of Luke, I was happy to pack for her. One of us deserved to leave LA with her heart intact.

Chapter 40

WITHIN DAYS OF ANNIE'S *PEOPLE* article being published, Drew showed up at our door. We'd been back from California for almost a month, and Luke had spent nearly every day of that month at our house. Annie had stayed quiet about their relationship, but I'd seen some hand-holding and even a kiss. Still, when Bryce opened the door and Drew stood there, my stomach dropped. His dark hair was perfectly disheveled and his beard perfectly scruffed, and I had no idea if Annie would be swept off her feet again.

"What are *you* doing here?" Bryce asked, knocking a piece out of Drew's confident facade.

"Bryce!" I scooted him out of the way and opened the door wider, but not wide enough to let Drew in.

"Hi, Drew."

"Hi, Emily." The corner of his mouth twitched, attempting to smile until I shot it down with a look. "Is Annie here?"

"Maybe, but I doubt she wants to see you." At least, I hoped she didn't. It had been a while since I'd asked if she was still in touch with him.

"I doubt it too, but I'd like to apologize to her in person." The sad look in his eyes couldn't be faked. I opened the door wider and waved him into the kitchen.

"Bryce, go get Annie."

"She went somewhere with Luke." He directed his answer at Drew, and there was no mistaking his reluctance to let Drew anywhere near his sister. Drew was a foot and a half taller than my brother, but I would have put my money on Bryce if it came down to a brawl between the two of them at that moment.

"Why don't you text her to see when she'll be back." I set my jaw and raised my eyebrows to let him know it wasn't a request.

We heard voices at the door almost as soon as I said the words, and Annie and Luke walked in laughing, which came to an abrupt stop when they saw Drew.

"What are you doing here?" Her words echoed Bryce's exactly, but her reaction didn't. She crossed the room and gave Drew a tentative hug that he returned with more enthusiasm. Annie pulled back long before he was ready.

"I read the article in *People*." He glanced at us and leaned closer to Annie. "Can we go somewhere and talk?"

"Sure," she said slowly. Her eyes drifted to Luke's.

"I'm gonna take off." Luke's eyes couldn't hide the hurt his voice covered.

"You don't have to," Annie answered while Drew took a territorial step closer to her.

"Yeah, I do." He nodded and put on his hat.

"Call you later?" Annie asked him.

He gave her a noncommittal tilt of his head and left.

"Let's go upstairs, Bryce." I led him out of the kitchen and to his room, but there was no way I was staying there. I bribed him to stay with promises of extra video game time; then I crept back down the stairs to listen. The wall blocked them from view, but I could hear most of what they were saying.

"My roommate stole them; I told you that." There was a pleading to Drew's voice I'd never heard before.

"You also told me you were going to erase the pictures." Annie's voice was firm.

"I know. I was going to, but I missed you so much I couldn't."

I rolled my eyes at that.

"You missed me so much you couldn't talk to me for four months?"

"I was too embarrassed. I was broke; I didn't have a job. I felt like a loser, and here you are this famous actress. I left to forget you because I knew you could do better. But it didn't matter where I went. I couldn't get you out of my head. I still love you, Annie."

The silence that followed had me sending my sister telepathic messages. *Stay strong, Annie. Stay strong!*

"The thing is, Drew," I breathed a sigh of relief when I heard her conviction, "if you tell someone you love her, you don't pressure her into doing things she doesn't want to do, and you don't just disappear—"

"I swear you don't have to worry about that anymore. I'll do whatever it takes to earn your trust again."

"That's sweet. It really is." She paused, and so did my heart. "I don't think I trust myself when I'm with you, and I know I don't like myself. I appreciate you apologizing in person for what you did to me—"

"I told you, it wasn't my fault," Drew interrupted, his voice rising.

"You may not have done it on purpose, but you're to blame. I forgive you, but I'm not stupid enough to forget it. For the first time in a long time, I'm actually happy. What I had with you was exciting, but it wasn't happy. *I* wasn't happy. I'm not going to do that to myself again, Drew."

I wanted to clap. So I did. Very, very quietly.

"Is this because of Luke? Are you choosing a balding cowboy over me?"

"I'm choosing *me* over you. But I'll tell you that it's Luke who built me back up when you almost destroyed me."

"Whatever. If you want to throw your life away, you're not the same girl I met nine months ago. That girl was fun, ready for anything. Luke's boring is rubbing off on you."

Drew's angry tone scared me. I stood up in case he tried anything. My pulse raced and pounded between my ears, making it hard to hear what Annie said next.

"You should go now." Footsteps sounded, and the back door creaked open. I held my breath, waiting for Drew's heavier footsteps to follow. Finally they did. As soon as the door shut, I closed my eyes and did a happy dance.

"Have you been up there the whole time?" Annie's voice brought my dance to a stop mid-booty shake.

"Yes," I admitted then crept down the stairs even though I'd already been caught.

"So you heard everything?" Annie put her hands on her hips and stared me down.

I nodded again.

"I was pretty good, wasn't I?" A wide grin appeared.

"You were pretty awesome." I hugged her tight until she pulled away.

"I think I'd better call Luke."

"Good idea. He's a great guy, but . . ."

"What?" She raised her eyebrow like she knew what was coming.

"You're only eighteen. Take it slow."

"Almost nineteen. And I don't think Luke knows any other speed." She gave me a reassuring pat on the back. "Was Bryce eavesdropping too, or should I tell him he can come out?"

"He can come out," I answered, ignoring her eavesdropping comment.

*   *   *

A few days later, as LaRell and I were getting dinner ready, I got a call from an LA area code. I almost let it go to voice mail since I didn't recognize the number, but my curiosity got the best of me.

"It's Rachel," came the short reply to my hello.

"Oh, hi. How are—"

"After everything Jason and I have done for you, how dare you talk my brother into converting to Mormonism?" she blurted out, "Do you have any idea what this has done to our family?"

"What are you talking about?" I interrupted.

"He just told us he's getting baptized!" She yelled loud enough that I yanked the phone away from my ear.

I glanced at LaRell then stepped outside and shut the door behind me.

"Rachel, I don't know anything about this. The last time I talked to Joel was at your wedding. He didn't say anything to me about wanting to get baptized, and he hasn't said anything to me since." My voice rose to be heard over hers.

"Don't lie to me. I know you had something to do with this. You know my father told Joel he won't have anything to do with him if he does this? My mother has already lost one son, and now she's losing another one." The more Rachel talked, the more hysterical she got.

"I'm really sorry, Rachel. But whatever choice Joel is making is his own. I didn't have anything to do with it." My heart was pounding, but I kept my voice calm. I was determined to keep my cool.

"But you're the one who introduced him to the missionaries. You're the one who started this whole thing."

"I'm the one who gave him up because I knew what *he* would have to give up to be Mormon!" I lost the composure I'd fought so hard to regain and burst into tears. "You can blame me if you want, but the person you need to have this conversation with is your brother. It's his decision. I had nothing to do with it."

I hung up before she could say anything else. I sank down to the cement step, its concrete coldness quickly seeping through my jeans. I took some deep breaths until I couldn't hear my blood pounding in my ears anymore and stared at my phone, trying to process what Rachel had said. Joel was getting baptized. Baptized. *Joel.*

And he hadn't told me.

I stood up and walked inside, avoiding LaRell's questioning look. I went back to chopping the vegetables for the minestrone soup, working extra hard on the onion so I had something to blame for my tears. When my phone rang again, I hesitated picking it up for fear it was Rachel again.

"You want me to see who that is?"

I nodded.

LaRell picked it up off the table and showed me the screen. Becca's name was on it. I groaned. There could only be one reason she was calling, but there were a hundred different reactions she might have. I didn't want to take a chance I'd get the same reaction from her that I'd gotten from Rachel. I couldn't take another call like that. I shook my head, and LaRell set the phone back down. It dinged seconds later letting me know I had a voice mail.

I let dinner and my guests keep me from listening to the message until I could shut myself in my room and listen in private. The sadness in Becca's voice convinced me to call her back without hesitation.

"Emily?" Becca answered.

"Hi, Becca. I got your message." I braced myself for whatever she had to say.

"Have you heard about Joel?"

"His baptism? Rachel called me." I noticed there was no "Joel *and me.*" Rachel hadn't mentioned Becca either.

"Oh boy, how did that conversation go?"

"Not so good." I laughed and felt more at ease. She didn't sound angry. "How do you feel about it?"

There was a long pause, and I thought I heard a sniff. "The missionaries challenged me too, but I can't do it." Another long pause, another sniff. "I still have so many questions, and if I did convert, it would only be for Joel."

"If you don't have your own testimony, you're smart not to make that commitment. It's a pretty important promise." When she didn't respond, I asked another question. "Why didn't he tell me about his baptism?"

"I don't know. My guess is that he doesn't want you to think he's doing it for you." She sniffed, and I didn't know what to say, so I waited.

"He doesn't love me, Emily."

Those weren't the words I expected.

"What do you mean? He asked you to marry him." I knew Joel well enough to know he wouldn't have done that on a whim.

"He cares about me, but he doesn't love me. I'm not his soul mate. I'm not the person who was meant for him. And I'm starting to see he's not the person for me. Especially if he's serious about converting to Mormonism."

I was torn between trying to comfort her and my own feelings for Joel. I didn't know what I believed about soul mates, but if she was telling me Joel wasn't hers, why would I try and prove her wrong?

"So have you told him that?" I asked.

"Yes." Sniff. "It's the second hardest thing I've ever done."

"I'm really sorry, Becca." I held my breath. Breaking up with Joel couldn't be the only thing she'd called to tell me.

"You know what the hardest thing I've ever done is?"

"Um, no." This conversation was taking more surprising turns than a *Dr. Who* episode.

"Telling him you're his soul mate."

"You told him what?" I sank onto my bed.

"You're in love with him, right? I'm not wrong about that."

I didn't have to think about my answer, but it took me a half a minute to work up the courage to say it out loud, and when I did, it came out as a whisper. "You're not wrong."

"Good, because I know he's in love with you, and I care about him too much to see him unhappy. He's giving up everything to join your church: me, his family, maybe his career. I know he's not doing it *for* you, but he needs you."

It took so much effort to hold back the flood of emotions threatening to crash over me that I couldn't respond.

"Are you still there?" she asked.

"Yes. I don't know what to say." I stared at the floor, taking in everything she'd said. But a tingling that had started in my toes was spreading through the rest of my body.

"Say you'll be here for him."

"Of course," I answered, my mind going blank to every thought but how I would get there.

"It's Saturday at five. At the church off Beverly."

"You're sure he wants me there?"

"I'm sure he *needs* you there more than he even knows. I've known Joel for a long time. I know from the way he looks at you he's in love with you. I can tell by the way he talks to you and about you—"

"Why are you telling me this instead of him?" I interrupted.

"He's scared to death of getting hurt. He knew how his family would react when he told them about his decision, but he's still crushed. He can't handle losing anyone else."

"Why are you doing this?"

She waited a long time to answer. "Believe me, it's not easy. It kills me to let him go again. But I also don't want to try and make a relationship work with someone who's in love with someone else."

"You really believe that?" I asked. I wanted to believe everything she was telling me, but I couldn't understand why she wanted to set her fiancé up with someone else.

"Trust me. I thought about just breaking up with him and letting you two figure out for yourselves how to get together, but I'm also a big believer in karma. If I get you two together, maybe I'll find my soul mate. He's out there somewhere," she said with an exaggerated sigh that made me laugh.

"I'm sure you'll find him."

"Yeah. I just hope he's good-looking," she said and laughed again.

I laughed with her, but I couldn't talk through the tears that had escaped and were rolling down my cheeks. I was overwhelmed by her generosity and filled with excited anticipation. At the same time, my heart hurt for him and everything he was about to lose. And another part of me was afraid he'd change his mind about me and the Church before we ever had a chance.

"Thanks, Becca."

We hung up, and I took a few minutes to let everything sink in. Then I got on my laptop. I had plane tickets to buy.

Chapter 41

My plane touched down at LAX Saturday afternoon two hours before Joel's baptism. My stomach didn't land with it. It kept that dropping roller coaster feeling long after I'd deplaned. It was still there as I walked into the chapel as the service was starting. The room was fuller than I expected, and I recognized many of the faces from the YSA ward I'd been in. Joel was sitting on the front row and didn't see me sit down in the back.

The speakers were two of the elders who had taught Joel. Apparently he'd gone through a few sets. They both had a lot to say about the number of questions Joel had and how they both had to get to know the Old Testament better in order to answer them. The second elder spoke about the opposition Joel faced from family and friends as he investigated the Church and decided to get baptized.

"I admire him so much. I don't know if I could do it. But he's doing it because this Church is true. Joel is my hero." The elder spoke with the knowledge and certainty of an eighteen-year-old, and I couldn't help but wonder if the missionaries who had taught my dad thirty years ago had the same confidence in him and his testimony.

I pushed that worry aside. That fear had kept me from Joel for too long. I hoped Joel would be more committed than Dad had been. I hoped he wouldn't ever think the pressures of being a member of the Church outweighed the benefits of living the gospel, like Dad had. I hoped he wouldn't be a number in that too-high percentage of converts who fell away. I hoped all of these things because my biggest hope was that, wherever his journey took him, I'd be there with him.

The bishop dismissed everyone to the font, but I waited until the room filled before I went in. I didn't want to distract Joel from the covenant he was about to make. He didn't see me until after the confirmation as he stood to bear his testimony. A line formed between his eyebrows when he saw me, but then it gradually smoothed as a smile spread across his face.

His testimony was short and sincere. He focused on prayer and the very clear answers he'd received to every question he'd asked, including the one about whether to convert. He also was confident his relationship with his family would be healed because he'd been promised that in a blessing and in his confirmation. Everything he said increased my confidence in his commitment to the gospel.

The exuberant ward mission leader gave the closing prayer, and after the amen, people filed out to congratulate Joel. I hung back and waited. Our eyes drifted to each other over and over until finally the last person had hugged him and shaken his hand. He walked toward me, and I stood, gripping the back of the bench to keep my balance, unsure my shaky knees would hold me up much longer.

"Hi," we said at the same time. An awkward second passed before he held out his arms and we hugged.

"How did you know?" he asked when we broke apart.

"Your sister," I said, and his eyebrows shot up. "And Becca." His jaw dropped.

"Do you want to get out of here?" he asked, and I nodded. "They're having a fiesta thing tonight to welcome me or something, so I can't go far." He grabbed my hand and led me through the people still milling around in the chapel and the hallway. We went outside to a little alcove where we could have some privacy. Dusk was settling in, and the air hung wet and heavy with recent rain and a hint of saltiness from the ocean.

He let go of my hand, and we sat on the cement ledges next to each other. I shivered as the last of the sun disappeared and the night air set in.

"Cold?" he took off his jacket without waiting for an answer and handed it to me. I wrapped it around my shoulders, breathing in his musky scent.

"So Rachel and Becca both told you?" he asked. "How did that go?"

"Umm, not so good with Rachel but really well with Becca. Which one do you want to hear about first?" I pulled the jacket closer and shivered again, partly from the cold, mostly from anticipation.

"Let's start with the bad," he said after thinking about it.

"She's really mad, especially at me. She thinks I'm the one who talked you into getting baptized—"

"I told her you weren't. I told my whole family you weren't. That's part of the reason I didn't invite you—in case they showed up, you wouldn't be here to blame."

"I think she's just hurt. And scared. They don't know what to expect, and they don't want to lose another brother and son. I get why they're mad."

He nodded and kept his eyes glued to the ground, pain etched on his face. "I can't tell you how hard that was, Emily." He looked up at me, close to tears. "There's no way I could have done it if the answer I'd gotten hadn't been like a smack in the face."

"Give them time. They'll come around." I rubbed his arm to comfort him.

"I know they will, but things won't ever be the same. I'm just praying they'll be better." He sat up and took a breath. "Tell me about Becca. I can't believe she called you. She was more hurt than my family."

"She said you needed a friend here and I should come." I didn't know how much more I could say. I'd planned it all out on the plane. I would tell him how my feelings had grown stronger even though we'd been apart. I'd tell him everything I'd been holding inside. But suddenly, sitting across from him in person, I didn't have the courage. If Becca was wrong about his feelings for me, I'd risk losing his friendship too.

"She was right. When I looked up and saw you, it made everything okay. You should have told me you were going to be here." He reached out and squeezed my hand. But it was more friendly than romantic and made me doubt his feelings for me even more.

I nodded and took a deep breath. I was leaving the next morning. I had to tell him what I couldn't keep in any longer. "Joel, Becca told me she broke up with you because she wasn't your soul mate." I paused and met his eyes. "She thinks I am."

When he blinked and nodded instead of reacting with surprise, it gave me courage to go on. "I don't know if she's right or not. I don't even know if I believe in the whole idea of soul mates, but I know I've spent a year fighting my feelings for you for stupid reasons. I know I should have thrown out all the plans I'd made and the criteria I thought you needed to meet and just listened to my heart. I'm here as a friend, if that's what you want. But I want so much more than that—"

He stopped me with a kiss that lasted longer than my speech. And then another. And another. And none of them lasted long enough to make up for the days we'd spent apart and the months I'd wasted trying to make my life look a certain way instead of putting it in God's hands.

"I've got plenty of friends," he said when we broke apart.

I smiled, all my worries washed away, except for one. "How are we going to do this with you living here?"

He stopped me with another kiss, deeper than the first. Every part of me was wrapped up in that kiss, my heart, my head, my soul. I let go of my worries and fell into his kiss, trusting things would work out even without a map to show us which direction we were headed.

About the Author

BRITTANY LARSEN LIVES IN ORANGE County, California, with one husband, three daughters, one white dog, and one black cat. She would rather drive all the way to Utah than fight the traffic to LA, but occasionally she'll make the sacrifice for great Korean BBQ. At least she did one time. Mostly she spends her days in "active" wear staring at blank pages on her computer screen, wishing for words to magically appear.